"Action packed and full of adventure."

NIAMH

"This series continues to go from strength to strength."

NADIA

"I couldn't put it down."

SAM

"I was on the edge of my seat the whole time I was reading it."

DAWN

"It has a brilliant plot which keeps you guessing to the end AND truly fantastic."

BEN

WELCOME TO THE
SHAPESHIFTER UNIVERSE

- - -

When Dax Jones first showed up in my head, skinny, dark-eyed and restless, I had no idea how much he was going to mean to me. As a journalist I interviewed a lot of celebrities. They were fun—but the best stories I ever got were not from celebs. They came from normal people whose lives had been suddenly changed in some unexpected way. They were the *real* deal.

So Dax showed up kind of ordinary. And yet not. His name is a clue. Half ordinary, half extraordinary. I wanted to write about supernatural stuff but not in a wifty-wafty way. I wanted to imagine it as I believe it really would be. So I played the 'what if' game. What if you changed shape one day? Just shifted into something else? In this world—here, today. *Right now* while you're reading this. Look around you. How would people react if you were suddenly holding this page open with the claws and snout of a fox?

Ready to find out? Just sit back and enjoy the ride . . .

For my boys

OXFORD
UNIVERSITY PRESS

Great Clarendon Street, Oxford OX2 6DP
Oxford University Press is a department of the University of Oxford.
It furthers the University's objective of excellence in research, scholarship,
and education by publishing worldwide. Oxford is a registered trade mark of
Oxford University Press in the UK and in certain other countries

British Library Cataloguing in Publication Data
Data available
ISBN: 978-0-19-274609-2

1 3 5 7 9 10 8 6 4 2
Printed in Great Britain
Paper used in the production of this book is a natural,
recyclable product made from wood grown in sustainable forests.
The manufacturing process conforms to the environmental
regulations of the country of origin.

THE SHAPESHIFTER
GOING TO GROUND

ALI SPARKES

OXFORD
UNIVERSITY PRESS

1

Something was tickling his feet. His bare toes had come into contact, buried under the quilt, with something odd. Something tickly.

Dax Jones turned from right to left in bed, a pale lilac light beginning to filter through his closed eyelids. Flipping his pillow over for some pleasing coolness, he rested his cheek again and instinctively pushed his feet down once more. Something tickled.

With a spasm of shock, he jerked back his feet and shot upright in his bed, nearly knocking his head on the low shelf that clung to the wall with metal brackets. Dax's heart raced. Something weird was in his bed. Something very weird. He flickered on the edge of shifting, but needed his hands to pull back the quilt.

With a deep breath he leaned forward, seized the pink bedding, flicked it back—and almost screamed when he saw the eyes. Staring, blue, unmoving. Lifeless eyes in the face of a severed head. It was the silky blonde hair which had tickled his toes. Dax didn't scream. He shuddered and leapt to his feet, banged on the wall, and bellowed 'ALICE!'

His eight-year-old half-sister arrived rather too quickly, making Dax instantly suspicious. 'What?' she asked, innocently, pulling her pink dressing gown around her and frowning with fake concern.

Dax narrowed his eyes at her and then pointed to the head in his bed. It still stared, motionless, at the ceiling, a waxy smile on its lips. Blood-red lipstick had smeared across the curve of one rigid cheek.

'Oh! There you are, Barbie!' cooed Alice, and tucked the head under one arm, like the ghost of Anne Boleyn, a naughty smile on her face. The almost-life-sized plastic doll's head was set upon a shoulder-shaped pedestal and sold in great numbers to little girls who wanted to play at hair and make-up. It was usually to be found on Alice's dressing table, festooned in ribbons and hair clips and smothered with glittery eye gel and strawberry scented lip gloss. It was disgusting at the best of times, but to think he'd had his *toes* on it. He grimaced with revulsion.

'The next time you do that, I'll put it in Dad's vice and turn the lever until its eyes pop out!' growled Dax at his sister but she was already running out, giggling.

Dax shuddered again and looked around the small room that had been his sleeping place for the last few weeks. Once it had been his: khaki green, damp, and dark. Since his departure to Tregarren College last year, though, Alice's mum, Gina, had swept in and redecorated it in shades of lilac and pink. Shortly after, Alice had swept in and stuffed the room full of dolls. Dolls of all shapes and sizes simpered down from shelves on the walls, pouted up from little wicker chairs in the corners and grinned madly through the pink net curtain at the high windowsill. Baby dolls, teenage dolls, ballerinas, belly dancers, funky street kid dolls, medieval queen dolls, and more and more baby dolls. Whatever Dax did in this room, he had a rapt, staring, smirking audience. And if he ever *did* hit his head on the shelf over the bed, one of them went 'I love you more than bunnies!' and gave an insane gurgle.

Dax flopped back into bed with a groan and eyed the gap above the windowsill dolls, where a narrow top window flipped outwards behind the pink net curtain, allowing some fresh air in. He felt a flicker again and took another deep breath. Not to gather his courage this time, but to squash his desperate urge to shift and get outside the house. He'd been back here for what seemed like an eternity, since he and his friends had fled the wreckage of Tregarren College. And, as the new college wasn't quite ready, it would be at least another two weeks before he could get away from Alice and her dolls and Gina and her tight, suspicious smile.

Gina was his stepmother. She wasn't a wicked stepmother. She wasn't a nice one either. It had been some time now since he'd had to endure all the little spiteful acts that had shaped their relationship for the last eight years—poking and slapping, undermining his confidence, throwing out his favourite possessions, and banishing him to the garden for any reason she could think of; sometimes for no reason at all. Dax had been only four when he met Gina, just a few months after his mother had died. Gina had arrived so *thoroughly* in his life, replacing the mother he had already begun to struggle to remember, and supplying a sister in less than a year. Dax's dad had got a job on the oil rigs not long after. He was never home much; he seemed to be happier in the company of the North Sea.

Of course, Alice and Gina had got used to having both the men in their family at long distance over the past year. Dax wished they could get used to it again. Soon. He missed Gideon and Lisa and Mia—and it was so hard to talk to them on the phone. You never knew who might be listening. Dax sighed and got up again. He tugged the pink net along the taught wire that held it, allowing a more normal colour of daylight through, and scenting wild creatures on the breeze that wandered in; creatures foraging in the woodland some way off behind the back garden boundary. He sucked the air in hungrily and then glanced at his bedroom door. It was early. Gina wasn't even up yet and she usually had a lie-in on a Sunday. Alice probably wouldn't bother him again for a while, now that her doll's head joke had gone so well. He might have half an hour or more . . . long enough?

Dax wrestled with his conscience and tussled with his instincts. Then wrestled with his conscience again. He leaned across the narrow room to a chest of drawers and eased the top drawer open. Inside it lay a folded piece of thick white paper, bearing a governmental crest. Below it was a list of instructions. Non-negotiable instructions, which he read again.

1. Please remain calm and relaxed and enjoy your break at home.

2. DO NOT, under any circumstances, display your COLA abilities to anybody—indoors or out.

3. If you have ANY worries or concerns contact your allocated counsellor IMMEDIATELY, at any time (24 hours) on the number advised.

4. Remember to call in at weekends to Control (on weekdays your tutor will call in on your behalf).

5. REPORT immediately any changes in your physical or emotional health, to your allocated counsellor.

6. If you suspect, through accident, that your COLA status has been revealed to anyone other than those who already know, contact Control IMMEDIATELY.

The information ended with an assurance that a new base for the Colas was being organized as swiftly as possible, and the new college term would begin in the early autumn. Dax knew it was happening fast. All across the UK, more than a hundred twelve-and-thirteen-year-olds were in danger of revealing their incredible secrets at any moment. At first he was amazed that the government department in charge of looking after the Children Of Limitless Ability seemed so relaxed about the situation. In the last two years a collection of children had suddenly begun to display the most incredible powers—healing, vanishing, creating utterly convincing illusions, telepathy, telekinesis, clairvoyance. All the stuff you thought only happened in books and films, had begun to happen—to *actually* happen—to these children only. One of the Colas could even shapeshift into other creatures.

Dax listened across the landing for noises from Gina's room. Nothing. He closed his bedroom door quietly, still weighing up the risks. Of course, by now he knew that the government wasn't really relaxed about the situation at all. Since the Cola's remote college in Cornwall had been destroyed, measures to find a new, safe, and suitable location would have been pushed through at top levels, at top speed. The Colas were being tutored at home and kept out of harm's way until the new location was ready. And if they *did* misbehave the government would know. *Immediately.* Dax knew this. He could hear it. Not just in the occasional extra click on the telephone line, but in the very air around him.

More wildlife scents cruised across from the window and Dax folded the crested paper and put it back in the drawer, sliding it shut. Half an hour, surely. Half an hour. If he went from here, it was only Alice and Gina he had to worry about—and sooner or later they were going to have to know anyway. Did he dare? He closed his eyes and focused on the electrical pulses of communication in the air around him. Yep . . . it was Mike and Dave on duty today. Mike, who liked to do crosswords, and Dave, who liked to talk, quietly, about his girlfriend troubles. In the street at the front of the house they would be camped, as still as they could be, in the dark blue Transit van that had been parked a few doors along since mid-May. Dax grinned. They still didn't understand what it was they were expected to report back about . . . if they ever saw it.

'Well,' mumbled Dax to himself, making a decision as he pulled on his jeans, T-shirt, and trainers, 'they might see it today. If they're looking.' Just like that, he'd decided. And with barely a thought he had already shifted. He was at the window in a second, balancing on the thin metal of the frame, his piercing eyes taking in the tiniest detail of any movement in the garden, the wasteland beyond and the dark wood that lay behind the allotments. He dropped down two feet to the concrete outer sill, paused to read the air, and then shot into the sky.

2

It was incredible to think that this was only the third occasion that he had done this. As the earth fell away beneath him and wisps of light early-morning cloud whirled away from him, Dax felt a joy that was unique to this moment. To shake off the lumpy, clumpy weight of human form and shift into the fastest falcon on the planet was every bit as dazzling as it should be. Had he been able to shout he would be bawling YEEEESSSSS!!! with a throat thick with emotion. As it was, he let out a shrill avian cry of *Creeeeee—Creeeeee—Careet!*

When the houses below were matchbox small, he flipped into a stoop, curling his peregrine body into a corkscrew dive which cut through the warm rising air that wanted take him back up. His plummet back to earth was so fast that the air around him seemed to turn pink, but when his eyes adjusted to the wider view, the detail snapped back into sharp focus, even at 140 miles per hour. Below him lay the awkward curve of his road, the grey roofs of the houses dull in the morning sun. A snake of green rectangles were the gardens and a paler green landscape adjoining them was the wasteland. This in turn became a patchwork of allotments, and sprawling in to the east of these was the dark loveliness of the wood.

Across the tapestry of land he could see a hundred or more creatures stirring, foraging; some already running in fear. A pair of pigeons flapped frantically towards the cover of the woods. Dax's cry of joy had been a death siren to them, and he knew, without a moment's doubt, that if he chose to pick one off in mid-air, he could do it as easily as collecting a pebble from the beach. Pigeons were fast and evasive, but Dax, the peregrine falcon, saw everything played out before it had even happened, such was his speed.

And he did think about it. He hadn't killed yet, as a falcon. No falcon mother had taught him, but he knew precisely how to hunt. The pigeon would whirl and wheel and try to dodge him, but he would seize it in mid-air with his raptor claws. Together they would tumble to earth in an embrace of death and as they went, his talons digging in tighter with every hopeless struggle the pigeon made, he would dip his beak into the rainbow grey feathers on its collar and snap its spinal cord. His prey would be dead before they hit the ground and there he would cover it with the flecked grey mantle of his wings, like a protective parent, for a second or two, before breakfast.

The pigeons were in luck today. Dax thought he might well hunt before he returned to the doll-filled bedroom, but not as a falcon. He pulled out of his dive and arced through the humid rising air above the allotments. The steaming compost heaps made a heady smell and mice and voles scurried into their depths in panic. Dax coasted low above the wigwams of bamboo cane with late runner beans curling around them, past weather-beaten sheds and bulging water butts, and landed on the low branch of an oak at the edge of the woodland. He waited a while, roosting, scanning for any early gardeners, runners, or dog walkers. Nothing. Good. He was exhilarated, but tired and hungry. Dax flew to the woodland floor and shifted from falcon to fox.

The joy was more gentle than for his falcon shift; he was used to it, but he knew the fox was his truest form. He might eventually learn to shapeshift into anything, but his first instinct would always be to the fox. DaxFox trotted through the woodland, scaring a whole new batch of animals. Woodland dwellers had little to fear from a peregrine; a peregrine hunts wide open areas, cliffs, fields, and clearings, but the fox could be almost anywhere. Dax felt faintly guilty. He should have sneaked downstairs and eaten a little breakfast before he'd escaped the bedroom. That way the rabbit he was after could have lived a bit longer. But now he knew he *had* to hunt. Not just because he was hungry as a fox, but because he would be *famished* as a falcon, and possibly not even able to fly back into the house. The soaring and stooping and corkscrew aerobatics had cost him a huge amount of energy. No real peregrine would do it for fun.

So Dax paused at the edge of a small clearing within the wood, still and silent, watched the rabbit for a while and then pounced. He killed it instantly, the boy inside him still experiencing a pang of guilt. He ate fast and efficiently, leaving little for the woodland scavengers and being careful to wipe his snout and paws on the dry, tussocky grass. The first time he had hunted he had shifted back to a boy, only to find Owen staring at the caked blood in his hair. Eugh!

The meal did its magic. Dax felt a surge of strength and gazed around him happily. Perhaps half a mile away a vixen was out with her almost full-grown cubs. He could scent them clearly. No dog-fox registered, which was just as well. He wasn't in the mood for a fight with the local bloke. He turned away from the fox family, first sending a pulse of calm and indifference in their direction, just in case. Although he had never been able to exactly talk to another fox, he could pulse out messages to other animals—and they to him. A sort of mixture of raw telepathy and scent, he suspected. Smell was vital in the wild and it had been one of the first changes he had noticed, just before his first shift into fox form the previous year. Yes—scent and telepathy—he'd experienced it more than once now. In fact, it was entirely possible that a vixen had saved his life earlier that year, when she had shot past in a blur of red and pulsed GO! at him, seconds before a pack of foxhounds and huntsmen on horseback had thundered through.

Dax went for a walk, relishing every step. As a fox he felt every muscle, sinew, organ, and tendon working in perfect rhythm. All was as it should be: the air playing with the white spray of whiskers that fanned delicately from his snout, the sticks and leaves massaging the soft grey-pink pads of his paws. The woodland relaxed around him, its inhabitants seeming to sense that he was well fed and not interested in further hunting now. The colours and textures sang out to him. It seemed like such a long time since he had been in this form in a wood. Florets of brown and yellow fungi grew in pretty scallops around old logs; clusters of jewel-bright berries glinted in the pale golden shafts that reached in past the trees, oak bark ran like a frozen river, shining black beetles rafting through the green and brown currents.

A bell sounded from far away: the town clock carried through on the still air. Eight chimes. Dax paused, one paw raised and his ears cocked. Eight o'clock. He sighed, emitting a whispery growl. He really should get back now. He must have been gone twenty minutes and at any time Alice could bash back into the doll's annexe, or Gina could rap coldly on the door and tell him to take a shower and make it quick. The fox sighed again and ran to the edge of the woodland, leaping up and shifting in mid-air to the falcon. The falcon whirled clear of the trees, but made no attempt to do aerobatics this time. Dax scanned the houses and gardens and the road below him and spotted the roof of the dark blue Transit van. He knew it was a bad idea, but he just couldn't resist it. How likely was it that Mike or Dave would be looking up at the sky right now? Dax grinned to himself, inwardly, and flew softly down to the van, landing on the grooved metal rack on its roof, careful that he didn't clunk his talons against it. Even so, he heard Dave say, suddenly, as if roused from sleep, 'What was that?'

'What?' said Mike, slurping a drink from a plastic cup.

'Ah . . . nothing,' concluded Dave. 'I think I was nearly asleep then. I hate this job.'

'Yeah, well . . . could be worse,' muttered Mike, but he didn't describe exactly how it could be worse.

'Kid never goes anywhere anyway,' grumped Dave. 'Must be one of these computer geeks or something. Never goes anywhere.'

'No—no computer. We'd have picked it up,' said Mike. 'He's into wildlife stuff, isn't he? Keeps a bird. Feel sorry for that bird. Fancy being cooped up all day when you're, like, a wild animal? It's not right.'

'Yeah, right—tell me about it,' said Dave, with feeling. 'You know what?'

'What?' said Mike, although he didn't sound as if he wanted to know.

'I could really do with a bag of Maltesers.'

Riveting though the conversation was, Dax knew he should really go. Besides, he could pick up stuff from Mike and Dave even in the house, sometimes, in certain weather conditions, when he shifted to a fox. Once, when Gina and Alice had gone out, he had stayed behind and sat in the hallway for an hour, in fox form, just listening in on Mike and Dave. He liked Mike and Dave better than Martin and Philip, who were the other shift. He actually felt sorry for them—he couldn't imagine a more boring job than being on government surveillance outside his house. He'd given up resenting it some time ago, when he realized they even had to follow him down to the shopping centre with Gina and Alice. Dax found it utterly tedious going out with Gina and Alice and it actually made him feel slightly better that some other poor mugs had to suffer it too.

He had never tried to catch Mike or Dave out—or the other two men paid to watch and listen to him. It didn't seem fair. They weren't aware of his special abilities and they were only doing their job. Today, though, he was in a slightly rebellious mood. His flight and his hunt had put humour back into his heart and as Dave continued yearning for Maltesers a funny idea arrived in his head. Instead of heading back over to his house, he flew silently down the road to the corner, where the newsagent's was already open. He dropped into the litter-strewn alleyway at the back of it and shifted quickly into boy form, knowing there was some change in his jeans pocket. He sauntered round into the shop, making little eye contact with the teenager on the till, and bought a packet of Maltesers. Outside, he sidled back into the alleyway, took the edge of the red plastic packet in his teeth, and shifted with a leap back into the falcon.

He was dragged down by the packet in his beak much more than he expected and was glad he had to hold it for only three seconds. Swooping along the quiet road he dropped the packet with pinpoint accuracy onto the windscreen of the Transit. He just heard the exclamation from Dave before he whipped up and away and whirled tightly around to the back of the house. He shot straight in through the letterbox window and landed on the scratched metal frame of the bedstead. Immediately he shifted back to boy form and was on the floor, laughing fit to burst, when Gina came in, three seconds later.

'What's up with *you*?' she asked, her sallow face puckered with distaste.

Dax sat up and shook his head, still grinning. 'Just . . . um . . . thought of something really funny,' he said. He knew he had to be careful with Gina. She wasn't the bully she used to be, not since the government had convinced her that her stepson was a 'genius' and had taken him away for special education. Gina was canny enough to realize she might get some benefit from Dax's 'specialness' at some point—she also seemed to sense that he was different now. That he had some power, although she had no idea what it was. Nor did Alice. Not even his father knew, although Dax had tried to tell him.

No—Gina might not be as sharply unpleasant as she had been, but she still wasn't to be trusted. She and Dax had a strange understanding these days. They both knew that the other knew that things had changed. Neither sought to ask or explain—they just kept each other at a careful distance. Gina did the basic minimum for him: laundry and food and an occasional trip out with Alice. She never asked about his life and Dax never volunteered anything. It wasn't totally comfortable, but it was better than it used to be.

Alice was different, of course. She did ask questions, but she was eight and a girl and it was easy to tell her to get lost. One day though, he knew he *would* tell her—show her. He didn't get on with her but he did care about her. He would sooner show her than Gina. Gina would probably hit him with a broom and call pest control.

'You've got a call,' said Gina, flatly, ignoring his subsiding mirth. She pulled the walkabout phone from the pocket of her quilted orange housecoat and handed it to him, before retreating from the room and closing the door.

'Dax?' demanded a girl's voice. 'Dax? Oh, for heaven's sake. Tell me I *wasn't* in your stepmother's pocket. Oh—that's too revolting! I could hear the phone banging against her blubbery skin. Yuck!'

'Hi, Lisa,' grinned Dax. 'Nice to hear from you.'

'What *were* you laughing about?'

'Oh—I'll have to tell you later,' he sighed, sitting back on the bed and sending her a message in which Maltesers featured strongly.

Lisa Hardman giggled. 'You didn't!' she said.

There was a pause in which they both tried to work out two conversations at the same time. One conversation was the 'normal' one, usually extremely dull, which was being recorded by Mike and Dave in the Transit van. The other conversation didn't require cables and telegraph poles—that was the telepathic one, enabled by Lisa's incredible powers as a psychic.

Not everyone could send and receive messages

with Lisa in this way. Some of the Colas could manage something, usually in times of great need or stress, but only Dax, as far as he knew, could carry on a proper conversation with Lisa from the depths of his mind, across several counties. It was something to do with being a part-time fox, they reckoned. It was a bit patchy sometimes, and it definitely helped to make some other form of contact first, to kick it all off, which was why Lisa was phoning him and not just wafting into his mind unannounced.

'How is your dad?' said Dax, out loud. Maurice Hardman had been in a car accident earlier that year and was still recovering.

'He's good,' said Lisa, and then went on to talk about her dad's physiotherapy and the visiting nurse and all kinds of general stuff. If it sounded a bit lacklustre to Mike and Dave, it was because she was carrying on an entirely different conversation with Dax on the telepathic line.

Dax—you need to get here. You need to come and see me as soon as possible.

I can't! sent Dax. *You know they're watching me all the time!*

Look, Dax, she came back, testily, *it's not like I'm missing you or anything! This is important. I can't explain it now—it's too difficult with the talking out loud stuff. And I'm still not sure what it is . . . exactly. But it's to do with Gideon. You need to get here!*

At the sound of his best friend's name, Dax caught

his breath. Gideon had gone through such terrible times this year. He couldn't stand the thought of him having any more bad luck.

What? What about Gideon?

'Anyway, I'm taking him out for walks now,' Lisa droned on, out loud. *I told you! I don't know! Not yet! You need to be here. Stop arguing with me and shift your furry backside into a feathery backside and get down here!* 'He's doing really well. He'd love you to visit. Maybe we can ask Owen for a pass and get you down here.' Lisa knew full well that no such pass would be issued by Owen or any other Cola teacher. All Colas were grounded, for their own safety, until the new college was found.

'I'll see what I can do, Lees,' said Dax. 'I'd love to take off for a while, but I'm just doing as I'm told. I don't want to get into trouble.' *All right! I'm coming. Can't just yet though. Too late today. I'll leave at first light tomorrow—should be with you for breakfast. Can you hang on till then?*

'No—we mustn't get into trouble,' agreed Lisa, vapidly. 'But maybe you'll be allowed.' *Yes—OK. That'll have to do. I'll try to find out more. My shoulder's like a block of ice but it would help if someone would just SAY what's up. God, they're annoying me today!*

Dax grinned. When Lisa got messages from the spirit world (and, as the most powerful Cola medium, she got a lot), they could often be as tangled and confused as they were persistent. When she had first got her 'gift' she had fought against it and refused to co-operate. The spirits queuing up for her services seemed to lean on her left shoulder, because whenever a particularly powerful vision or message came through, it would get so cold it would ache. Dax could picture her now, in her beautiful manor house hallway, on the phone, rubbing her shoulder fiercely and glaring into the beyond.

'I'll ask Gina and Owen and let you know,' concluded Dax, for the benefit of Mike and Dave's recording equipment.

'OK—call me back! Bye!' Lisa hung up with a last pulse of telepathy. *First thing, Dax! First thing!*

Dax put the phone down and found his hands were shaking. What was happening to Gideon? He wished he could phone him and ask, but he couldn't. Even if he knew about something being wrong, Gideon probably couldn't say. He, too, would surely have worked out that all their phone conversations were being monitored. And anyway, if Lisa didn't know what the problem was, it was highly unlikely Gideon would. Lisa was a psychic, a clairvoyant, a medium, and a dowser. Gideon was a telekinetic. He could make your telly dance around the hallway, but he couldn't hear spirits talking or see into the future.

Dax couldn't see into the future either, but the present was beginning to bother him. Yesterday he could just about manage being stuck at home with Alice and Gina. Today was going to be a lot harder.

3

Sundays were often drawn out and dull at home. This one was no exception. Dax turned down the offer to go to the out-of-town superstore with Gina and Alice and settled down to read a book on bushcraft which Owen had given him for his last birthday. Owen had been the first adult to see Dax shapeshift, nearly a year ago. He was part teacher, part government agent: a strange mix of authority and friend. Dax owed his life to Owen—and Owen probably owed his life back to Dax after the adventures of the past few months.

Owen had made it his personal mission to educate the Colas in how to look after themselves—Dax, Gideon, Lisa, and Mia in particular. This didn't mean keeping their teeth brushed and learning to open a tin of beans. When Owen showed them how to look after themselves it was much more thorough than that. Owen took it upon himself to teach them bushlore: how to find food and shelter and warmth, away from towns and cities, deep in the woods. At first, Dax had thought Owen's extra curricular lessons were just for fun and a way of bonding with his strange charges, but as time had gone by he had begun to understand Owen's thinking.

'People fear anything that's different,' Owen had once

told him. 'And nothing gets much more different than a Cola. And among Colas, nothing is much more different than *you*, Dax. At some time, you may need to get away from people.' Dax was the only shapeshifter. There had been another, a boy who became a wolf, but he had been killed before he even made it to Tregarren College. That left Dax. There were one hundred and nine Colas and only one of them could shapeshift.

Other things Dax had in common with the rest. Not one of them, for example, had a living mother. Every single Cola had lost his or her mother by the age of four. Nobody could work out why, and there were no clues to connect these women in any way, except that their deaths had been swift but unremarkable. The Cola mediums had all—of course—tried to find out something from the spirit world, but nothing ever came back to them. No Cola mother had ever made contact.

Dax flipped over a page of his book and studied a picture of men making an underground oven. He thought, again, about the network of children all over the UK, and wondered how they were all filling *their* time. He could imagine the Teller brothers entertaining each other with their amazing mimicry, Barry sneaking about his home invisible, Spook Williams lording it around his house, demanding extra sequins on his ridiculous magician's cloak.

The Children Of Limitless Ability were all around the same age, and had been found right across the country (only one had been discovered abroad, but she had been born in England) and from all types of backgrounds. There was Gideon, who lived in a two-up, two-down council house on the outskirts of London with his dad and there was Lisa, who occupied a luxurious mansion in Somerset with hers. Lisa and her dad had a pony and a thoroughbred Arabian mare. Gideon and his dad shared a budgie.

Some of them had brothers or sisters; some were raised by grandparents; some had kind new stepmums as well as dads. Some, thought Dax with a downbeat of sadness, had dads who were never there. He turned over another page of the bushcraft book, which had been written by an expert who had travelled the world, scraping survival from the North Pole to the Sahara with his wits and a well-packed rucksack. Robert Jones loved his son—Dax was sure that he did—but he also seemed to fear him. Since he had become a shapeshifter and a Cola, Dax had seen his father only three times, and had never yet managed to explain to him what had happened, never managed to share the amazing transformation in his life.

Robert Jones just kept sliding away from him. As if he already knew but could not bear to have his thoughts confirmed. *Soon*, thought Dax, *I have to tell him soon. Or I'll show him. He's back next week and I WILL show him.* Robert Jones had sent his son some money and apologies—and a promise that they would spend some time together as soon as he got back.

Dax realized he wasn't reading the book; much of it he knew by heart now, anyway. He snapped it shut and paced into the hallway. Two hours had ticked by since his illicit fly-past over the Transit and his chocolate delivery. He grinned, wondering what Mike and Dave had made of it, and shifted into a fox so he could settle on the doormat and listen in.

At first, all he heard was the buzz and whine of all the electrical equipment in the back of the Transit van. It astonished him that Mike and Dave could sit there with it all day and not get earache but, of course, to the human ear it was barely detectable. After a minute he heard Mike rustling what sounded like a newspaper and Dave sighing.

'I think we should report it,' said Dave. 'No—I really think we should.'

'What? Maltesers from heaven?' dug Mike. 'That'll get the Special Ops team down here at the double. Deadly chocolate bombing incident . . . ' He sniggered.

'But it's weird. It's definitely *weird*,' said Dave and he sounded tense and worried. Dax felt a little guilty. 'They said watch, follow, stay on top of the situation. They said, also, watch for a *bird*. Any sign of an unusual bird. You know, maybe something that takes messages or something . . . ?'

Mike sighed. 'Yes, mate. I got the brief too, you know. We haven't seen a bird.'

'They also said,' persisted Dave, 'anything unusual. *Anything*. Anything odd. And if Maltesers from the sky, minutes after I said I wanted some, isn't odd, I don't know what is.'

'Fine,' said Mike. 'Call it in. Go on . . . '

Dave sighed. 'You'll back me up on that then? You'll say that's what it was.'

'I didn't see it—I only heard it,' said Mike. 'You said it was Maltesers, not me. Could have been anything; something chucked by a kid or dropped by a crow.'

'Exactly!' said Dave.

'Ssshhh!'

'Exactly,' said Dave, more quietly. 'A bird!'

'Did you see it?'

'No.'

'Any other evidence?'

'Well, yeah. There's definitely a bag of Maltesers under the front wheels, I know that. It slid down the windscreen. But seeing as we're not meant to be in here, I don't see how I can pop out and get it.'

Mike was beginning to laugh wheezily now. 'Hey, you know what?' he sniggered, putting on a very bad American accent. 'You're right. We gotta suspect Maltesers situation here! We gotta call for back-up! Get the Feds over to head up the Snack Disposal Squad!'

Dax began to feel *very* guilty. He'd only done it to cheer Dave up, but now he realized it was a stupid thing to do. He shifted back to a boy and returned to his book, wishing the day would move faster. At least on weekdays his tutor filled up the long hours. An elderly but very bright man called Mr Gibbs, he would drill Dax through all his school subjects thoroughly at a makeshift desk in the dining room. Dax liked him, and sensed that he knew about the Cola powers his pupil possessed. He always touched on wildlife subjects with a broad smile and a knowing glance. He also checked Dax in every day with Control, and was entertainingly snippy with them when they kept him waiting too long on his mobile phone.

Dax had made his own call to Control earlier that morning, while Gina and Alice were watching TV. He was required to give a pass code and answer a set of security questions and the person on the phone concluded every call with the same advice: 'If you have any concerns or fears, call us *immediately*, Dax.' Dax now had plenty of concerns and fears, since the phone call from Lisa, but it didn't occur to him to call Control. One thing he had learned in the past year since he had joined the Cola Club, was that not everyone in authority was necessarily on his side. He had spent a suspicious spring this year, in the last weeks before Tregarren College was destroyed, convinced that sinister tests were being carried out on all of them. He'd even gone so far as to stop eating and drinking at the college, until he'd discovered what had been making everyone tired and washed out. Nothing to do with the college at all, as it had turned out. Everything to do with poor Gideon.

Alice and Gina returned with their shopping and the day dragged on. In the evening they ate curried chicken in front of a TV quiz show and Alice threw stupid answers through mouthfuls of rice.

'What is the capital of Australia?' intoned the host,

seriously, beneath his improbably blond hair. 'Is it A: Sydney; B: Alice Springs . . . '

'Kangaroo!' shouted Alice. 'Bamboo . . . Cake.'

Dax had to laugh. Sometimes he could quite like Alice, in spite of her doll thing.

' . . . or D: Wellingt—'

There was a pop and a tinkle as a lightbulb blew in the hallway and the house was suddenly silent and in darkness. Dax glanced around, surprised, and Gina said a rude word, before putting her dinner tray down on the floor and pacing across to the window to look outside. She cursed again. 'All the lights are out,' she said. 'Must be a power cut.'

'Oooh—can we get the candles out?' asked Alice. 'We can tell ghost stories.'

'No—it'll come back on in a minute,' said Gina, but it didn't. Ten minutes later they were sitting around a candle in the kitchen and trying to get the radio tuned in properly. It ran on batteries. The local radio station was obviously equipped with a back-up generator, because it was still broadcasting, and taking calls from excited listeners about the power cut. It seemed that a huge area, across three counties, had gone dark, and battery-powered burglar alarms were going off everywhere. The head of the local fire and rescue department arrived on air, pleading with the public not to call unless it had a genuine emergency.

After the next song, a spokesman for Southern Power was on, explaining that there had been some kind of major incident involving the power grid. Was it terrorists? the presenter prodded urgently, but the spokesman either didn't know or wasn't willing to say.

The power still wasn't on by the time Dax went to bed, but he had other things on his mind. He planned to leave as soon as it was light. He knew it was breaking all the rules, but it might even be possible to get back again before he was missed. His tutor didn't arrive until ten, and Gina usually had her hands full with getting Alice off to school. Sometimes they didn't bump into each other until late morning.

Realizing, though, that he might not be back, Dax switched on his torch and found some paper and a pen. *Dear Mr Gibbs*, he wrote, because he couldn't imagine confiding in Gina or Alice, *I have had to go out for a while, but I will be back again as soon as possible. I apologize for keeping you waiting, and I promise I'm not doing anything risky* (he felt a twinge at this: it wasn't strictly true). *It's a really important thing—please wait for me for as long as you can before calling Control. I will explain when I get back. Yours sincerely, Dax.*

He folded the paper and wrote *Mr Gibbs* on the back. He guessed Gina would find it and read it before she handed it over, but it didn't really give anything away. He hoped that Mr Gibbs would wait a while for him in the morning if he didn't make it back in time. He put it on the chest of drawers, got into bed and willed himself to sleep until dawn. He would wake on time: he never needed an alarm clock these days.

In fact, he woke a little before dawn, with a purpose that led him out onto the landing, creeping past Gina's and Alice's bedrooms and easing silently down the stairs to the kitchen, where he found the power was now back on. He didn't have the time to hunt today, so he must eat before he began his journey. Dax found cold chicken leftovers in the fridge, a packet of ham, some fruit juice, and a banana. He stuffed them all quickly, his heart already hammering with excitement and fright. He washed the food down with the last of the juice and let out a shaky sigh of satisfaction, before creeping back upstairs again. Back in the dolls' annexe, he ignored a hundred or more glassy eyes staring at him and got dressed. From under his bed he pulled out a small green backpack. Inside it was his emergency stuff: stuff he'd had on hand all summer. He hadn't seriously thought he'd need it, but the events of the last year had made him prepare for the unexpected. In the backpack was a change of clothes, a torch, a waterproof pocket mac, a cap, a folded sheet of lightweight plastic, a ball of string, a box of matches wrapped in clingfilm, a metal water flask, a knife in its leather sheath, some money (not much), and another survival-type handbook which he'd bought the last time he went out with Gina and Alice.

Dax slipped the backpack onto his shoulders and buckled the straps across his chest. He knew it would go with him. Anything he wore simply shifted along with the rest of him. Stuff that he was only carrying in his hand would fall—unless it was possible, as in the case of the Maltesers, for him to hang on to it. Shifting to a fox, he had never tried to carry anything, but backpacks had gone as seamlessly to fur and skin as the rest of his clothes. It was to do with his awareness of himself and what he looked like to others, he thought. He had had endless discussions with other Colas about this: about why his clothes didn't drop off him every time, and why he didn't shift back shivering stark naked, whimpering for pants. He was deeply relieved at the convenient way it all worked.

Fingers of sunlight had now thickened into broad bands of pink in the east, and although he would be flying west, he knew it was light enough now that the warm thermals of air were already lifting away from the earth and a steady breeze was pushing towards his window. Good. Before he shifted to a falcon, however, he went to DaxFox, checking quickly with his astonishing hearing that the nightshift was safely in the Transit and not taking a quick tour of duty around the house (they did this from time to time, and Dax heard them on every occasion). No. He could hear Philip murmuring quietly on his mobile phone, amid the usual clicking, buzzing, and humming. His partner was singing a pop song softly to himself. What a dull life!

Dax was about to shift from fox to falcon when he suddenly froze. There was a noise out on the landing and suddenly one of the thin strips of dim light around his door fattened to a wide column, revealing the silhouette of Alice.

She froze, and her mouth fell open as she watched the fox turn and stare back at her. In the pale glow of the dawn, Dax could see her pupils growing huge and dark with disbelief. He had to think quickly. Yes—yes, he meant her to know at some point. But not now! Not now!

Dax shifted swiftly to a boy. He smiled at Alice. 'Eeeee—beeebbeee—hair band, cheese,' he said, smiling madly. 'What a pram on my head. You are dreaming, my dear sister. Go back to bed. Frog. More frogs. Bed time. Where is my exam paper? You've eaten it.' Amazing himself with his ability to sound so completely nuts in a crisis, he steered the confused eight-year-old around and propelled her back to her room. At her door, she turned and stared at him again, her mouth still open in wonder. 'Still dreaming. Fox, frog, fish and dog; go back to sleep,' he advised, gently, and Alice nodded slowly and then closed her door.

Dax shifted immediately and shot through the bedroom and out of the open window before he could lose his nerve.

4

Dax had flown long distance only once before, from the bottom of Cornwall to the top of Hampshire; a flight that had exhilarated and exhausted him. He had slipped free of the grasp of the Cola Club protectors seconds before the coach full of disorientated children was set to leave the flooded ruins of Tregarren College, choosing to fly home instead.

He could still see Owen's disbelieving face and Gideon's amazed but delighted grin in the half second before he shot away. He was in his own town hours before the coach would have arrived, but a grim-faced Owen had raced ahead in a sleek black Mercedes to check that he had made it home. Dax had been roosting on a lamp post at the end of his road for some time, wondering when to knock on Gina's door, when he saw the car and realized it was Owen. Wanting to spare his friend and mentor the awkwardness of questioning Gina, he had swooped down low as soon as Owen got out of the car, and led him away from the house, and round to the wasteland at the back.

Owen deserved this; deserved better in fact. On his long journey back, following the rugged lines of the Cornish and then the Devonshire coast, Dax's exhilaration had given way to guilt. He wouldn't change the situation, but he did feel a bit bad about Owen. As he flew across the soft rolling hills of Dorset and skirted the dark green canopy of the New Forest, turning north, he decided to apologize to the man who had first found him and taken him away from his bleak life with Gina and Alice to join the other Colas; who had pulled him back, literally, from the edge of death; who had looked out for him. Owen worked for the government, but there was no doubt that he genuinely cared for the Colas. Dax trusted him more than any other adult he could think of.

He had waited, turning in the warm, early afternoon air which rose from the wasteland, until Owen stood still, his rough-cut, wavy hair lifting in the light breeze, and then raised his leather-jacketed arm like a practised falconer. Dax dropped onto it, taking care not to dig his talons in too tightly. There was no need, of course—he could simply have dropped low to the tall grass, coasted into the woodland, and shifted back to a boy. But he wanted Owen to get a proper look at the magnificent thing he had shifted into. Charcoal grey feathers on his back, tail, and wings gave way to grey-and-white speckled bars across his chest and down his feathered legs; pure yellow glowed around each round black eye, and also dusted his talons. During his long flight he had roosted, briefly, high on a church spire in Exeter, and had found time to inspect himself in the mirrored glass window of a tall office building opposite. He was a fine specimen, as fine in bird form as he was in fox form.

Owen still looked annoyed, but his justifiable mood was buffeted away by wonder at the bird of prey on his forearm. 'God alive,' he had murmured. 'God alive, Dax . . .'

After a few more seconds of amazed study, Owen took a deep breath, blinked, and then set Dax down on a chunk of concrete in the weedy grass. He looked around him, but Dax already knew there was nobody in sight. He had shifted to a slightly nervous looking boy, perched on the edge of the concrete. And apologized.

Now, as the sky behind him grew brighter and the green and gold colours of the Wiltshire valley drifted below him, Dax guessed he'd be apologizing to Owen again soon. He hoped whatever Lisa had to tell him would make it easier. He *had* stuck to all the rules for weeks and weeks. Well, mostly.

It was fully daylight by the time he found himself on the Hardman estate, coasting high across the woods where he had once been hunted by dogs. He had thought he might have to land on Lisa's bedroom window ledge, but he should have guessed she would not be there. A swift movement sixty metres below him was Lisa's blonde ponytail, flicking from side to side as she ran hard along the perimeter of the large estate. She was dressed in dark blue running trousers and a matching zip-up top and the glint of the silver detail on her expensive running shoes was visible to him even at this distance. Lisa glanced up and saw him almost immediately, even though he hadn't sent out any telepathy to her. She was getting good . . . really good.

She stopped (a rare thing for Lisa once she got running) and laughed out loud in delight. This was the first time she'd had a proper look at him in falcon form. Like Owen, she held out her arm for him to land on, but he went to the wooden post of the perimeter fence and she looked put out as he landed. He dropped down to the grass and shifted swiftly, so he could explain.

'I would've taken a large chunk out of your arm if I'd landed on that,' he said, tugging at the thin material of her sleeve.

She nodded grudgingly and then stared back at him in wonder. 'Oh wow, Dax! I mean . . . wow!' He grinned. It was definitely a wow moment, he couldn't deny it. 'Go on—shift back,' she urged, her dark blue eyes sparkling with excitement. 'I didn't get a proper look!'

'I will,' he said, 'just as soon as you've got me some breakfast.'

She looked put out again and seemed about to say something waspish to him, but then she noticed how shaky and pale he was looking. 'OK,' she said. 'Come on—Marguerite's got a full English ready.'

Dax sighed with delight and walked after her, wishing she hadn't come quite so far from the house. She began to run back again and instinctively he slipped into fox form to keep pace with her. He was still exhausted and hungry, but it was better than trying to lumber along as a boy.

Just as they always did, they synchronized into a comfortable jog and began to communicate without speech. *Have you picked up any more about Gideon? Do you know anything yet?* sent Dax, already picking up the scent of frying bacon from the house.

I'm getting a bit more now . . . let's get back and eat and I'll try to explain, she sent back. He didn't think she was being evasive. He knew that she was now picking up his exhaustion and hunger and had worked out, quite rightly, that he couldn't possibly concentrate properly until he was sorted out.

Dax shifted back to boy form at the grand stone archway of the mansion's front door. Maurice Hardman knew about his shapeshifter powers—had seen him as a fox, in fact. The staff, though, had not. Dax knew them well enough to think they would probably—from the calm butler, Evans, to the warm and passionate Spanish cook and housekeeper, Marguerite—take it all in their stride. He felt, though, that he should show respect to Lisa's father and not spring any shocks on the household without permission.

Maurice Hardman was waiting for them at the breakfast table and smiled warmly when he saw Dax. 'How are you, Dax?' he beamed. He was looking slightly thinner than when Dax had last seen him. One pink scar across his chin and another snaking into the grey hair at his left temple were visible reminders of the car crash that had almost killed him in April. His hands, though, were steady and firm, gripping the financial section of the newspaper he always had with him at breakfast.

'I'm great!' grinned Dax, sinking happily into the

chair at the breakfast table, which was already loaded with warm stacks of triangled toast, dishes of butter, pots of tea and coffee, and jugs of milk and fruit juice.

'He's exhausted and hungry,' said Lisa, sitting down opposite him. 'Get some toast down you, Dax. The rest is coming.'

'The rest is here!' called a proud, sing-song voice, and Marguerite arrived to place a hot round plate in front of him, heaped with crispy slices of bacon, eggs, mushrooms, beans, sausages, grilled tomato, and fried bread.

Dax murmured his delight and took up his knife and fork. 'Thank you so much,' he whispered and Marguerite walked away smiling.

'I hear you shift to a falcon now,' said Maurice, leaning across the table in fascination and Dax nodded and mumbled, 'Reregrin ralcon,' through a mouthful of bacon. Maurice looked triumphantly at his daughter. 'What did I tell you?' he said. 'A peregrine! I knew it! The fastest and the best! Did you know that peregrines are the fastest bird on the planet? Did you? They commonly do more than 140 mph when they're in a sky dive. Some people believe they can even do 200! Can you believe that? A peregrine! Dax—you have to let me see you fly. You have to!'

Dax nodded, laughing through his breakfast, already recovering his energy.

'What does it feel like?' asked Lisa, her voice oddly reverential, as if she were in a church.

Dax shook his head and rolled his eyes and kept on eating. He sent her a scene of the planet from a mile up in the atmosphere: the curved patchwork of the Somerset countryside seen through a haze of blue, and wisps of white cloud; a view so wide and rich and fluid and unframed by an aircraft window that it was barely possible for the human mind to process. He also sent her the feeling of the warm thermals holding up his wings as he turned gently beneath the morning sun. Lisa gasped and sat back in her seat, her hands dropping to her lap. Her eyes looked moist.

'Pretty good then,' her dad observed.

As soon as he had finished his breakfast, Dax wanted to sleep, but there wasn't time. It was now well past seven, and if he was going to try to get back and avoid being caught out, he would have to go soon. He took a deep breath, pushed his empty plate away and picked up the mug of warm tea with both hands. Then he sent, *Now—I can concentrate now*, to Lisa. She nodded and Maurice glanced between them.

'Sorry, Mr Hardman,' said Dax, suddenly ashamed. 'I get so lazy sometimes. I was just saying I can concentrate now. Thank you for my breakfast.'

'Not at all. In fact—I'll leave you both to it,' said Maurice, getting up, patting Dax on the shoulder and tucking his paper under his arm. He walked away slowly, with a slight limp. 'But I want to be there for take-off when you head back, mind!'

'Of course,' grinned Dax. 'We'll call you.'

When Maurice was gone Lisa sighed and rested her elbows on the table. 'I've been getting it for three days now.'

'Three days?' said Dax. 'Why didn't you call me sooner?'

'I didn't know what it *was* at first!' snapped Lisa. 'You *know* it can be like that sometimes. Especially when it's about my friends or family. The more important it is to *me*, the more foggy it is when it comes through.'

'I know,' sighed Dax. 'I'm sorry. I know. Just tell me what you're getting.'

'OK,' she said, softening her glare. 'It was just images and noises and a sort of smell at first. Crackling light and dark and a kind of earthy, pavement-y smell— and a rumbling, shrieking, almost metallic noise. Like something . . . like something *twisting*. It's hard to explain. I thought about the Eiffel Tower once or twice, but that doesn't really make sense. It wasn't the Eiffel Tower . . . at least there's nothing in the news about that. But it wasn't *meant* to be that anyway. Big. Metallic; concrete and earth and *crackling*.' She sent him a pulse of the experience, but it was vague and dark and faint, and Dax felt her words were probably doing a better job of explaining it.

'So what has it got to do with Gideon?' he asked, taking another gulp of tea.

'A few hours after I got that, I got a smell, while I was out on Chrysler. Not the kind of smell you normally get out horse riding. It was really, really strong.'

'Yes?'

'Chocolate.'

Dax gave a hoot of laughter. Gideon absolutely *loved* chocolate. He could eat bricks and bricks of it. Whenever Dax had had a hard day, he could always rely on Gideon to sit down next to him and hand him a battered chunk of chocolate—he seemed to have some on him at all times. 'Chocolate!' repeated Dax, still chuckling. 'That'll be Gid, then!'

Lisa didn't return his smile. She looked at the tablecloth and began to rub her left shoulder.

'What?' said Dax, suddenly very worried. 'What else?'

'I got down and tied Chrysler up, because I knew one was coming,' she said, quietly.

'One what?'

'An episode. One of the stronger ones. Most of them, you know, don't slow me down at all. I just make a note, if I need to—fill in the SCN slips at Tregarren.' Dax nodded. At college all the mediums had to fill in Spirit Communication Notice slips whenever they took a message from the beyond, and a staff member had to check and sign it before it could be delivered; Lisa produced more SCN slips than any other Cola.

'Sometimes,' Lisa continued, 'I know when they're going to be stronger than average. If I get a really intense smell, that's a sign. Or if I go numb and tingly from my left shoulder right down to my ankle. If I don't get myself somewhere safe, ideally sitting down, I can end up getting hurt.'

Dax gaped at her. She had never told him this before. Lisa was incredibly independent and frequently rather rude to the spirit community which chose to use her as a link with the earthly one. She had hated her 'gifts' when they first arrived, disrupting her privileged life and taking away her popularity with the other rich little girls at her school. By now she had come to terms with it, but she was still quite impatient with the amazing abilities which fate had dropped into her lap. Never, though, had she allowed Dax to know that her visions and premonitions had the power to physically drop her in her tracks.

'Stop *looking* at me like that!' she glowered at him, and he realized he was still gaping. 'It's just a precaution! All I've ever got so far is a bruised cheek and a cut lip. And it hardly ever *is* that strong. But this one was . . . and I could tell, so I tied Chrysler up and sat under a tree and just breathed in chocolate gas for about five minutes, and then it came. More of the metallic and concrete and earthy stuff . . . more of the crackling and twisting. Then just Gideon. Gideon sitting alone in a circle of blue lights. And . . . wires and stuff around him. Nothing else. No other people. Wires. And . . . ' Lisa's face crumpled and her voice thickened; her hand went to her throat and she hitched in a breath before whispering, ' . . . *despair.*' Dax stared at her, horrified. He'd never heard the word spoken like that. As if the two syllables were plummeting away into darkness, away from all that was light and warm and good. He put his mug down with a clatter, his hands shaking.

After a few moments, he said, 'Anything else?'

Lisa was looking past him, into the air, and frowning slightly, as if she were planning to paint what she saw and was measuring up.

'Gideon,' she said again. 'He's in trouble. We have to get him somewhere safe. We have to do it soon. It could be . . . days . . . less. I think we may have a day.'

5

Dax stared at Lisa, aghast. 'A day? We've got to get Gideon—and we've got *a day*?'

Lisa continued to stare into the air over his shoulder. 'A day. Not much more. They'll be coming tomorrow—I'm sure of it.'

'Who? Who'll be coming? Lisa—we have to call Owen.'

Lisa's eyes suddenly snapped on to his. 'No,' she said. 'Not Owen. We don't call Owen.'

Dax was dumbfounded. 'Why not?' he said, at length.

'I keep seeing . . . I mean, feeling . . . Oh, I don't know exactly, but it's a really strong feeling, that Owen must not know.'

'Owen is one of us,' said Dax.

'You didn't think that in the spring, did you?' she countered, raising one eyebrow at him. 'You thought he was trying to poison us.'

'I was wrong.'

'Maybe—maybe not. But leave him out of it until we've got Gideon—then we'll try to work it all out.'

Lisa stood up. 'You have to get back. Then you have to get out again at the end of the afternoon and go to Gideon's place. You have his address?'

Dax nodded, and then shook his head, holding up both hands. 'Wait! He's going to have people watching him, same as me.'

'I know,' said Lisa. 'It's a good thing they don't bother with the likes of me, or they might be here by now, after *you*. But it seems like only the telekinetics, glamourists, and shapeshifters are worrying them. All the sweet little mediums and healers are safe enough.'

Dax nodded, slowly. He and Lisa had reached this conclusion during their complicated double conversations on the phone, some time ago. All the Colas were being monitored by their home tutors and calling Control daily, but only the 'risky' ones had the twenty-four hour surveillance going.

'You have to get Gideon to persuade his dad to take him out after his tutor's gone. They have to go to the Angel Centre,' explained Lisa.

'The Angel Centre? Where's that?'

'It's a shopping centre about ten minutes' drive from Gideon and his dad's place. He'll know it. Once you get him there, with his dad, we have a chance of getting him away. You have to get him away from his dad and down to the car park. I'll be waiting there in a car with Evans. He's borrowing his brother's taxi. Then we can get him away—back here at first, and then we can work out what to do next.'

'You've really thought this through, haven't you?' said Dax.

'I haven't been able to *stop* thinking about it for the last twenty-four hours,' sighed Lisa.

'Have you tried to contact Gideon? You know—telepathically.'

Lisa shook her head. 'I have tried, but he doesn't pick it up. He doesn't know what's coming. Dax—I think you have to go now. My tutor will be here soon, so yours will be, too. How are you going to manage that, if you're late?'

Dax told her about the note he'd left for Mr Gibbs. 'He's a good bloke. I think he might not tell on me if I'm just a bit late.' Lisa looked sceptical. 'Well—we'll just have to hope,' concluded Dax, standing up. He picked up and shouldered his backpack.

'You OK to fly all that way back?' asked Lisa, anxiously. 'It's such a long way.'

'I'll be fine,' said Dax. 'You'd better get your dad. I promised him a take-off display.'

Maurice Hardman followed them out on to the sweeping gravel driveway and Dax shook his hand. 'I'll be seeing you back here soon, then,' said Maurice, 'with Gideon.' Dax nodded. 'I don't know what all this is about,' continued the man, 'but if I've learned anything from my daughter over the past couple of years, it's that she is rarely wrong with her premonitions.' He glanced at Lisa who smiled, sadly. 'I think I know somewhere we might take you all, if the powers-that-be come looking for you. After that I'm sure we'll find a way to work it out.'

Dax liked to hear a grown-up voice saying these words. He wished he could squash the flicker of doubt that ran through him. He had a bad feeling about the days ahead and the urge to go to Owen was very strong. He wouldn't, though. Not until they'd got Gideon and worked out what the danger was. Maybe Lisa would agree that they could call him then.

Dax shook off his thoughts and prepared to shift. 'OK,' he said, grinning at Lisa and her dad. 'See you.' He turned into the breeze, ran a few steps and then leapt upwards, shifting instantly into the peregrine falcon. As always, a rush of joy accompanied him high into the air. For his audience's benefit he wheeled around low over the stone fountain in its circular pool in the middle of the gravel driveway. Lisa and her dad whooped with excitement and looked utterly amazed. He did a second arc around the pool and then took off like an arrow, high, high into the sky. He had to get high to find the fastest route through the air. He must get back as soon as he possibly could. His tutor would arrive at the house in a little over two hours.

It was twenty minutes past ten when Dax shot back in through the window. The pink netting was still tugged to one side and his talons grazed the curly blonde nylon hair of a baby doll as he swooped in and landed on the metal bed frame. He shifted instantly and shrugged off his backpack. He was sticky with sweat and shaking with fatigue, but there was little time for gathering himself together. He glanced around quickly and saw that the letter to Mr Gibbs had gone. Should he just walk down, casually, and hope for the best? No! Dax realized, with a gasp of irritation at his stupidity, that he had to be *outside*. When Gina or Alice had found his note earlier, they would have assumed he'd sneaked away to be on his own somewhere outside. He could hardly materialize indoors now. Wondering if he still had it in him, Dax squeezed his eyes shut and shifted once more into the falcon. He flew to the window, checked quickly around him, and then winged it down the garden and dropped to the compost heap behind the shed. Five seconds later a tired-looking boy walked back up the garden and opened the kitchen door.

Gina was there, making a cup of tea, most likely for Mr Gibbs.

'And where do you think *you've* been?' she snapped, the moment she saw him. Dax closed the kitchen door behind him wearily.

'I'm sorry,' he said. 'I had to get out for a bit. I really needed some fresh air.'

'*Really important*, was it?' sneered Gina, squeezing the teabag against the rim of the china mug with a spoon and flinging the small hot missile into the pedal bin. 'You are such a drama queen, Dax. I found your note. Anyone would think you were leaving the country. Well, I just hope you're not in trouble, boy. It's nothing to do with me, if you are. I do my best for you—but you're a law unto yourself. Go on—' She suddenly flapped her hands at him. 'Go on—you've kept him waiting long enough. You'd better get in there and apologize. I'm coming through with tea in just a minute—but don't think *you're* getting any.'

Dax took a deep breath and walked through the hallway. He paused at the dining room door. Something was odd. He could smell it. Through the slightly open door, he could see his letter resting on the table, and long fingers drumming across it impatiently. He didn't need to see the hand to know who it belonged to. His sharp fox sense of smell told him exactly who it was waiting in the dining room, and exactly the mood that person was in.

It was Owen. And Owen was angry.

Dax took another deep breath, trying to steady the sudden quake in the pit of his stomach. Mr Gibbs must have called Owen the minute he'd read the letter—and Owen had come immediately. He gritted his teeth. Why couldn't they just give him the benefit of the doubt for half an hour? There was nothing else for it. Dax pushed the door and walked into the dining room. Owen was sitting on one of the dining chairs, tipping it back in the way that always gets children told off. As soon as Dax entered the chair thudded back onto four legs and Owen stood up. As he pushed the dining room door shut, his eyes raked quickly across Dax, missing nothing: the pallor, the sweatiness, the shake of exhaustion, and the mutinous set of the boy's mouth.

'How far?' he said, his face closed and tough. In his black leather jacket and black jeans he looked like an assassin.

Dax studied his hands and said nothing, but he was shrinking away inside himself. He hated—*hated*—seeing that expression on Owen's face. The anger was bad; the disappointment was far worse.

'C'mon, Dax. I want to know. How far? And how long, for that matter? How long have you been playing dare with the boys outside?'

Dax was startled. He realized Owen was talking about the men on surveillance in the van. 'It—it's not like you think,' he mumbled, sounding weak and pathetic. But it was, in a way. His flight yesterday, before the urgent call from Lisa, was all about playing dare. It had been stupid.

The door clicked open again, and Gina came in with Owen's tea and a plate with three Jammie Dodgers on it. It almost made Dax laugh—hysterically— the way she set it down and simpered at Owen. Her eyelashes *actually fluttered*! Dax suddenly realized, with a revolting certainty, that she fancied Owen. Owen was tall and well built, weather-beaten and good-looking, with arresting blue eyes, which he turned on Gina now, with a tight smile. 'Thank you very much, Mrs Jones,' he said. 'I think Dax could do with some too, if you don't mind.'

Gina shot Dax a *look* but she quickly returned Owen's smile. 'Of course. And call me Gina!' She fluttered back out of the room and Dax and Owen *almost* shared a knowing look. But the situation was too grave and the ghost of the smile on Owen's face vanished swiftly. He sat back down, picked up the letter and turned it over between his fingers, thoughtfully. 'You haven't answered me yet,' he said.

Dax sat down too. 'Honestly,' he said. 'It was just these

last couple of days. Something . . . something came up and I had to get out. On my own. Without Dave and Mike.'

Owen blinked. 'You even know their *names*?'

'Well—yeah. They do talk to each other, you know. And all the electrical gadgets make such a racket. I don't mind really. I know why you've got to do it. I wish you could just trust me, though.'

'Trust you,' said Owen. He reached into his jacket pocket and retrieved something which crackled slightly in his hand. 'Trust you—not to do anything silly?' He raised his hand and dropped a battered bag of Maltesers onto the table.

Dax felt himself blush from his throat to his eyebrows. He buried his face in his hands and through his fingers his voice came out muffled. 'They told you about *that*?'

'Yes. They did. They were under instructions to report anything unusual. And chocolate deliveries from heaven count as unusual in their line of work. Dave did say he was very tempted just to eat them and not mention it, but he really felt it should be reported. Dax—what the hell were you thinking of?'

Dax raised his crimson face but couldn't meet Owen's eyes. 'I'm sorry,' he said, and meant it.

Owen sighed and took a gulp of tea. Gina returned with another mug (chipped and with a crack) for Dax. No biscuits. As soon as she'd gone, Owen pushed the plate of Jammie Dodgers over to him. 'Get them down you, for God's sake! You look like you're about to pass out.' Dax ate them gratefully, but without much pleasure.

'What's happening, Dax?' said Owen, more calmly now. 'Why are you going AWOL? I came here to tell you off for a quick flight round the neighbourhood, only to find you vanished. I imagine you've been a bit further than the corner shop this time.'

Dax opened his mouth to tell Owen about going to see Lisa, but there was a pulse of memory in his head. Lisa had said he mustn't speak even to *Owen* about her warnings over Gideon. Dax could not believe Owen was anything to do with any threat to their friend—but maybe he was involved without knowing it. Dax needed to be sure before he said anything. It went totally against his instincts, but he knew he would have to lie.

'I—I was going a bit crazy,' he said, looking hard into his tea. 'Have you seen my room?' Owen nodded and grimaced. 'Well—it's all Gina and Alice and dolls and Gina and Alice and dolls—and . . . '

'I get the picture,' said Owen.

'I really have tried to be normal—for weeks. I admit I've shifted to the fox sometimes, when I've been on my own in the house, but nobody's seen me.'

'Are you sure about that?'

'Of course,' insisted Dax. 'Gina and Alice don't know yet. I just don't . . . trust them enough to show them yet. I suppose they'll have to know one day, but I want my dad to know first.'

Owen nodded.

'Anyway,' Dax went on. 'I just got really wound up and I couldn't help it. I had to have a little fly around the woods. I was really careful . . . right up until the Maltesers bit. I just perched on the van for a while, heard Dave going on about them, and then . . . well, OK, it was a bit stupid.'

Owen sighed. 'And this morning? Were you planning to drop in a Cadbury's variety pack this time? A box of Milk Tray? A small hamper from Marks & Spencer?'

'No—I just needed to get out again. I was always coming back, but . . . ' He saw the letter still in Owen's hand, and realized it was going to be difficult to explain. His mind worked furiously for a plausible explanation and the shelf behind Owen's chair provided it just in time. A small collection of his nature books were stacked on it, including the one on British birds. There was a page on peregrine falcons and their habits.

'I needed to get to the sea, you see,' he heard himself lying. 'I think it's the peregrine thing. Like, I need to get to the woods for the fox thing, but that's quite easy and at least I can smell the wood from my window. Peregrines like to be by the coast, though. I first shifted to a falcon by the sea, remember? It's like . . . an instinct. I just kept thinking I needed a little bit of time by the sea.'

Owen nodded slowly and Dax wasn't sure whether he was accepting this. He pushed on anyway, loathing himself as the lies multiplied.

'So I flew down to the south coast. Along the New Forest shoreline and over to the Isle of Wight. I didn't know how long it would take, so I thought I'd better leave Mr Gibbs a note . . . just in case.'

Owen drained the last of his tea and stood up. He looked hard at Dax and, again, Dax couldn't be sure if he believed him or not. The lies burned inside him. Eventually Owen said, 'OK. Fine. But it stops here—now. Do you understand me?' Dax nodded. 'No. You don't,' said Owen. 'I don't think you understand me at all. Why do you think those poor guys are stuck out there every day? For fun? Do you think all I'm worried about is you going off on little sightseeing tours? Right now, we have about three weeks to go before we can get all the Colas back under one roof, under proper protection and guidance. You're all dotted across the UK like unexploded bombs. Sooner or later, one of you is going to blow it for all of us. You don't like the constraints you're under now? You have *no idea*, Dax, how hard it is for me and Paulina Sartre to convince the government that your freedom and your normal life is as important as your safety.

'There are people that I work with who think the logical thing to do with Colas is keep them in an underground bunker—for the good of national security. Fortunately, these are not the people I'm answerable to. But right now, I can see their point.'

Dax gulped. Owen sounded way too serious.

'You also have no idea how many pigeon fanciers there are in Hampshire.'

Dax blinked. He didn't know *what* Owen was talking about.

'Peregrine falcons are the most efficient pigeon killers on the planet,' explained Owen. 'And some pigeon fanciers have been known to shoot or poison peregrines, to protect their racing stock. Remember that, next time you fancy cruising down to the coast.' He stuffed the letter and the Maltesers back in his pocket.

'Don't give me any more cause for concern, Dax. Please.' And he strode out of the room, down the hallway, calling goodbye to Gina as he opened the front door, and was gone.

6

Dax felt small. Unworthy. He hoped that Lisa could justify to him why he had just spun a total fiction to someone whose opinion mattered to him more than anyone else he could think of.

Mr Gibbs had been sent home for the day, Alice was at school, and Gina was cleaning the house noisily, bashing china and cutlery around in the kitchen and then vacuuming so vigorously she chipped paint off the skirting boards. Dax had no idea what *she* was so worked up about.

He sat on the stairs and tried to think above the racket of the vacuum cleaner. No more shifting, if he was to do as he was told. He tracked back carefully through his conversation with Owen and was relieved to find that he hadn't actually promised, at any point, that he wouldn't shift again. At least he wasn't going to break his word—and if Lisa was right about whatever warnings she was getting, then he could explain to Owen later why he couldn't bring him in on it. He looked at his watch. If he was to carry out Lisa's audacious plan, he guessed he would need to go at about three o'clock. It would be a good time to exit, as Gina would have gone to fetch Alice from school, and he would arrive at Gideon's, if his falcon-flying calculations were correct, at about 4 p.m. Gideon's tutor would have left, and he would be able to ask his dad about going out to the shopping centre. If Dax could persuade him that it was important enough.

There were altogether too many 'ifs' in this plan, thought Dax. He would have to get a really good lunch inside him for yet another flight. A tremor of anxiety ran through him when he thought of Owen. Cheating his trust felt so bad. Yet, if Lisa, who also looked up to Owen, felt this was necessary, he couldn't take the chance.

Gina went out at the end of the morning, telling him to get his own lunch. Dax smothered a grin: it was exactly what he'd been hoping for. 'Will you be back before getting Alice?' he asked, casually.

'Probably not,' she said, shortly. 'But if I do come back I don't expect to find you watching TV and lounging around. Do some study or something. If you get in any more trouble they'll sling you out of your posh school before you even get to the new one, and there's not enough room for you around here all the time.'

Dax couldn't agree more. Gina had received information from the government about the wrecking of Tregarren College in a 'freak storm surge', explaining that the new premises were being fitted out immediately. She hadn't a clue that every student and teacher had almost been wiped out on their last night in Cornwall; almost certainly would have been if it hadn't been for Dax, Lisa, and Luke. Luke had been the one who really saved them though, thought Dax, his throat tightening with sadness as he saw again Gideon's twin brother, his face a mask of pain, holding back the sea as it hung above them all, giving them time to flee while his sister clawed at his hair and screamed with fury. Seconds later, both were gone, along with the college, and Gideon was an only child again.

Dax made himself a double cheese toasty, using four bits of thick bread and nearly half the cheese in the fridge. He washed it down with a mug of tea and then followed that with two bananas. He'd have to get a few more snacks down before three o'clock. He had two hours yet to fill. His backpack was ready and he'd pored over the map of southern England several times, double checking where Gideon was, and memorizing landmarks that he'd be able to see from the air. He'd been to Gideon's house once before and remembered there was a children's playground in the park opposite. That would be a help.

He checked his bag again and then sat on his bed, ticking over with anxiety and excitement, wishing the time away. When the doorbell rang he jolted. After a few seconds, he ran down the stairs and peered through the spyhole. A bespectacled face loomed up at him as if on the back of a spoon. Dax chuckled with amazement and yanked the door open. 'Clive! Wow! I didn't know you were back!'

His old schoolfriend grinned and shuffled self-consciously with pleasure at seeing Dax again. 'We got back last night and it's a teacher training day at school today,' he explained, pushing his black-rimmed glasses up his nose a notch and scratching his mousy hair. 'I was hoping you'd still be here. Thought you might have been sent on to the new school.'

'Nah—it's not ready yet. Come in! I've got so much to t—' Dax abruptly shut himself up and then shook his head meaningfully at Clive. 'Kitchen,' he said. 'I'll make you a cup of tea.' Clive followed him in and watched, perplexed, as Dax put the washing machine into a spin cycle and started bashing kitchen utensils around. Over the weeks Dax had worked out that if the guys outside were doing any kind of electronic sweep of the house, listening in, the kitchen was the hardest place to pick up anything. Too much metal, machinery, and general hubbub.

Clive knew about Dax—he was the only person (other than a reporter called Caroline Fisher) in Bark's End who did. He had witnessed his friend's second ever shapeshift, after he'd been chased into the school basement by bullies and Dax had run in to help him. The anger which had crashed through Dax at the sight of his poor, beaten-up friend, bullied just for being clever, had brought about the shift. In those days, he'd had no control over it at all. The bullies were astonished and terrified to find themselves under attack from a wild animal, and mystery had shrouded the truth of 'The Beast of Bark's End School' ever since. Clive had had a much easier time afterwards. One of the bullies never came back and the other turned into what Gina would call 'a perfect lamb'. Well, he was heard to bleat occasionally, anyway.

Clive sat down at the kitchen table and stared at Dax. 'Go on!' he said. 'Do it!'

Dax, glancing around to check that neither Mike nor Dave were on a tiptoe trail around the house, quickly shifted into the fox. Clive stared, his mouth falling open. He'd seen it before, but never ceased to be utterly transfixed. At first he'd been afraid, fearing that Dax was some kind of dark shaman or an evil 'skinwalker', which he'd learned about from reading the shapeshifting legends of the Navajo indians. He closed his mouth, gulped, and nodded.

'Now the second one,' he said and Dax leapt, still as a fox, up onto the other kitchen chair, putting his paws on the back of it. As he shifted, he felt his talons tighten for a steady grip and the vision of the room around him flexed into something he could probably never explain to his friend. The depth and detail of what he could see was beyond any human capability. From the ants scrambling along the kickboard of the back door to the starling two miles away to the east, flickering in the top pane of the kitchen window, Dax saw every living thing that moved—and knew precisely how fast it would need to be to escape him.

Clive's mouth was agape again. Dax flew back to the floor and returned to boy form as he landed. 'Did you know,' began Clive, breathlessly, 'that the peregrine falcon could be the fastest animal on earth? They've been clocked going at more than 140 mph! And that when they dive, they don't just dive—they can corkscrew and go even faster than gravity! And they can snap their prey's spine with a single crunch of their beak! And that—'

Dax laughed. 'Yeah! Yeah—I looked them up too.'

'And their eyesight!' went on Clive, caught up in his marvelling. 'They see everything about ten times faster than we do. If you, like, throw me a ball, then I'll have a split second to see it and catch it. Well—not *actually* catch it in my case, obviously.' Clive was as rubbish at games as he was brilliant at science. 'Well, a peregrine can see it, work out how big it is, what size it is, what trajectory it's on, if it's dead or alive, whether it's heavy or light, how much it cost down Woolworth's and *still* have time to read the paper before catching it! That's how fast they are. Wow! Have you been out flying since you got back?'

Dax nodded, biting his lip. He thought he could safely tell Clive about what was happening, but since he'd got the warnings from Lisa he was worried about saying anything to anyone. He didn't want to put his friend in danger. 'Come on,' he said, checking his watch. 'I've got about an hour before I have to go out. Let's go for a walk. I need chocolate and stuff.'

They ambled down the road, past the dark blue Transit van with its hidden occupants, and Dax tried not to look at it as they headed towards the corner shop. He knew that Mike and Dave would have to get out shortly and shadow him if he went too far from the house. By the time they'd come back out of the shop with pockets full of sweets, and turned towards the small recreation ground near the senior school where Clive now went,

Dax's professional shadows were in place, discreetly tailing them. Dax was relaxed about it. At least they were getting some exercise today.

As he and Clive lolled around by the metal mesh fencing at the edge of the rec, Mike was checking over a car with a For Sale sign in the back, while Dave had walked straight past them and was now easing himself into the doorway of an estate agent's and studying house prices. They were actually quite good, thought Dax, because nobody else ever seemed to notice them. They were nondescript men in nondescript clothes. You couldn't do the job if you stood out, he guessed. It wasn't their fault that he had souped-up senses. He even knew what they smelt like.

'How was Poland?' Dax asked Clive, who had just returned from a holiday out there. Only Clive's parents, intelligent and remote, would take him on holiday to Poland.

'Not bad,' said Clive. 'Cars are a bit weird.'

'Made anything recently?'

'Hmmm—not much. An irrigation system for my Venus flytraps. Solar-powered. So when the sun really gets hot and they start drying out, it also fills up the batteries and then flips the switch for running the water.'

Dax shook his head, grinning. Clive was a genius. He had no Cola powers but his brain for science and engineering was incredible. He was in top sets for every subject at school, and had even represented the county in a British Association of Young Scientists contest that year—winning, of course, with his water-powered engine.

'Hey! Boffin!' Two boys, who looked about fourteen or fifteen, vaulted over the fence and walked past them.

'Hi,' said Clive, smiling weakly and flapping a hand at them.

'Got any dough, Boffin?' said one, peering down at them. 'I'm out of fags.'

'No,' sighed Clive. 'You know I haven't. I never have any money.' This was true enough. It never occurred to Clive's parents to give him any.

'Well, why don't you make one of your machines, and get it to churn out cash?' said the other boy, shoving at Clive's leg with his foot.

'Yeah, one day,' said Clive. He was trying to be cool, thought Dax, and making a much better job of it than he used to. The boys, obviously from his school, weren't like Toby and Matthew, their old junior school bullies. They didn't seriously have it in for him; Dax could smell no violence on them. But they were bored and bothered by his cleverness and would pick him apart in seconds if they felt like it.

'That would be cool,' said the second boy, and sniggered. 'You think you can be cool, eh, Boffin?' Clive said nothing and Dax watched silently, weighing up what was happening.

'Yeah—he's well cool,' said the first boy, but as if he were talking to a toddler. 'Look at his clothes!'

Dax winced for his friend. Clive was wearing a faded

yellow T-shirt with a cartoon hedgehog on it, brown corduroy trousers, and brown clunky shoes. He had never had the faintest idea about fashion and really had no notion at all that he ever looked eccentric.

'He's cooler than you'll ever be,' said Dax, suddenly, stung for his friend. He felt Clive tense next to him, willing him to shut up. The two boys looked at each other and grinned. Here was entertainment. They both sat down, cross-legged, on the rough grass by the fence.

'Go on then—how's he cool?' asked the first.

'Well, he's already working for the government, for a start,' said Dax, wondering what on earth he was doing, but apparently unable to stop himself babbling.

'Yeah, right!'

'Yep. It's true. You'd better not pass this on.' Dax looked at them hard and saw that their expressions of disbelief were faltering just slightly. He looked back at Clive. 'Sorry, mate,' he said. 'Can we trust them? Are they all right?'

Clive stared at him as if he'd gone bonkers, and then looked back at the two older boys. 'Yeah,' he said slowly. 'They probably are all right. You still shouldn't have said, though.'

'It's the science stuff,' said Dax, leaning towards the two boys. 'You know about that, right?' They nodded, uncertainly. 'Well, he's hit upon something so—so *incredible*, that they've had to bring in protection for him while he works on it.'

'Yeah, right,' said the first boy again, tittering, but looking around him at the same time.

'Don't believe me?' said Dax. 'See that guy over by the car, behind me? *Don't* turn your head—be careful!' They both moved their heads slowly, staring agog at Mike who was checking over the tyres of the car now.

'Now look—slowly—to the right. Is there a fair-haired bloke by the estate agent's?' They looked and nodded now, mouths falling open. 'That's them. Don't approach them. Just watch. We're trusting you, because I think Clive needs other people to look out for him, too. I can't be around much and I'm not at your school.'

The boys were staring at him now, amazed. He didn't know if it would last. 'We're going now, but you stay here and watch,' said Dax, getting up and pulling Clive to his feet. 'Keep watching them and you'll see, they'll start to tail us back down the road. Like I said—*don't* approach them. You'll blow their cover and Clive will get it in the neck. And you'll look out for him, yeah? At school?'

The first boy looked directly into Dax's eyes and his mouth set firm. 'All right,' he said. 'We will.' Dax and Clive turned the corner of the fencing, back onto the road, and walked back. The older boys stayed where they were, watching, absorbed. And sure enough, discreetly, a minute later, Dave and Mike walked back behind them.

As soon as the front door was closed, Dax and Clive collapsed, hissing and snorting with laughter, onto the floor. Dax laughed so hard he was in tears. 'You sh-shouldn't . . . h-h-have done that!' gurgled Clive.

'They believed me! Mike and Dave did a perfect job!'

Clive sat up and mopped his face with a cotton hanky

with a C embroidered on it (there was no hope for him, really). 'I've got to get back,' he sighed, happily. 'Will I see you later this week?'

Dax's laughter subsided as he remembered what he had to do next. He didn't know when he'd see Clive again. 'I don't know,' he said, truthfully. 'Clive—if . . . if you don't see me for a while, just . . .'

'What?' said Clive, suddenly picking up Dax's tone. 'What's happening?'

Dax looked at him for a few seconds and then said, 'Stuff's always happening to me, these days. I never know what will be next.' He got up and rested his hand on the door latch. 'I'll see you, though. Soon, I hope. Look after yourself.'

Clive looked at him soberly. 'I know stuff's always going to happen to you,' he said. He reached inside Dax's collar and found the chain with the key, underneath, which he pulled out and weighed in his hand for a few seconds. Dax blinked. He hadn't thought Clive had noticed, but the boy looked from the key to the eyes of his friend and said, 'Remember, though, you need people like me, too.' It was an odd thing to say.

Clive left and Dax went up to his room and ate all the sweets and chocolate in his pockets, although it was the last thing he felt like doing: his stomach was clenched with nervous excitement. He didn't write another note. He put on his backpack, opened the window, and checked his watch once more. 3 p.m. It was time to find Gideon.

7

Gideon had been through an amazing and terrible year. As Dax found the warm thermals and rose high above the Hampshire countryside, he wondered, again, how his friend was coping.

In the spring, Gideon had discovered that he had a twin brother—the quiet, untalented Luke. Days later, the entire college had been astounded to meet their *sister*. After twelve years on the planet as an only child, Gideon had abruptly found himself one of three. He had loved it. Dax had not. The arrival of the triplets brought with it an uprising of jealousy in Dax which still made him squirm with shame, but his troubled instincts about Catherine— the third of the Reader children—had proved to be horrifyingly correct.

Catherine's Cola power had been her ability to leech off the others—although none of them had realized it for a long time. Catherine was so sweet and friendly, given to hugging and kissing—and all the while she was literally sapping the energy and the talent from the Colas around her, showing off first one paranormal trick, then another. It seemed that physical contact was all she needed and nobody understood why they felt so exhausted after an encounter with Gideon's bright and sparkly new sister.

Catherine may have been friendly and charming, but she was also insanely jealous—and capable of much worse than theft. Because she couldn't keep hold of her stolen abilities, she had decided to kill off every Cola she stole from in one terrible evening, so she could own their powers permanently. She would have been successful, but she didn't know about Luke. Nobody had known. Luke had shown no Cola power at all, but when the moment of death for them all arrived, he had simply erupted with telekinetic talent. He had saved every Cola and all the Tregarren staff from being swept to their death by a twisted, raging sea. Quiet, ordinary Luke saved them all.

But nobody had saved Luke. He and Catherine had both been lost under a deluge of seawater and tumbled ruins. It made Dax's throat tighten to think of it even now; more, to remember Gideon's face when he had heard that he was, once again, an only child.

Across the summer months, at home with his dad and the daily tutor, Gideon had made a good effort not to dwell on what he'd found and lost and their regular phone conversations had been cheery and full of silly Gideon humour. Only occasionally, when a silence reigned for a second or two longer than was usual for Gideon, did Dax detect the sorrow that rode on his back, breathing heavy grey vapours of despondency onto Gideon's shoulders. This was the image Dax received, during those occasional silences, and he wished badly that he was a healer, like Mia, and could send some comfort.

Now, shaking off the grey vapours image, Dax

reminded himself that he had a mission of a more practical kind. He had to get Gideon away—and with Gideon's own set of government agents undoubtedly watching, it wasn't going to be easy. First he must persuade Gideon that it had to happen, when he didn't even know why himself.

Within an hour he was hovering over the recreation ground opposite Gideon's small terraced house. He turned a wide arc around the green below him and coasted down towards the yellow brick house, trying to remember where Gideon's bedroom window was and hoping that it was open. The front window was closed, and Dax thought it was Gideon's dad's in any case. He flew over the ridge of the roof and down to the top of the shed in the back garden. Here he turned and scrutinized the open window at the back. He was sure it was Gideon's room. He could hear a radio in it. He took off and landed again, a second later, talons gripping the plastic windowsill tightly. Gideon was playing a console game and listening to the radio, looking greenish in the light from the monitor on his small desk. Dax paused and watched his friend for a moment, fondly noting the familiar tufty blond hair, sticking out in all directions as if he'd just rolled out of bed. He shook his feathers and then politely commented: 'Careeeet.' It was a peregrine greeting.

Gideon swung round in his chair and then his eyes and mouth widened in surprise and delight. *'Dax!'* he whispered. Dax waited a while before shifting, knowing that Gideon wanted to take in his bird form—he'd only seen it once, from a distance. Gideon grinned and marvelled, stepping across to the windowsill to touch his fingers lightly on the grey and white feathers around the falcon's yellow-rimmed eyes and then trace the vicious but perfect curve of its beak.

When he stepped back, Dax shifted to a boy, sitting on the windowsill—and then stepped across and whacked up the volume on the radio. The surveillance equipment somewhere nearby was prickling in his ears. 'Hello, mate,' he said, leaning close to Gideon to be heard. 'Get your stuff. I've come to get you out of here.'

Gideon wasn't as surprised as Dax had expected. Lisa had called him, he'd said, and attempted a strange conversation about very ordinary things. All the while he'd been speaking to her he'd been aware of her buffeting his subconscious with warnings. He didn't pick up telepathy like Dax did, but when Lisa really put her mind to it, she could get *something* across to almost anyone. It was just a question of whether they could work out what it was.

'So that's what Hardman was squawking about in my brain,' he muttered, after Dax had brought him up to date on the events of the last two days. 'She doesn't know what's up, though, does she?'

Dax shook his head. 'Come on! Since when have the spirits been *that* helpful to any one of us? It's never anything nice and clear, is it? We always have to work for it.'

'It's the Loved-Ones' Buffer,' said Gideon, unexpectedly.

'What?'

'Lisa explained it to me once. The Loved-Ones' Buffer is the interference you get when you actually *care* about the people you're trying to help, she said. The more you care, the harder it is to make any sense of the stuff that comes through. That's why she's brilliant at helping people she doesn't care about, but a bit rubbish when it comes to us. Quite touching, really. LOB.'

Dax grinned. It was a perfect explanation. Then he steadied his face and said earnestly: 'She told me they're coming to get you. She didn't say who, but I get the feeling it's the government.'

'The government? But they're the ones watching out for me! That's what the tutors and the Control business is all about, yeah? And the phone tapping. To make sure we stay safe . . . So why should I be bothered about the government?'

Dax shook his head and tutted. 'Gideon! Don't you remember? When I first got to Cola Club *you* were the one saying "Ooo-er! They won't let us on the internet! They're scared of us! They think I might bring down a jet!" You *loved* it. And now you don't believe it.'

Gideon was silent. He turned around and snapped the computer game off and then sat heavily back in his chair, looking a bit queasy. 'Why now, though?' he murmured, half to himself as the radio thumped out a cheesy 80s hit.

'I don't know. Something's changed,' said Dax, leaning closer and talking even lower into his friend's ear. 'And whoever it is coming for you, government or not, it's not a good thing. That's what Lisa's picking up on. We have to go. This afternoon. Now.'

'What about my dad?' asked Gideon.

Dax thought for a moment. 'Trouble is, Gid,' he said, 'I think he might try to stop you. I don't know if he'll believe us. If he decides to stop you, we're done for. We need his help to get to the shopping centre.'

'The shopping centre? This is hardly the time for buying stuff!' snorted Gideon.

'Lisa will meet up with us there,' said Dax. 'We have a plan. You just need to get us to the shopping centre; your dad needs to drive us there.'

'Us? How are we going to get *you* there? He's going to want to know what's going on.'

'I know,' said Dax, who'd been working out the finer details of the plan during his flight. 'I'll shift back to the falcon and you'll have to hide me in your backpack. Along with all the stuff you might need—a torch and a change of pants and so on.'

Gideon nodded. He began to gather his backpack stuff—a few notes and coins from his piggy bank, a torch, a woolly hat, a mac, and some underwear and socks—and two big bars of chocolate from his bedside drawer. He looked pale as he put the backpack on his bed.

'Just have to go and convince Dad now,' he mumbled, looking very unsure. 'You really think this is necessary?'

Dax nodded gravely. 'You might want to write him a note before we go. Find a way of getting it in his pocket or something,' said Dax. He realized that it was much harder for Gideon to cut and run from his father than it was for him to desert Gina and Alice. Gid's dad was great, and had also suffered much in the past few weeks, with the discovery and then the loss of two more children. 'It probably won't be for long. Just until we can find out what's happening . . . ' He knew he was babbling. He hadn't a clue what was going to happen next. There was only one plan in his mind, and it involved the key on a chain around his neck.

Gideon found some notepaper and scrawled: *Dad—please don't worry. I'm with friends and I'm safe. Something weird is happening and I'm safer away from you for a bit. I'll let you know what's going on as soon as I can. Please—please—don't tell anyone I've gone, for as long as you can.*

Love Gideon

'It won't take them long to know you've gone,' said Dax. 'You're under surveillance, you know.'

Gideon looked astonished. 'What—men in vans and stuff? Watching *me*?'

'Well, they've been watching *me*—and you're much more of a risk than I am. So, yeah—out in a van or maybe in the top floor of a house over the road. I can hear them now, and I'll hear them following us as we go. And I'll smell them when they tail you on foot. Don't worry. We'll find a way to lose them.'

Gideon was looking even more nervous now. He took a

deep breath and focused hard on his bookshelf. A stack of hardbacks on it rose steadily, perfectly balanced, into the air. They almost touched the ceiling, and then, just as steadily, sank back down to rest on the shelf. Dax realized it was a kind of meditation for Gideon. He was impressed. His friend's control had grown much, much stronger. Gideon blinked and lifted his chin, looking more like his old self. 'OK,' he said, opening his bedroom door. 'Here goes.'

The inside of the backpack was dark and cramped and smelt strongly of old plimsolls. Gideon had obviously been using it for sports gear of some kind. Dax sank his talons into the balled-up socks and kept his head down, peering out of a gap beneath the strap at the top of the bag. Gideon had carefully placed the backpack between his feet, in the passenger footwell of the car, and the engine rumbled through it as Gideon chatted to his dad about some CD he wanted to buy with his pocket money. Fortunately, Michael Reader had agreed that a wander around the shopping centre would do them both good. He was an IT consultant and working from home while Gideon was back. He was weary of his desk.

'What d'you want to bring your bag for?' he asked, and Dax tensed, his talons snagging deeper into the socks.

Gideon replied, 'Oh, I wanted to bring my money in it. I've got a lot of coins and they make my pockets go funny.' It wasn't very convincing, but Gideon's dad seemed to accept it.

Gideon had no intention of spending any of his money on CDs. He knew he might need every penny once they were on the run. Soon the car was parked and Gideon was carefully shouldering the bag containing his best friend. Dax could see the bright lights of the shopping centre and hear the babble of the late afternoon crowd. Although his sight, as a falcon, was breathtakingly sharp, his hearing and scenting were nothing like as good as when he was a fox, so he couldn't yet detect the agents who were undoubtedly tailing them.

'Gideon, why are you wearing that hat in here?' asked his dad, bemused. Gideon was wearing the woolly hat from his backpack. It had ear flaps and a peak and made him look a bit like a lumberjack.

Gideon laughed and said, 'Dad! Don't you know *anything* about what everyone's wearing these days? This is cool!'

'Looks pretty hot to me,' came back a wry murmur, but Gideon kept his hat on, and he had very good reason to. He convinced his dad to stop for a burger and chips at one of the fast-food outlets on the top floor. As they sat down he began to sneeze, loudly, jolting Dax sharply in the bag still on his back. *He's really giving this his all*, thought Dax, struggling to stay upright.

'I think I'm coming down with a cold,' said Gideon, before launching into another fit of nasal explosions. He picked up some napkins and snuffled into them. 'Oh-oh!' he said. 'Dose bleed!' Dax caught a whiff of ketchup and marvelled at Gideon's quick thinking. 'No—you waid here wid da food,' Gideon was saying. 'I'll just go doo da doilet. Back idabit. Ged subbor dissue . . . '

Dax could picture what was happening, bumping along on his friend's back. Gideon was stumbling off, still sneezing occasionally, holding the tomato sauce spattered napkins to his nose. He made straight for the gents and headed into a cubicle. As soon as the door was closed he shut the lid down on the toilet and hoisted Dax out of the bag, wincing as his best friend's talons bit into his balled fist. He said nothing, but did a couple more sneezes and added a fluey groan. Dax shifted quickly and awkwardly in the small space and the boys silently got to work. Inside a minute, with Gideon still faking the occasional sneeze and snuffle, they were in each other's clothes. Gideon was now wearing Dax's aged jeans and pale blue T-shirt, his peaked cap on his head and old trainers pinching slightly on his feet. Dax, meanwhile, wore Gideon's baggy black jogging pants and black trainers, his bright green sweatshirt, and his ludicrous lumberjack's hat. Dax handed over his green backpack, and picked up Gideon's red and blue one. He also collected the squadgy mound of ketchup-stained napkins, along with another roll of toilet paper. They grinned at each other. Gideon was about to open the door when Dax held up his finger and shook his head. Instantly, he shifted to a fox, sitting on the toilet lid, and listened.

He immediately picked up the interaction of the men who were on surveillance duty for Gideon. They were not, thankfully, *in* the toilets with them, but one was posted immediately outside, as far as Dax could tell. In fact he could smell the low-level stress on the man, but there was no high alert; the men obviously felt everything was under control. Good. He shifted back.

'Right—I'll go first. The car's down on the ground floor level—by the lifts—OK? It's a black taxi. Tell them to have the back windows open,' he whispered to Gideon, who was jiggling about excitedly. He opened the cubicle door and Gideon touched his shoulder. Looking back, Dax saw the note Gideon had written to his dad; he hadn't given it to him yet. Damn! He took it, not sure he could deliver it.

Dax stepped outside. Nobody else was in the gents, which was a great relief. He picked up the large rosette of ketchuppy napkins and mashed them into his face, snuffling just like Gideon, the hat pulled down low over his brow and covering his dark hair completely. He was glad he and his friend were roughly the same height and build. As soon as he was out he was aware of one of Gideon's shadows on his left, reading a paper by a drinks vending machine. He turned sharply right and headed back in the direction of Gideon's dad. Michael Reader was still at the burger bar table, eating chips and idly looking around. Dax headed back to him, clutching the note in his hand, and as soon as he drew level with the man, shoved the note right in his pocket.

'Sorry,' he burbled, through the sticky mess against his face. 'Got to go.'

Before Gideon's dad even had time to react, Dax took to his heels. He pelted across the food outlets floor and straight towards the escalators, deliberately knocking over a chair as he went. Helpfully, Michael Reader stood up and yelled, 'Gideon! Gid! What the bl—?'

One second later a man in a grey jacket and jeans shot past him and tore after Dax. Perfect! Dax threw himself down the escalator, abandoning his napkin mask and squeezing past shoppers and their bags. He jumped the last six steps, hit the lower floor running and sprinted down the wide indoor avenue of fashion stores and boutiques. In the middle of the shopping centre was a glass and chrome spiral staircase, mostly for show, but used by shoppers who couldn't be bothered to wait for the lifts or the escalators. Dax made straight for it, now aware that Gideon's second shadow was closing in on his right. He hurtled up the steps, turning up and up in a tight corkscrew, battling past people and ignoring their sharp rebukes as he bashed into their bags and shoulders. He could smell the hot urgency now pulsing up from the nearest man pursuing him, but didn't look down.

Back up a level, to the food outlets floor, Dax now headed left to a balcony area that held a row of tables with umbrellas, where people could sit outside, drinking coffee and eating cakes while they looked across the town. He sprinted past them and leapt up onto the railing at the far end. On the other side of this was a long trough of plants which trailed ornamentally over the edge of a fifteen metre drop to the street below. He heard women scream and a man shout and willed himself not to look back. They had to believe he was Gideon. Dax dropped onto the plants beyond the railing. Another shout rang out, and the rapid chatter of a two-way radio perhaps three metres from him. Dax took a deep breath and then leapt off the balcony.

8

They *had* left the window open and the engine was idling. It was just as well. They needed every second. Dax had shifted the moment he judged he had fallen out of view and then upended himself into a classic peregrine corkscrew, falling faster than gravity should allow, to pull up a metre from the pavement and shoot sideways through the open arches of the car park beneath the shopping centre. He flew like an arrow between concrete pillars, inches below the undulating ducting and cabling of the low ceiling and found the cab, its black bodywork painted orange by the cheap strip lighting. He entered the car so fast that he crashed into Gideon's shoulder. Before he'd even had a chance to shift, the electric window had slid up and the car was moving. Lisa was in the front seat next to Evans, turning to stare back at him in awe.

'You did it! You both did it!'

'Well, what did you expect? Of course we did it!' said Gideon, looking cocky and impressed with himself, but not quite managing to stop his teeth chattering or to stop puffing. He'd had to run as fast as Dax, down the back stairs, to get to the car. He'd only got in thirty seconds before the falcon shot into his shoulder. Dax shifted, let out a shaky sigh, and sank back into the leather seat. His heart was racing so fast he thought it might burst right out through his chest.

'You all right, mate?' said Gideon as they left the car park and sped away onto the ring road that led west.

Dax nodded, still breathing hard. 'I just threw you to your death,' he grunted.

Gideon grinned, then a more sober look fell across his freckled face and his pale green eyes dropped to his hands. 'Do you think Dad'll know . . . that I'm OK?'

'Of course he will,' said Dax. 'I shoved your note in his pocket just before I ran. Did you see those men take off after me?'

'I saw one,' said Gideon. 'I didn't really believe you until I saw him go. It was like something out of James Bond. You should've seen his face.'

'Well, *you* shouldn't have!' said Lisa, tartly. 'You should have been keeping your head down and getting right down to us!'

'I *did*!' protested Gideon. 'I got here, didn't I?'

'Hmmm,' said Lisa. Dax could see she was very anxious. Her dark eyes glittered with agitation and she kept fiddling with one of her blonde plaits.

'What now?' said Gideon.

'We take you back to Somerset,' said Lisa.

'But won't they think of looking there?'

'We're not going to the manor,' said Lisa, rolling her eyes. 'We're not *completely* stupid, you know. There's a flat in Taunton. My dad'll meet us there and we'll work out what to do next. The main thing was to get you away.'

Gideon grinned at her and folded his arms. 'My saviour!' he sighed. 'Anything else coming through the LOB yet?'

'No—the LOB doesn't apply where you're concerned!' she said, narrowing her eyes at him. 'Stuff has to come through the SLOB for *you*—the Sadly Lame One's Buffer.'

Dax laughed. It was good to hear Lisa and Gideon bickering again. He had missed it. They drove on for several minutes before a siren sounded and two ambulances and a police car flashed by in the eastbound lane. They all caught their breath.

'They were quick,' said Dax. Lisa looked anxious again. This didn't bother him. What *did* bother him was that she was rubbing her left shoulder and looking past him. He and Gideon exchanged glances and waited.

Lisa said nothing but her eyes grew hazy and opaque and when she spoke, it was with a worrying slur, as if she was drunk. 'Evaaansh,' she said.

The butler, who had remained silent but alert since Dax had arrived, shot her a concerned glance. 'Miss?' he said, changing up a gear.

Lisa swayed slightly and then wiped her brow. 'We have . . . ' She broke off and then flopped back in her seat, raising one hand to the hanging strap above the cab door. Her hand shook and then gripped it tightly, as if she was trying to wrestle back control from whatever was channelling through her. Gideon and Dax sat forward, worried. Lisa coughed and sounded like herself again. Her words came out sharply.

'Turn round, Evans. Next exit. We have to go back.'

'Go *back*?' exclaimed Gideon. 'Are you *nuts*? We've only just escaped! The centre will be crawling with . . . er . . . Special Branch or something! Won't it, Dax?'

Lisa turned round again and there was a fine sweat on her face, although her colour was normal. 'No. Not to the centre. We're turning round at the next exit—and off at the one after that. I think. I'm pretty sure. I . . . I thought it was only Gideon we'd come for, but it's not.'

'It's not?' queried Gideon.

'No. Sorry everyone, but we need to head back towards London. We have to get Mia.'

The monolithic grey slab rose from a cheerless landscape of tarmac and stunted grey trees.

Dax couldn't believe Mia lived in this block of flats; that a life force as warm and lovely as hers could be contained in something so cold and ugly and functional. The windows that allowed a little light out of the block were all of the wire mesh variety: safety glass. They looked like rows and rows of cages.

'What floor is she on?' asked Dax, as the cab engine idled behind them and Evans waited in the front seat, tense and watchful. Gideon walked across to a steel panel on the wall beside the entrance to the block. Squinting past a smear of what might have been ice cream, he counted twenty floors, each with eight flats.

Lisa said nothing. She just paced a slow circle, as if in meditation, over the uneven slabs of paving and their polka dots of spat-out chewing gum. Then she raised her eyes high—almost to the top of the building. 'Floor seventeen,' she said, and pointed to a window which glowed an orangey-red shade through its drawn curtain. 'I don't know the number, but I'll know it when I see the front door.'

'How do we get in?' said Gideon. 'It's got an intercom thing, and you have to punch in the number of the flat you want.'

'If we wait,' suggested Dax, 'someone will come out and we can slip in past them.'

They walked to the automatic sliding doors that stood between them and the twenty floors of Meredith Mansions (a more ludicrous name for this miserable stack of dwellings Dax couldn't imagine), and waited. Within a few minutes people came. Boys—about their own age, wearing droopy jeans, sweatshirts with hoods, and trainers. Four of them swung suddenly down on the steel banisters from the stairwell above and loped across the dirty stone floor of the lobby. They stopped when they saw Dax, Lisa, and Gideon waiting on the other side. They exchanged conversation and very soon, amid the stench of disinfectant, urine, and cigarette butts that flowed out from under the doors in a steady draught, Dax picked up excitement and aggression. Oh no. They didn't need this.

The shortest boy, who had a square jaw and a practice moustache (it looked like a fluffy layer of dust on his upper lip) spread out his arms and stepped towards the door. It slid open automatically. 'Wanna come in?' said the boy, grinning. As they stepped forward, he waggled his finger and stepped back. 'Ah! Ah! Ah! Not without the password!' The door slid back again. The boy and his mates laughed and waved at them. Then dusty-lip boy moved forward again and repeated his performance. 'Got the password?' he said again as the door slid shut once more.

Dax shoved his foot into it and it stopped and reversed. The boy and his cronies whooped, ready for some entertainment. Gideon and Lisa stepped in beside Dax and he could sense their impatience. Dusty-lip boy stood in their path. His three mates ranged around him, blocking the way to both the lifts and the stairs.

'I said "password",' said dusty-lip boy. He grinned again, but the scent of violence on him was building, and Dax realized he had picked up a stick, snapped from a mop head which was sinking back into the murky disinfectant in a caretaker's bucket under the stairs.

Dax sighed and glanced at Gideon, who was scowling at the four self-appointed gatekeepers. 'First me, then you, OK?' he said and all four boys looked around at each other making 'Whooo-hooo!' noises of pretend fear.

Dax stepped towards dusty-lip boy. 'We need to find a friend. You are in our way. I am asking you nicely to move over.'

He locked his eyes onto the boy's and did something he'd only recently realized he could. The Alien Thing.

In the weeks that led up to his eventual shift to a falcon, before he'd known he could be another shape, Dax had done the Alien Thing without even knowing it. Lisa told him about it later. It was in his eyes. He could *think* falcon, but *not* shift, and when he did so, his eyes changed, for just a second. They flicked into two glittering black beads surrounded by yellow—and then back to ordinary brown again. It was seriously spooky, said Lisa, and, having tried it out in front of the mirror, Dax agreed with her. It made him look like an alien.

He didn't need to do the Alien Thing twice. At the first go it left dusty-lip boy gaping in fear. The moment he let out his gasp, the stick he'd been carrying swung out of his fist and twirled around, as if he had suddenly decided to audition for the majorettes. He shrieked and staggered back and Gideon began to grin, despite his intense focus on the mop handle. He sent it a foot above their dazed, upturned faces, and then began to turn it horizontally, like the rotor blade of a helicopter. As it speeded up, the foursome stood hypnotized beneath it with their mouths open.

'Come on,' said Lisa. 'Stop showing off. We haven't got all day!'

The lift lurched to a stop on floor seventeen without any ping to announce their arrival. Lisa turned immediately left and led them down a narrow corridor with walls of grubby cream stippling. She ignored a blue door on her right and went directly to a dull red door, facing them at the far end. They paused, huddled in front of it, and looked at each other, then Lisa took a deep breath and pushed the doorbell.

Silence reigned as they waited, nervously, for the door to open and a slice of their friend to come into view. There was light through the high, frosted safety glass in the door, but they detected no movement. Lisa rang again and this time called out, 'Mia! It's us! Open up!'

Dax heard a thud and a noise like someone stumbling. Feet shuffled across the carpet on the other side of the door. 'Someone's coming,' he said. 'It's Mia.' He caught her scent, but felt uneasy. It wasn't quite right. It seemed ... soured, somehow. With a shiver, Dax began to realize that Lisa had had very good reason to make them do a U-turn.

Something struck the other side of the door, dully, and a shadow was cast up on the high window. A muffled voice begged: 'Go away. Please ... I'm sorry, I can't. Just ... go away, all of you.'

They looked at each other, aghast, and then Lisa pounded on the door. 'Mia! It's me! Lisa! You *have* to let me in.'

'I can't. I can't see you.' A dragging sound gave Dax the vivid image of Mia sliding wearily down the other side of the door. He felt desperate. Mia was fragile. She always had been. Maybe she hadn't been looking after herself. In her first term at Tregarren College she'd nearly killed herself by healing too much and too often and not knowing how to release the pain she collected inside her. Surely it couldn't be happening again?

'Shall I break down the door?' said Gideon, looking as sick with worry as Dax felt.

'No—wait.' Dax looked around him and back down the corridor to the lift lobby. A square sealed window gave onto a bird's eye view of the darkening estate. Above it was a narrow ventilation strip, with slats of glass which lay open at an angle. 'Wait here,' he said. 'I'm going in to get her.'

He turned and ran back along the corridor, leaping into the air halfway down it and shifting seamlessly to falcon. He heard Gideon's gasp of amazement and remembered that this was all still very new to his friend. He spread his wings into an arrow shape and shot out into the cool air of the early dusk. He wasted no time, banking tightly around the corner of the tower block, and flew along the wall, past the opaque glass of the stairwell and along to the window they had seen from the ground. His memory hadn't let him down—the shallow top window *was* open, although a curtain was drawn across it.

He landed deftly in the narrow gap and then dropped inside to the sill with a scratch of talon against plastic. He paused, wondering whether to fly through the gap in the curtains or whether to just shift to a boy and jump down. He needed to listen first, so he did neither, but became the fox. The sill was deep enough for him to keep a grip, although from the other side of the curtain it must have looked most peculiar, as a fox shape suddenly formed in the cheap red nylon, crackling slightly with static.

He'd made the right choice. Instantly he could hear everything in the flat. Mia was still by the front door, crying almost soundlessly in a way that made his heart contract. Another human lay sleeping heavily in another room. The radio played old songs very quietly in the kitchen and a clock ticked slowly on the wall in the room he had just entered. The sounds didn't trouble Dax half as much as the smell. He didn't doubt that the flat was spotless; he could smell kitchen cleaner and bathroom spray and wood polish. But another smell lay beneath all these bright chemical facades, like an illness. Which it was.

Dax jumped down and padded across the swirly red carpet, past the battered leather sofa and through the doorway, turning into the hall. Mia was indeed crumpled at the foot of the front door. She looked thin and there were dark shadows under her eyes. Her face was puffy and sallow and her fingers, when she raised them to her mouth at the sight of Dax, trembled badly. He could see she had been trying to hold on to her determination to keep them all out and he at once scented a hot red shame in her, followed by a weakening. She wanted their help— she really did. Why wouldn't she let them in?

'Dax,' she whispered and stood up unsteadily. 'I didn't . . . I don't . . . '

Dax shifted and stepped towards her. He took her arm and pulled her away from the door, so he could open it and let the others in. She made no attempt to stop him. She just turned away and walked back down the narrow hallway, in the terribly stooped, defeated way he'd only seen in homeless people, and disappeared into the sitting room. Lisa and Gideon plunged through the door like a torrent of anxious water. Lisa hurtled after Mia and Gideon stared at Dax.

'What's up with her?' he asked, but Dax shook his head. He thought he knew, but he didn't want to say.

Mia was sitting on the leather sofa, hugging her knees and not looking any of them in the eye. 'I'm fine,' she insisted, perhaps unaware how ludicrous she sounded. She had never looked less fine.

Dax knelt in front of her, shifted back to the fox, and raised his snout to the air. In a second he was back as a boy again, and his throat was full of anger. 'It's not you, is it?' he said, his voice hard, because if he didn't keep it that way he knew it would crack.

Mia snapped her eyes on to his and hissed: 'You don't know what you're talking about, Dax! Leave it alone. I told you, I'm fine. What are you all doing here anyway?'

'We're here for you!' said Lisa. 'Something is wrong here. I thought you might not know it, but you do, don't you? Look at you! What have you been doing? How has your tutor let this happen? How come Control hasn't come in?'

'My tutor has been ill,' said Mia. 'She's been off with flu for the last week. And no—I didn't try to heal her. I haven't seen anybody else, so leave me alone. Lisa—I'm fine!'

'Will you *stop* saying that!' shouted Lisa and there

was a thud from the next room along, and Mia's eyes, a lovely violet that looked faintly tinged with yellow today, widened.

'What's all this, pet?' A man stood in the doorway. He was tall and well built, but his shoulders curved inwards. His dark hair was pillow-squashed and his eyes, pale violet blue, like his daughter's, were still bleary from sleep.

'These—these are my friends,' said Mia, flushing. 'You know . . . from the college. Um . . . Dax, Gideon, and Lisa.'

The man regarded them with surprise and then nodded. 'Pleased to meet you all. You've been good to my girl—'preciate it.'

Dax stood up and looked at the man levelly. It could not have been obvious to anyone who didn't have a fox sense of smell, but the patterns that curled in and out of his nose told an unworthy story.

'How are you?' said Dax, suddenly and seriously, and the man started.

'I'm well, lad,' he said, with a trace of a Newcastle accent.

'Better than you should be, I reckon,' said Dax, coldly.

'Dax!' Lisa nudged him from behind. Mia just stared at him, the flush on her puffy face deepening.

'What you getting at, son?'

Dax felt his fingers curl into fists. He didn't want to lose it, for Mia's sake.

'How much did you drink last night, then? Or . . . '

He took a deep breath and his mouth twisted with distaste. 'Maybe it was lunchtime.'

Mia's father stared at him. He said nothing.

Dax swung back round to Mia. 'You're coming with us,' he said, and heard Owen's tone in his young voice.

Mia shook her head. 'I can't,' she said, pushing a lanky strand of hair off her face with a hand that still trembled. 'He needs me here . . . he—'

'So he can get drunk and then just pass the hangover to you!' Dax was shouting now; he couldn't stop it. Gideon and Lisa were looking horrified and Mia covered her face.

'He doesn't mean to! He doesn't!' came Mia's muffled protest. 'He can't help it . . . he's been so sad and so lonely and it's not his fault. He never asked me to take it.'

Dax opened his mouth to shout again, but he was cut off. Mia's dad stepped towards her and sat down next to her.

'Your friends are right,' he said and Dax's mouth snapped shut again in surprise. The man looked up at him, his eyes very shiny. 'You're right, son. She's no business being with me. I can't look after her and she . . . she tries too hard to look after me. Aw, lass,' he gave Mia a fierce hug and sniffed hard, 'you're so like your mother. More and more every day. It makes me so happy but it makes me so sad. I need to sort myself out. I'm too weak; I'm messing you up, aren't I?' Mia shook her head, but he took a deep breath and looked at Lisa. 'Go and get her stuff,' he said. 'There's not much. It's all in her bedroom.

You'll take her to your dad's, right? Look after her?' Lisa
nodded.

They led Mia to the front door and soon Lisa emerged
with a small holdall of Mia's clothes, shoving a worn
toothbrush in a zip pocket. Mia hugged her dad and
said he had nothing to be sorry for, but that wasn't really
true and they all knew it. It was the most dismal goodbye
Dax had ever witnessed. They slipped quietly out into
the unwelcoming corridor and as the others headed for
the lift shaft, Dax paused and went back into the flat.

Mia's father was in the sitting room, fiddling with the
needle stylus of an old vinyl record player, which gave
out harsh static coughs as his fingers made contact. He
let the needle drop to the grooves of the old black LP and
it crackled into some familiar opening bars. He didn't
look at Dax but he spoke like a man in a sleepwalk.

'It's not right, what they did. I don't mean what made
Mia what she is. She's amazing—a gift to the world. But
my Jenny? Why take her back?' He was crying as Elvis
Presley began to sing. 'Why take her back?' he gulped at
the ceiling. And then he closed his eyes and began to sing
in a cracked voice along to 'Return To Sender'.

9

The lobby was deserted as they emerged from the lifts, but the mop handle lay on the floor and Evans was walking nervously up and down outside the sliding doors.

'Miss—we have to be quick!' he said urgently, as soon as they stepped outside. 'Those youths came running out shortly after you went in and I believe they were going to call for some reinforcements.'

As he said this Dax caught a flicker of movement to his left and realized there were enemies hiding in some stunted bushes. He heard urgent hisses and smelt the dangerous combination of fear and anger. 'Go!' he said and they all tore across the uneven paving to the car, which Evans had, fortunately, left idling.

Lisa and Gideon dragged Mia into the back seat and Dax hurled himself into the front beside Evans just as a dozen or more boys hurtled towards them. They were holding sticks and iron bars—one had a bike pump and threw it hard as the car powered away. It cracked against the back window and Mia screamed. Evans drove like something from an American cop show, and in less than thirty seconds they had cleared the estate and were pulling back onto the main trunk road and heading west again. The sound of police sirens chilled them all into silence. Dax glanced back at Lisa but she shook her head. She seemed to think they'd got away cleanly, but Dax reminded himself of her LOB. He couldn't get too relaxed.

'What if those kids tell the police or something?' said Gideon, gnawing his lower lip.

Dax had been thinking just the same thing. He knew that their little display of weirdness had been a very bad idea. There just hadn't been any other way at the time.

'Nobody will believe them,' said Lisa. She had taken a hot flask from a bag in the back footwell. 'Evans—do you mind if Mia has some of your coffee?' she said.

'Of course not, miss,' came the reply. 'It's sweet though—and strong.'

'Good,' said Lisa and poured a hot dark stream into the plastic cup as the car moved smoothly along the road.

Mia took it and drank, screwing up her face. 'Do I look horrible?' she murmured hollowly into the plastic cup.

'Yes,' said Lisa. 'But we'll sort you out, you silly mare.'

'It really wasn't his fault, you know,' mumbled Mia, sadly. 'Don't be hard on him. He didn't know I was healing him.'

'I know. I'm sure he didn't,' said Lisa, although not one of them believed that.

'Why didn't you get rid of the—the hangover stuff,' said Gideon. 'Didn't you learn how at Tregarren?'

'Yes,' mumbled Mia into the plastic cup, 'but it's really hard with people close to you. It's hard to help them and then it's hard to let the symptoms go. And I'd run out of all my incense and stuff for smudging. I couldn't ask Dad for money for more. He can't afford it.'

Smudging was one of the techniques healers used to clear all the toxic stuff away from them after they'd been helping someone in pain. It involved burning aromatic herbs and twigs and incense to clear the air. It looked like a load of nonsense and smelt like a dodgy pizza sometimes, Dax and Gideon had agreed. But it seemed to work.

The car glided along the dual carriageway and for a while they were quiet, each of them trying to take in the enormity of what they were doing. Eventually though, Mia finished the coffee and spoke.

'What's happening? This isn't just about me, is it? Something is happening.'

'I've been having . . . um . . . premonitions,' said Lisa. 'About Gideon mostly. Not good ones.'

'OK—so why are we driving west? Shouldn't we be going to Control back in London? Or meeting Owen or something?'

Lisa sighed and Gideon said, 'She thinks they're something to do with it. That's what she thinks. We don't know if she's right, but . . . '

'But you can't take the risk,' Mia finished. 'What about your dad, Gideon? Did you tell him?'

'No,' said Gideon. He looked very troubled. 'We couldn't. He would have tried to stop Dax and me. But . . . maybe . . . you know, maybe we could just drop back to my house before we go? We're just about going past the turn-off to my estate now—and he could be back there by now, maybe . . . ? We could explain—set his mind at rest?'

'No way,' said Lisa. 'Don't be an idiot.' Gideon said nothing more. He knew she was right.

A few seconds later Lisa was asking Evans to turn again—not towards Gideon's house, but into a service station.

'Miss—I do think we need to make haste,' said Evans, still polite and quiet despite his *Starsky and Hutch* moment a short while ago.

'I know, I know,' said Lisa. She shivered. 'Just have to stop.'

Evans nodded and the car slid into a service station and parked. Lisa began her shoulder rubbing again. 'Oh no,' groaned Gideon. 'What now? Spook Williams tied to a railway line?'

'Well, I'd leave him there if he was,' snapped Lisa, of their old Cola enemy, but she was leaning over to the window and peering up out of it with a look of concerned fascination.

'Go on then!' urged Gideon. 'If you need the loo, get out!'

But Lisa shook her head impatiently and continued to stare out of the window. 'Here!' she murmured, with amazement. 'It started *here*.'

'What are you on about?' demanded Gideon.

'Wait here!' Lisa had thrown open the car door and

run across the brightly lit tarmac between the petrol pumps before anyone could say a word.

'Wait here!' repeated Dax, and then bounded after her. She was now loping up a dark, wooded slope, away from the pool of artificial light.

'What are you doing? Are you mad?' he panted, racing up behind her.

'It's here!' she said again. 'It started here.'

At the top of the slope, in a dark tangle of small trees and thick scrub, Lisa was trying to find a way through. She located a gap in the leaves and sticks and Dax saw there was a small rough footpath which began at the crest of the slope and wound down to some land behind. He also saw a strange blue-white glow coming up from the path. It troubled him. A lot.

'Lisa—wait!' he shouted and ran along behind her.

'It's here—it started here!' she was still saying. 'And it followed a path . . . it came in south-east. It was trying . . .' She suddenly stopped and turned to look at him, her face pale in the weird blue-white light. 'It was . . . I . . . I don't know.' Her face screwed up with frustration and she shook her head. 'Look!'

Dax looked. Below them was the source of the light. Five large vehicles, dark and shiny, stood parked around an open field. Mounted on each vehicle roof was a huge round spotlight, and each spotlight was trained on an immense tangle of thick metal struts. Coils of cable lay in huge wooden reels, piled near the concrete base from which the metal struts tumbled in a tortured shape. Dax realized that more cable lay stretched and snagged across the spot-lit grass. Several figures moved among this strange sculpture, apparently trying to set it to rights. Too late, Dax realized that at least two of them had turned and were looking up the slope to where a boy and a girl were staring, transfixed, their faces radiant with the unnatural glare.

He yanked Lisa back up the path by her elbow, ignoring her yelp of protest. He gritted his teeth as he saw the two men running towards them. He heard again the crackle of two-way radios. 'Go! Go!' He shoved Lisa hard ahead of him, but she seemed to have realized what was happening now, and shot back up the slope with Dax at her heels. They almost fell down the other side and back into the pale yellow light under the service station canopy. Evans was standing anxiously by the driver's door.

'Get in! Get in!' yelled Dax and Evans jolted and got in. The noise of the two-way radios was getting closer and Dax didn't dare look back. What had they done? What had Lisa led them to?

For the third time in an hour, Dax hurtled into the black taxi. He slammed the door shut and Evans pulled away fast, but not fast enough. Two men in dark suits slid down the slope and just stood watching as the car moved back onto the road, barking the registration number into their radio communicators. Dax groaned. He should have known it had gone too well; had been too easy. He could hardly believe it, but they had literally run right into a bunch of government agents, he had absolutely no doubt. Now Lisa's confused warnings were starting to make some sense. Dax could not think of a force on earth—certainly not in the UK—which could tease and pluck and twist a thirty metre solid steel electricity pylon into a tangled mess of metal.

Except a very powerful telekinetic.

And there was a whole government department who knew this.

'What? What?' Gideon was shouting over and over as the car tore up the road again. Dax shook his head and stared back into the rear at Lisa.

'We can't go back to Somerset now,' he said. 'You know that, don't you?' Lisa nodded miserably.

'I can take you somewhere else,' said Evans but Lisa and Dax looked at one another and sighed.

'You can't,' said Dax. 'They've seen the number plate. They'll trace this taxi to your brother—and then to you, and then to us.'

It took a lot of arguing to persuade Evans to drop them off. He pulled into the darkness beneath an overhead railway bridge and was still remonstrating with Lisa when they shut the doors, toting their bags away from the road.

'You have to keep going,' said Lisa, pulling the straps of her designer silver duffel bag over her shoulders. 'Go and park the car somewhere a few miles from here . . . then . . . hire another one or something, and go to Bristol Temple Meads station. We'll meet you there. There's a railway station just over this embankment.'

Evans looked very unhappy. 'I'll leave the car and come with you!'

'You can't! They'll find the car and then work out where we've gone,' pleaded Lisa. 'You have to keep going and draw them away! We're depending on you!'

He looked desperate, but finally nodded. 'All right— but you call me, the minute your train gets in,' he said, glancing around anxiously for signs of whoever it was who would be following. Lisa took out her tiny mobile phone, switched it on with a chime and a pink twinkle of light and smiled at him. Then she gave him a quick hug and deftly slid her phone into his jacket pocket. Evans got back into the car and drove off, unaware.

'What d'you do *that* for?' gasped Gideon as they stood back in the shadow of the bridge.

Lisa looked at him and sighed. 'Don't you ever watch TV?' she said. 'They'll be tracking my mobile phone signal—no question. That's why I had it switched off.'

'Off?' Gideon stared at her. 'How could they track it if it was switched off?'

'Well, they couldn't when it was *off*, obviously! But now that it's *on*—they will. They'll work out who the car belongs to and then who was borrowing it, and then that it was me helping you get away—and that I've got a mobile—and then they'll track it.'

'But . . . ' Gideon struggled to make sense of her words as they began to climb up the grassy slope away from the road, still in the shadow of the railway bridge.

'But that means they'll just track Evans to Bristol . . . and when we get off the train to meet him, they'll be there.'

Lisa sighed again. 'We're not *going* to Bristol, stupid!' Dax grinned. He had worked this out, but it was funny to hear Lisa lecturing Gideon. 'The last thing we need now is to be anywhere near Evans or my dad. And the last thing Dad or Evans need is to know where we really are. Remember—there are other psychics than me! Dad and Evans will never talk, but they could still get it out of their heads.'

'Oh . . . ' Gideon looked worried. 'Is anyone going to tell me, then, what happened back there?'

Dax looked over his shoulder and into Gideon's confused face. 'Gid,' he said, 'um . . . have you had any funny dreams recently?'

'Yeah,' said Gideon. 'I dreamt the milkman wanted to leave me a note—so he did it with a sort of collage of leaves over the back garden. The leaves said "Your cat is dangerous." And I don't even *have* a cat! Then I was at my old junior school and I had no pants on.'

'Ri-ight,' said Dax. 'No bendy metal dreams then?'

'You what?'

'No scrunching up giant electricity pylons in your sleep?'

Gideon looked panicked. 'No! Tell me what you saw . . . '

They walked away from the railway and along the main road towards a coach station that Lisa had spotted.

'I'd rather go by train,' she said, 'but now that we've told Evans we will, it's best that we don't.'

'Oh no,' groaned Gideon. 'I hate coaches. They make me sick. How far are we going?'

Lisa looked at Dax. 'I don't know. How far, Dax? Where's your place?'

'My place?' Dax echoed. He hadn't spoken to anyone—ever—about the Owl Box.

Lisa smirked. 'It's been bobbing about in your head all day. You've got a bolt-hole, haven't you?'

Dax grinned. 'We're going to Exmoor,' he said. 'If we can get a coach that goes there.'

'It's to do with that reporter, isn't it?' said Lisa, suddenly, as if this had only just occurred to her. 'Whatsername? Caroline thingy.'

'Caroline Fisher,' said Dax. 'Yes.'

Lisa and Gideon and Mia looked at each other and then back at Dax, perplexed. Caroline Fisher was a tenacious reporter who had tracked Dax all the way to Tregarren College in his first term and threatened to expose all the Colas to the public. She hadn't known, then, what she was getting into. The principal of the college had allowed her into the grounds, shown her around—and then sent her off to her death.

Patrick Wood had been a glamourist—an illusionist, like Spook Williams—and his power to make Caroline Fisher see a bridge across a marsh when it wasn't there had led her into a treacherous bog. Dax, Gideon, Lisa, and Mia had saved her life, seconds before she drowned in mud. With her thanks came her silence—she had pledged never to reveal the Cola Club secret.

'She said I shouldn't trust everyone at Tregarren,' said Dax, simply. 'And she sent me a key to this place—the Owl Box. It's somewhere on Exmoor. Said it was there for me if I ever needed it. I never thought I would.'

Dax had never seen Gideon quite that colour before; his skin was normally pink and freckly but it now had a definite green tinge. He shot Lisa a worried look across the aisle, but she was busy arranging Mia and some rolled-up jumpers so the girl could lean into the corner made by the coach seat and the window and try to sleep off the remains of her dad's hangover.

Dax fished around in the pocket of Gideon's jeans (they hadn't yet changed back into their own clothes) and found a few lumps of chocolate and—yes!—a tiny foil-wrapped cylinder which promised four or five Polos. He undid it and waved it under Gideon's nose. 'C'mon. Eat one of these and keep looking out of the window,' he urged and Gideon grimaced, but took a mint and popped it in, before staring doggedly out through the smeary glass as the motorway went by in a dark blur.

Dax was anxious that Gideon wasn't sick. Not just for Gideon's sake, but for all of them. The coach was only half full but he thought they had managed to get on without really getting noticed. Lisa, who had a lot of cash on her, separated into wodges of notes in five or six different pockets, had bought their tickets. They could only get as far as Exeter on this coach, but they would be able to find another one to Exmoor from there. Once she'd handed out the tickets Lisa had wandered off for the twenty minutes they needed to wait, taking Mia with her.

'I'm going to get her some food and pep her up a bit if I can,' she'd said to Dax and Gideon. 'Then we'll get on to the coach separately from you. It'll help if we don't look like we're travelling in a foursome. Just in case . . .' She had looked anxiously around at a security camera, messing around with her hair as she did so, so whoever was monitoring wouldn't get a good look at her face.

Gideon had grinned and said, 'Look again, Hardman.' They all looked. The lens of the camera was shattered in the shape of a spider's web.

'Did you do that?' whispered Lisa, unable to stop her marvelling even in front of Gideon. He looked smug and shrugged.

'Better not do them all, though, Gid,' murmured Dax. 'It might get them thinking.'

Now, as he sat back and follow Gideon's gaze out into the night, Dax wondered again exactly who 'they' were. He didn't like the answer that kept knocking around in his head. 'They', of course, were the government. The image of the twisted-up electricity pylon flared into his mind and he saw again the way the men on the site had moved. Governmental types all moved that way—with economy and precision; sure of what they were doing and what their aim was. Even Mike and Dave, employed to saunter about like normal people, still had a similar way of moving. Or maybe it was something in their scent. Dax didn't know how he knew, but he was as certain as he could be that the twisted pylon site had been chock-full of special operatives. The suited men at the petrol station were unmistakable. They must have been investigating the ruined pylon—that was no ordinary accident. He remembered watching TV with Alice and Gina on Sunday night and the sudden blackout that had lasted several hours. It fitted. It fitted with the whole sequence of events, from the moment Lisa had called with her telepathic demands.

How would *he* react if he were in the government and heard that a pylon had abruptly been wrenched out of its foundations and scrunched up like a Curly Wurly on a hot day? How long before the people that ran the Cola Club project got a call? He glanced nervously at Gideon who was working his mouth around the Polo and looking a bit better. Gideon had taken the news calmly and simply shrugged and said, 'Well, it wasn't me! Blimey! I'm not *that* good. Yet.' But he'd been quiet for a while now and Dax thought it was probably not just because he felt sick.

'Gid,' he ventured. 'You would tell me . . . if . . . '

Gideon looked round at him. 'If what? If I'd started squishing up electricity pylons for a hobby?' Dax laughed and shook his head, but Gideon turned round fully to him and lowered his voice. 'I'm not stupid, Dax! I know I've been a bit dumb this year, with all the Luke and Catherine stuff—but that was mainly because she was leeching all the energy out of me, remember?'

Dax nodded. 'I know,' he said. 'I know.'

Gideon continued, 'You know you all thought it was me that night in the dorm, when all the windows smashed?' Dax nodded again, remembering the weird awakening to a shower of shattered glass. 'Well, that wasn't me either, was it? It had to be Luke. And anyway, I don't *do* the dreaming thing. That's *your* thing!'

Dax smiled tightly. Dreams *were* his thing. In them, across the last year, he had been left messages by the wolf—the first shapeshifter, a boy like him, who had died as a wolf, thanks to Tregarren College's first principal, Patrick Wood. The wolf had warned Dax in dreams, and later in apparitions, of two big threats to him in the past year.

'So what's happening in *your* dreams, Dax?' prodded Gideon.

Dax sighed and shook his head. 'Nothing,' he said. 'It's only Lisa who's been getting anything and she's had the LOB.'

'The SLOB? The Sadly Lame One's Buffer?'

'She doesn't think you're lame,' snorted Dax.

'No—she just thinks I'm an idiot.'

'She thinks everyone's an idiot. She's a brat, remember?'

'Yeah, she is. But that mobile phone thing was cool.'

'Yeah—and your security camera thing was cool. Unless it just shattered when it saw your ugly mug.'

Gideon shoved him and laughed and Dax felt better. He needed Gideon to be as Gideon-y as possible right now. 'But you can work it out, can't you?' he went on, quietly. 'They're going to think it's you. Unless one of the other teles has suddenly got a lot more powerful. You were always the best. Did you get a power cut last night?' Gideon frowned and then nodded, looking more and more worried. 'Yeah—we did too,' said Dax. 'Maybe that pylon thing is what caused it—and it's close to where you live, isn't it? There aren't any other teles around the south, are there?'

Gideon shook his head. The closest telekinetic Cola was in Gloucester somewhere, and that was Paul Lewis, who could only bend spoons the last time they saw him.

'Why aren't we talking to Owen? We should be talking to Owen,' said Gideon.

Dax fiddled with the shrunken foil parcel of Polos. 'Lisa said no.'

'Why? Who made her boss?'

'I don't know,' said Dax, again. 'She got that pylon thing bang on, didn't she? Took us straight there! And she got Mia right too. I don't know why she's got a problem with Owen. She won't say. She thinks he might be one of "them", I guess.'

'No way. He's on our side.' Gideon folded his arms. He glanced at Dax. 'Isn't he?'

Dax said nothing. He couldn't make himself believe that Owen *wasn't* on their side. He was probably hunting them down by now, though. He'd be furious with them, and worried about them. Definitely. But what would he do with Gideon if he found them? What would happen if they couldn't convince him that Gideon was nothing to do with the melted pylon? It was beginning to make his head ache just thinking about it, and worse, he couldn't get a chunk of Owen's last conversation with him out of his mind.

'There are people that I work with who think the logical thing to do with Colas is keep them in an underground bunker— for the good of national security.'

'Try to get some sleep,' he said, and closed his eyes.

10

'Dax! Wake up!' He was asleep with his chin in his hand, his right elbow on the arm rest. Lisa shoved his shoulder and his chin fell off his palm and his forehead smacked into the back of the seat in front of him. He made an annoyed grunt and Lisa hissed at him again, leaning back into her seat, so it wouldn't be too obvious that they were all together. 'Dax! Wake *up*! We're here!'

Dax nudged Gideon, who also grunted, and they scrabbled for their bags under their seats. Mia and Lisa were both fully awake. Dax felt relieved to see Mia looking a lot better. It was 11 p.m. and this was probably going to be their most dangerous time. Four twelve-and-thirteen-year-olds out at 6 p.m. on a September evening was fine, but this late was unusual and likely to prompt a well-meaning adult to ask if they were OK.

'We could do with Spook, really,' he found himself muttering, as they got off the coach and made their way to the more shadowy end of the coach terminal.

'You are joking!' said Gideon, and Lisa stared at him.

'No—I mean—we need an illusionist,' sighed Dax. 'We all need to look twenty-five.' Dax, Gideon, and Lisa all loathed Spook Williams—a very self-important glamourist Cola who could conjure up astonishing visions. And Spook loathed Dax, because Dax was immune to his illusions. Only Mia had any time for Spook, but Mia had time for everybody.

Gideon glanced around and spotted three different security cameras—all in the better lit areas of the terminal. Once he had them mapped in his mind, he stared hard at the floor and Dax saw, with an impressed shiver, each of the small torch-like electric eyes turn on its fixing, and face away from them.

'Should be OK now,' said Gideon.

Mia wandered across to a notice of timetables and peered at it. She came back looking worried. 'There isn't a coach for hours,' she said, with a tired shiver. 'There's one that goes north and stops at Minehead. It leaves at five a.m. That's six hours!'

Gideon was eyeing a line of taxis slowly edging along the far end of the terminal, collecting the late-night tourists and their bags. Dax shook his head, firmly. 'No cabs,' he said. 'Too easy for a cabbie to remember us, and where he took us.'

'Where are we going?' asked Mia. 'You do know, don't you, Dax? You *have* got somewhere for us?' She looked so pathetic that Dax felt a nervous twinge in his stomach. She was talking to him as if he was their leader and he didn't think he was. He looked at Lisa and she shrugged back at him.

'I need to get a map,' he said. 'All I know is that it's somewhere on Exmoor—and that's a big place. Where can we get a map?'

'There's probably an all-night convenience store around here somewhere,' said Lisa. 'C'mon.' She shouldered her bag. 'We can't hang around here forever. We'll get noticed.'

They trooped out in the wake of the last few coach arrivals and walked quickly past the brightly lit taxi rank, two more security cameras obediently twisting away from them as they went. Happily, Lisa's hunch was—as always—right and they found an all-night shop a few minutes away from the coach station. Dax went in and quickly found a tourist map of North Devon and a very detailed map of Exmoor, which showed roads and tracks for the benefit of walkers. He paid for them with some of Lisa's money and left with his head down, but Gideon had already twisted the in-store cameras around too, after casually glancing through the glass doors. Dax was amazed that nobody seemed to notice.

Mia was still shivering when Dax and Gideon met up with the girls under a tall hedge that sprawled high over the pavement and sheltered them in safe gloom. 'We need to get her somewhere warm until we come back,' said Lisa and they looked around to see where they might go. It wasn't a cold night: it was only mid-September and the summer was stretching into autumn—but it was getting cooler and Mia was still not well.

Dax sniffed the air and caught the soothing smell of a wood nearby. 'This way,' he said, and was surprised when everyone just followed him. It made that twinge go again. He didn't enjoy this feeling of responsibility. They reached the small copse in five minutes. Dax immediately felt the tension drain out of his shoulders as the tall oak and beech trees blotted out the slightly orange sky of the city. A cloak of quiet fell on them as they moved deeper in, and Dax and Gideon both took torches from their bags to guide the way. A long pine log lay on the soft woodland floor and here Dax stopped, rested the torch on the ground, and pulled the thin folded plastic out of his backpack. He spread it out and tucked it into the straight line where the pine log met the peaty ground. Then he put his mac on top of it. He looked at the others and saw Lisa was pulling a warm jumper out of her bag and Gideon was also hauling out his mac. They put the clothing down on the plastic and then Lisa took Mia's old fabric shoulder bag and squashed it down at one end.

'Pillow,' she said. 'Come on, Mia.'

Mia protested and said they should all sit on the makeshift bed, but they propelled her on to it, laid her down and tucked their other bags at her knees and feet, to keep out any chill.

'OK,' said Dax. 'You two sit on the log and take the first watch—till one thirty. OK?'

'What are *you* doing?' asked Lisa, folding her arms.

Dax grinned and said, 'Sorry. I'm the hot-water bottle.'

He shifted to a fox while Gideon muttered, 'Jammy!' and then curled up next to Mia, who laughed softly and said, 'Dax—you really do have your uses!' He would have been hideously embarrassed to have to do this as a boy, but as a fox it was matter of fact, just survival. Against warm fur, Mia's shivering gradually subsided and within minutes she was asleep. Dax listened to Lisa and Gideon talking quietly, set his mental alarm clock to 1.30 a.m., and then got some kip too.

He opened his eyes moments before Gideon looked at his watch and yawned, 'Wake 'em up! We need some sleep now.' Dax shifted back to boy and looked back at Mia, who was still asleep.

'Leave her,' he said. 'I can do the rest of the watch on my own.'

Lisa and Gideon glanced at each other and then Lisa got onto the woodland bed next to Mia. 'Don't even think about it, Reader,' she murmured.

Gideon shrugged and curled up on the ground next to Dax. 'You don't think you could do the fox thing for me, could you, mate?' he said, thickly, too tired to be embarrassed.

Dax grinned and shifted back again. He had intended to do his watch in fox form anyway. He sat up, shoving his furry rump against Gideon's back and felt his friend give way to sleep. He watched, silently, for three hours, enjoying the sounds beyond the occasional snore from Gideon.

A barn owl swooped low over him, her dish-like face ghostly white as she scanned for mice. A vixen padded into view just as the sky was turning paler in the east and stared at him for some time, confused by his casual hanging out with humans. He tried, as he occasionally did, to talk to her in his mind. He definitely *could* communicate with other foxes—and dogs—but not in any great detail. One word normally did it. The vixen's word was 'Odd', as she tilted her lovely snout to one side and studied him, before moving away in pursuit of a distant rabbit. A large spider walked over Gideon's leg and Dax ate it, instinctively. *Oh dear*, he thought. *That's such a nasty habit.* The three hours melted away and at 4.30, Dax shifted back to a boy and woke the others.

The booths were all closed, so they bought their tickets as they boarded the coach. They got on, again, in pairs, leaving two minutes before Dax and Gideon followed the girls. The coach was only a third full when it pulled away, mostly with a group of young American backpackers who were amazingly bright for five o'clock in the morning.

'They're going to a festival up in Glastonbury,' said Lisa, quietly, after staring hard at a couple of their fellow passengers. 'It would normally be only a couple of people on this coach at this time. That's really lucky for us. Hopefully we won't get noticed.'

Dax and Gideon settled into seats behind Lisa and Mia and downed cola and crisps that they'd got from a vending machine. Lisa and Mia were doing the same. Dax had studied the map and located the village, deep into Exmoor, that they needed to reach. The closest drop off looked as if it was about ten miles away from it, on the main Minehead road. He thought they could probably hike the rest of the way—and it might be quicker (and certainly safer) if they went cross-country.

Lisa turned in the seat ahead of them and peered through the gap in the head rests. 'I reckon they'll have found Evans by now,' she said, with a short, worried sigh. 'Do you think they'll . . . will they interrogate him?' She stared beseechingly at Dax.

'Probably,' he said, giving her a rueful smile. 'But he's tough. He can take it. And, of course, he really doesn't have a clue where we are, thanks to you. They'll work that out fast enough.'

Lisa nodded. She thought for a while and then said, 'Are we going to be able to do this?'

Dax and Gideon looked at each other. 'What exactly *are* we doing?' asked Gideon.

They were all silent for a while and then Mia surprised them by gently pushing Lisa aside and looking through the gap. 'We are doing what we're meant to do,' she said simply. 'We all know it. We'll work it out as we go along. Don't worry.'

A large pulse of healing warmth spun out of her for the first time since they'd rescued her. They all felt their skin prickle slightly and their eyes water. They travelled on for several minutes in contented silence before the doubts and worries began to return.

The roads were busier than Dax had expected—he guessed there must be a lot of people going to that festival further north. Lots of camper vans and spray-painted old cars with cheerful young people inside were travelling the winding A road. As the sun rose, Dax was studying the map, trying to make its unhelpful folds work into a neat package, when he realized that they were travelling more slowly. He glanced up and peered down the aisle of the coach, past the huge rucksacks of the travelling Americans and through the windscreen. He felt a thud of suspicion inside his chest as he made out a long snake of vehicles on the road ahead. The southbound lane continued to flow freely, but their side had now slowed to perhaps ten miles an hour. Lisa was looking too, now. She glanced at Dax edgily.

'I don't like this,' she said.

'You getting anything?' he murmured quietly, as Mia and Gideon peered discreetly over the seats and sat down again. Lisa wasn't sure. Gideon said it could be an accident. 'No sirens, though,' said Dax. He shivered at precisely the same time as Lisa. Not coincidence. Dax eyed the windows of the coach. They didn't open except for the ventilation strips at the top. He could fly out of those, no problem, but without being seen?

'I need to get out and spot what's happening,' he said to Gideon. 'You'll have to make a distraction at the front of the coach.'

Gideon nodded. 'Say when,' he said.

'Now,' said Dax and at once there was a cascade of hand luggage falling from the small overhead shelves above the front three rows of seats. The American travellers reacted with loud concern and then humour and before anyone had looked round towards the back, a falcon had shot out of a side window, unseen.

He rose high immediately, needing to clear the hill they'd been passing to see where the road curved on to.

The traffic had slowed to walking speed now, and Dax, as he rose above the pale green hill and coasted down over its far slopes, could see why. A mile or so beyond their coach the traffic was halted at a hastily arranged road-block. Blue lights circled wildly on dark vehicles parked on either side of the single carriageway that headed north and cars, lorries, and coaches were being diverted to the side of the road and boarded by teams of police. A large fluorescent sign on the back of one of the parked vehicles stated: POLICE INCIDENT—PULL OVER AND WAIT.

The team was working efficiently through the queue of confused motorists and truckers. Drivers and passengers were ejected from their cars and then allowed back in following a search which even included the boot. Lorry doors were being opened, three or four men at a time leaping into them and then cascading out with a curt head shake. They were wearing riot clothing, Dax realized, with a sick feeling in his rapidly beating falcon heart. This was 'them'. And if he had even doubted this for a second his ten-times-faster and ten-times-better vision picked out a single man who now stepped from one of the parked vehicles and raised a pair of binoculars to his eyes. The man scanned the skies and Dax flipped and plummeted behind trees on the lower slopes of the hill in three seconds. The man with the binoculars could have been anyone. Anyone at all.

Dax roosted on a spruce bough and wished for that moment that his eyes were only human. The man was Owen Hind.

11

It was a big risk, going back into the coach, but Dax had no choice. He had to get on so he could get them all off. He flew low, in the same direction as the slowly moving line of cars and scanned the heads inside the coach swiftly, making sure they were not looking around and likely to notice him. Only Lisa and Gideon were: both staring worriedly out of the window, scanning in all directions. Fortunately, Gideon spotted him as he hovered outside and quickly snapped his head back to the front of the bus. Dax heard the commotion as the hand luggage took another tumble and seized his chance. He was back on the seat and back as a boy, crouching low, before the first holdall was hoisted off the floor.

They all looked at him, alarm growing in their eyes as they read his expression. 'We have to get off,' said Dax. 'Now.'

'How can we do that without catching everyone's attention?' whispered Lisa. 'It's not a bus! We can't just ask to hop off here, in the middle of nowhere! We're lucky to have got this far—it's only because he's too miserable to care that he hasn't wondered what we're doing on our own, at our age.' She nodded towards the morose coach driver, a man in his fifties who looked as if someone had just shot his dog. He'd barely glanced at them when they'd got on, even as he sold them their tickets, but this good fortune couldn't last.

'You'll have to do something, Gideon,' said Lisa. 'Make something happen that gets everyone off. *Before* we get around the next bend.'

Dax nodded. 'Round the next bend and it'll be too late,' he agreed.

Gideon looked back down the coach and considered for a moment. He glanced out of the side window and at the verges of the road. Dax watched and felt a pulse of excitement as the cool focus abruptly slipped over his friend's face—Gideon was aiming. A pebble rose swiftly in the air beside the road, high above the coach and out of sight. Dax waited, holding his breath, as the coach rolled on slowly towards the bend in the road. Suddenly there was a loud crack. Everyone jumped and the coach driver let out a very rude word. The windscreen, just a bit smeary a second ago, was now a network of shattered glass, held intact by some kind of safety film but impossible to see through. The coach lurched to a halt and the driver punched the hazard lights button with another curse and put on the air brakes. He stared down the aisle at his passengers.

'Stay put,' he grunted. 'I'll have to call in to base and get another coach sent up.'

There were moans of frustration from the passengers. Gideon gritted his teeth. He'd stopped them but he still had to get everyone off the bus. And not draw attention to the four children. He looked around and then stared hard at the long chrome handrail which was suspended along the low coach ceiling above the aisle. He closed his eyes and his face reddened. This was going to take a lot of doing. Dax stared at Gideon as a faint sweat broke out on his brow. Then there was a metallic clang and the front end of the handrail struck the middle of the aisle by the front rows of seats. Someone screamed and everyone looked around nervously.

'I say we get off this freaky ride!' said one of the Americans and a number of people murmured agreement. The driver was out of his seat now, staring at his coach, scratching one armpit and murmuring. Then he jerked in shock as his rear-view mirror dropped heavily onto his steering wheel with a shatter of glass.

'All right,' he said. 'Everyone off! Stay on the verge.'

As everyone poured nervously towards the coach door, Dax hissed to Lisa, 'Go up the hill—say you need to go or something. Me and Gideon will go the other way and then I'll find you.'

Lisa didn't look back at him but she nodded as she propelled Mia ahead of her. Dax's heart was thundering with fear as he peered at the road ahead. They were perhaps fifty feet out of sight of the roadblock. What if the patrols started working their way along the traffic? They could emerge at any moment.

As soon as they stepped onto the verge, Dax and Gideon jumped across the low metal barrier, grabbing the moment of hubbub and confusion to get away and hoping they wouldn't be seen. Dax heard Lisa mutter that she needed the ladies and asked Mia to come with her as she too jumped across the barrier and headed for some bushes. Dax led Gideon along the path he'd seen from above, with low gorse undergrowth that made it possible for them to drop out of sight if they went to their knees.

'You can get up to the top unseen if you stay down,' he said and Gideon nodded, looking pale and scared.

'Are they definitely looking for *us*?' he said. Dax nodded. 'How do you know?' Dax couldn't bring himself to tell his friend.

'I know,' he said, grimly. 'Get going—fast—there's a wooded area to the west—that way,' he pointed. 'I'll find the girls and we'll meet you there.'

He shifted and soared away as Gideon began to crawl swiftly up the hill. Dax glided high and spotted Lisa's blonde head and Mia's dark one, hidden among the bushes further along. He dropped onto Lisa's shoulder, as lightly as he could, but she still yelped.

'Da-ax! You could file your nails once in a while!' she hissed, but he could feel her fear, shaking through her shoulder. He spoke to her telepathically. *Follow me—keep low. I'll fly ahead and show you the way.*

There were a couple of scary moments when Lisa and Mia were forced to break cover as they scrambled up the hill, dragging their bags and looking back fearfully to the road below. The passengers were mooching along beside the coach, talking in clusters. Nobody was looking up towards them, although a couple had walked further north along the roadside to find out what the hold-up was. They almost certainly *would* notice that the children at the back were gone by the time the new coach arrived, but, Dax noted with satisfaction, there was a mile or more of tailback behind the crippled coach and it would take a long time for the replacement to get there.

The driver had now knocked the shattered glass out of the windscreen so he could see, and moved the coach across onto the verge, leaving its hazard lights blinking. The slow traffic was edging past it and if the patrols did not move further down the carriageway, they might not see it for an hour or more. This could buy them precious time. Dax had no doubt that as soon as Owen spoke to the driver he would recognize Gideon's handiwork.

They found Gideon hiding behind a tree and Dax shifted back to boy shape. The four of them stared at each other. 'What now?' said Gideon. 'How far did we get? We must be miles and miles from the bolt-hole.'

Dax pulled out his map and tried to work out where they were. 'We stopped here—just before the Bampton turn off,' he said, tracing the network of roads with his finger. He continued to trace the direct route across country. 'I think it's about fifteen miles from here.'

'How do we do the next fifteen then?' said Gideon.

Lisa rolled her eyes. 'We walk! Dummy!'

Gideon stared at her, aghast. 'Walk? *Walk?* It's all right for you! You've got bionic legs with all that insane running you do, and Dax can just fly or do the foxtrot. But what about me and Mia? We're *normal*!'

'We can do it,' said Dax, trying to sound calm, although he could almost physically feel the threat that lurked just down the hill. 'We won't rush. There's no need. They won't track us here—not for a long while anyway. I can shift every hour and do a recce by wing; make sure we're not being followed.'

'You reckon we'll get there before dark?' said Gideon, looking severely doubtful. Mia was looking at her feet.

'It doesn't matter,' said Dax. 'If we don't we'll just make a shelter and camp out. Just like Owen taught us.' They all nodded and Dax knew he had to tell them. 'By the way . . . the roadblock— they were searching all the cars and lorries. They were in riot gear—you know, that black stuff with the puffy vests, and plastic visors.' They looked at him, appalled.

'For us?' whispered Mia.

There was a pause. Gideon took a deep breath. 'For me,' he said.

'There's something else you all should know,' said Dax, feeling as if he was in a bad dream. 'Owen was there.'

They stared at him and Mia put her hand over her mouth. 'Do you . . . do you think we should just go down there and find him?' she said, and Dax knew they had all been thinking the same. Imagine . . . this could end now. They could traipse down the hill and shout for Owen and be taken away by one of the black trucks and checked over, told off, looked after, and . . .

'... and then they could put Gideon in a concrete bunker, and we'd all live happily ever after,' said Lisa, as if she'd heard all of Dax's thoughts. Which she quite possibly had.

'How sure are you, Lisa?' Mia touched her friend's arm and stared at her. Dax expected Lisa to snap back, but she didn't. She just sank down and sat on the ground, cross-legged, her shoulders slumped.

'I don't know,' she mumbled. 'I don't know any more. I'm too tired and I've had some dead Irish bloke singing "Molly Malone" at me for the past three hours and telling me he lost three toes through frostbite. Like I CARE!' she shouted, staring hard at a pine tree a few feet away, as if the offending Irishman was serenading her from beneath its branches.

'So let me get this straight,' said Gideon, sitting down beside her. 'You *think* we should be fleeing for our lives—and that Owen's gone over to the dark side of the force and changed his name to Darth Hind ... and that I'm going to be encased in quick-drying cement and buried because I'm a threat to the nation—but you're not *sure*!'

Dax rubbed his hands over his eyes. This was not good. Not good at all. They were in a riptide. Should they trust Lisa? Or should they trust Owen?

'I'll go and see if I can get to him,' he said, quietly.

'Dax, no!' shouted Lisa, getting to her feet. 'I can see ... I see things. You and ... '

'You've seen things before and got hold of the wrong end of the stick!' accused Gideon, also back up on his feet. 'You thought Owen was going to kill Dax last year—didn't you? Only he actually saved his life!'

'What I *saw,*' said Lisa, through gritted teeth, 'was exactly right! Dax about to fall and Owen struggling with him! It was *right.* I just didn't understand what was happening.'

'Exactly!' said Gideon. 'You're not bloody perfect!'

Dax raised his hands. 'Enough!' he said. 'I'll try to get to him. Now. You stay here and stop arguing.' He glared from Lisa to Gideon. 'Keep quiet! They might send a patrol into the woods. I'll be back in a few minutes and we'll know what we should do.'

He ran to the edge of the wooded hilltop and shifted up and into flight. He flew in a low curve around the far side of the hill, coming into the roadblock from the north and scanning for Owen. He couldn't see him, but he made for the nearest dark van, and dropped down behind it. No visored head swung round, no muffled shout or urgent dialogue on a radio gave him away. He moved under the van and shifted to the fox, lying low on the tarmac, inhaling the scent of engine oil and petrol. Back in fox form, his vision shrank but his sense of hearing and smell shot up in power. Above the queries of the worried motorists and the barking commands of the search patrol, he could hear two men talking in the van above him; neither was Owen, but one was a man's voice which he thought he recognized.

' . . . best chance we've got,' said the voice, drily. 'If they're out here at all. He seems to think they are.'

'You think he's going to work straight on this one, though?' said another man; younger, Dax thought. 'He's too involved, that's what I say. He should be back at Control, not in the field. He's too involved to work straight.'

The first man gave a mirthless chuckle. 'Trust me—if you'd ever seen Hind slit an enemy throat you'd understand how straight he can work. The man's got ice for blood when he's in the field. Best operative I ever worked with.'

'Yeah—but these are kids.'

'No. They're not kids. They're Colas. Don't forget that. Hind won't. He'll do whatever has to be done.'

Dax realized his fur was standing on end. A wave of nausea washed over him. Only yesterday morning Owen had stood in Gina's dining room and Dax had thought he looked like an assassin. Yet still the words from the men above had shocked him horribly. Shaking, he shifted back to the falcon and took flight again. He didn't look back.

In the wood Gideon, Lisa, and Mia waited. Mia's face was full of hope. Dax flew to the ground and shifted. He didn't look any of them in the eye for a few seconds. Then he lifted his face to Lisa's and nodded. 'You're right,' he said.

They looked at each other, wordlessly. Gideon opened his mouth to speak but Mia touched his arm and shook her head. Dax picked up his bag and stepped away to the west. They followed him in silence.

12

It was quite easy going at first. There were a number of small paths winding through the countryside and nobody had any trouble following them. But after a while they led away high into the hills and were more exposed. Just as Dax was pausing, trying to work out whether they should leave the path and head into the thicker cover of the trees that ran along the bottom of the valley, he picked up a thudding sound in the air—almost felt it before he heard it. He glanced around at the others and then up into the sky. They followed his gaze, confused—they hadn't picked up the sound yet. Dax suddenly lurched off the path and began to run towards the trees.

'Come on!' he shouted and they followed hurriedly, jumping over mounds of grass and scrambling under the cover of the branches. They were only just in time. As soon as Mia reached them, a military helicopter rose over the top of the hill they'd just come down and began to fly, low, along the valley, like a huge, ugly, grey wasp. If they'd been five seconds later into the trees they would have been seen, and it would have been all over.

They huddled together behind bushes and peered out between the shivering leaves. The helicopter rotors thudded through the still morning air and grew quieter as the machine moved on down the valley. Just as they were beginning to breathe normally again, the thudding grew louder and the helicopter returned. It seemed to hang over their heads for a terrifyingly long time. Dax was about to shout for them all to run for it when it moved away again. They were still for another few minutes, staring at each other, fear holding them frozen and speechless.

Eventually Gideon said, 'This is like in the films! This is . . . this is too weird!' They all agreed.

'We'd better stay under the trees as much as possible,' said Dax. 'Follow the bottom of the valley, along the river.' Further down a small river meandered prettily. It would not be the quickest route to follow, but it was nearly all under cover, and Dax, having checked the Exmoor map again, knew that it led, eventually, to the area where they'd find the Owl Box. He felt the key under his sweatshirt again, anxiously, and then prodded everyone to move on.

'How far have we come, do you think?' said Lisa, as they climbed over fallen trees and picked their way through patches of nettles and bracken.

'Um . . . three miles, maybe. It's hard to tell,' said Dax. 'We'll just keep going as long as we can, and stop and make camp if we have to.'

He knew she wanted to know what he had learned about Owen. They all did. Mia was sensitive enough to realize that he couldn't speak to them about it yet and she had told Gideon not to ask (Dax had easily heard her whispering to him). Lisa knew how he felt too, although that didn't stop her trying to pick up the information from him telepathically. At one point, aware of the mental rummaging through his mind, Dax turned and shot her a cold glance. She looked guilty.

You may be right, sent Dax, *but I don't have to like it*. She looked genuinely downcast then.

Sorry, she sent back. *Just tell us when you're ready.*

The fact was, although Lisa could pick up flashes of information from most people, she couldn't actually get *in* to their heads properly unless they allowed her to. For most of the time she didn't remotely want to, but she'd got used to Dax leaving the door to his mind open, and was quite shocked to realize it was shut today.

As the morning wore towards midday, everyone was slow and irritable. They hadn't had enough to eat. They had meant to get food when they were dropped off by the coach, but now, of course, they had nothing. Dax cursed himself for not making everyone stock up at the shop in Exeter the night before. By midday, he thought they had probably not covered more than another three miles. The wiggly bends of the river took them in and out of their way. He was tempted to get them to cross whenever it was possible, to keep to a straighter line, but there were boggy areas and hidden drops and he shuddered at the thought of one of them getting injured. He didn't want Mia exhausting herself trying to fix anyone. She wasn't well enough yet. They must play it safe.

'Stop, everyone,' he said, as they reached a pretty glade where the sun broke through. Lush grass grew down to the edge of the river, which was shallow here and running busily across rocks and pebbles. 'We need to eat.'

'Eat what?' grouched Lisa. 'We haven't got anything, have we? We ate all Gideon's disgusting squishy chocolate at eleven o'clock.' She made an appalled face and Gideon huffed.

'At least I *shared* it with you!' he muttered.

'We need to make a fire,' said Dax. 'Small—high—smokeless,' he nodded towards Gideon, as he fished the matches out of his bag. 'You remember how?' Gideon nodded. 'Good,' said Dax. 'You and Lisa work on it and Mia—get some rest. Stay on the edge of the trees—and get right back in if you hear a helicopter again.'

'I don't need to rest,' protested Mia. 'I'm not ill any more—I'll be fine.' She was certainly better, but still frail and they all knew it. There was a defiant set to her mouth though, and Dax thought it might be better not to make her feel worse.

'Go on, then,' he said. 'Get some dry sticks—but *don't* overdo it!'

Lisa wandered over to him. 'You're going hunting, yeah?' she said quietly. Dax nodded. 'But what about Mia? She'll never eat rabbit, you know that.' Dax did know it. Mia was firmly vegetarian. It had been on his mind for the last hour.

'I'll see what else I can find. Just . . . don't let her wear herself out. And don't forget—*smokeless*!' Lisa narrowed her eyes and put her hands on her hips and was about to tell him his life story, so he grinned cheekily at her and shifted into the fox before she could get started.

He found and killed two rabbits within fifteen minutes, hunting the verges of the woodland where myriad creatures bobbed and ran. He returned to the full cover of the trees and then shifted back, depositing the rabbits carefully on the ground and surveying the woodland floor with great satisfaction. He was standing on a brown sea of beechnuts, strewn like a thick prickly carpet beneath a tall beech tree. He pulled the cap out of his backpack and scooped up great handfuls of the nuts in their spiky curling cases into it, until it was full. Then he tucked the nut-filled cap back into his bag and set off happily with the rabbits hanging limply from one hand. When he reached their small camp the fire was going well and—he noted with relief—without any smoke to give away their location. They had carefully chosen only the driest of sticks, stripping them of bark. Any moisture would have caused smoke.

'Dax—look!' said Lisa and pointed to a large white parasol of fungus, standing proudly out in the grass. Two or three others were grouped behind it. 'What do you reckon?' said Lisa. 'Mia thinks they're safe to eat.'

'Looks like a horse mushroom,' said Dax.

'It is,' said Mia. 'Let me go and get some, and I'll have something to eat too.' She eyed the dead rabbits forlornly.

'Get them—quickly—and I'll look them up, to double check. We *cannot* eat them unless we're a hundred per cent sure,' said Dax, sounding again like Owen. The thought made him wince inside. He didn't know how to feel about Owen.

Mia ran out from the trees and picked the fungi swiftly, haring back with four huge domes of pale white on thick stems with a collar around them. Dax checked them over, referring to the fungi section in his little book. As he handled them, they bruised easily, turning yellow-brown where his fingernails caught them. Beneath the parasols there were fine grey gills. Dax sniffed hard and got the reassuring scent of almonds. He checked them thoroughly for maggots, as the book instructed, and found them clean and whole. Perfect specimens.

Mia grinned. 'I'm right, aren't I? They are horse mushrooms!'

'Yep,' said Dax, taking a small chunk of one and popping it in his mouth. 'But I'm trying it first. If I start foaming at the mouth in the next five minutes, don't eat.' Mia laughed—a good, good sound—and shoved him, taking the fungi back from him.

Gideon had unearthed a shallow rectangular billycan from his bag. 'We can cook 'em in here. And we've got sticks ready for the rabbit. Bags Lisa does the skinning!'

Lisa took the rabbits from Dax with a sigh. She had done this before. 'I'll skin if you'll gut,' she said and Mia shuddered again, and turned away.

'Wait,' said Dax, smiling and pulling her back. 'Here's *your* main course!' He pulled out his hatful of beechnuts and Mia stared at them before beaming up at him in delight. 'I'll start shelling them and we can roast them in the fire,' said Dax, smiling back at her. It was a huge relief to have found a way to feed her. 'Can you get some water in my flask?'

She took it and slipped back towards the stream. 'See if you can find some sphagnum moss to filter it through,' called Dax, flicking the shelled nuts into a pile and she called back 'On it!' and held up a handful of dripping curly green vegetation which she had scooped from the boggier part of the bank. She hurried back quickly, keeping an eye on the sky.

By the time the rabbit meat was impaled on dry twigs, angled across the steady heat of the fire, the beechnuts and sliced mushrooms were roasting in Gideon's billycan in the middle of the fire. they filtered the water through the moss and then boiled it for several minutes and left it to cool, so they could drink it safely after their meal.

They shared the mushrooms, which tasted slightly stronger than the small field mushrooms which could be bought in supermarkets, and all but Mia ate every scrap of rabbit meat. Mia ate most of the roasted beechnuts, with little whoops—they were extremely hot. Afterwards they drank the cooled water from Dax's flask, quite sure that it had been boiled long enough to destroy any bugs. The moss had filtered out any dirt or grit or insects. It was mid afternoon by now, and they were all sleepy, but they couldn't afford to rest any longer.

Dax shifted to a falcon and did another circuit of the woodland as his friends cleared up the camp, burying the rabbit remains and destroying all evidence of the small fire. He could see no more aircraft. A few minutes' flight took him back to the Minehead road, where he saw that the roadblock had gone, and the traffic was moving normally again. He didn't know if this was good news or not.

Back at camp, he checked for evidence of their presence. They'd done a good job of scattering the damp burnt sticks deep into the undergrowth and covering the soggy black patch of ashes with fresh woodland litter. Nobody would spot anything unless they were seriously looking for it.

He led them all back to the beechnut crop and they worked together, carefully gathering as many as they could carry in their bags. It was now late in the afternoon and Dax was getting anxious. They hadn't covered nearly enough ground. He doubted they'd make it to the Owl Box before nightfall.

The nut gathering had shaken off their sleepiness and they all set out again with renewed energy, weaving along the river bank and looking for signs that they were getting closer to a village. Their adventure had become less scary, just as a result of a good lunch, but Dax was still weighed down with what he'd heard at the roadblock. He sighed, and determinedly put all thoughts of Owen out of his mind, especially the image that kept rising, unbidden, in his imagination, of a blue-eyed assassin, pulling his knife from his belt and slitting the throat of an enemy with efficient precision.

Consulting the map, Dax worked out that the Owl Box

wasn't actually *in* the village, which was called Tallock. They should arrive at it before they reached Tallock. It looked as if it was quite remote—because there were only two buildings marked off the road he had memorized for so many months. They appeared to be down a long track. Good. He hoped it was screened from view with plenty of trees around it.

As they pushed on, the valley *was* getting deeper and darker, with the river cutting down into it, its banks becoming steeper, and a canopy of bright early autumn leaves closing over their heads. Occasionally they spotted other walkers in the distance, and pulled back away from the rough path, moving deeper into the trees until the people had gone.

'Look!' said Gideon, as the afternoon began to stretch into evening. 'It's a disused railway line.' He pointed to a straight cutting through the valley, overgrown but still visibly the scar of an old track. As they got closer they could see that a few ancient wooden sleepers still remained, choked with vegetation and soil. Dax got the map out again and they all peered at it until they found a faint line with *Railway (Dis)* alongside it. It was the marker they had been looking for—the line cutting across the small river. Dax scanned the distance on the map from here to Tallock. He thought it was probably another five miles, along the river path. The light was beginning to fade and they were getting tired and hungry again.

'We won't get there today,' he said and they all groaned. 'We'll have to camp out again tonight—make a proper shelter. I think we should go on for another hour or so, and then get set up for the night before the light goes.'

They moved on quietly. Now that the excitement of the morning was so far behind them they were beginning to slow down, their limbs aching. Dax wanted to remind them that this was still really serious, but he could see they were too tired for a lecture. Besides, he knew that everyone was thinking about it: wondering what was going to happen next. He felt a peculiar sensation on the crown of his head and wondered if an insect had fallen onto it. He raked his fingers through his thick dark hair, but nothing fell out.

They found a good remote spot for the night's camp, on a high bank above the river where holly trees grew densely around them. As they had done several times before, in Owen's woodsman lessons, they found five stout long branches and built a loose wigwam, digging the bottom ends deep into the soil and knotting the top ends together with tough thin roots pulled out of the ground. Then they laid smaller sticks and soft branches all around the framework at angles, weaving some of the bendier twigs in and out. Finally they cut some supple spruce boughs from the lower parts of the trees, using their knives safely as they had been taught, striking always away from the body. Dax felt proud of them all as they quietly got on with the task. What would Owen think of them now?

'He'd be proud,' said Lisa, reading his thoughts, as

they all tucked the soft green boughs in a downward position so that any rain would flow off them, anchoring them into the twigs and patching any gaps with leaf litter. 'He'd be really proud. This is what he was always preparing us for. Exactly this.'

Gideon stood up from the fire he was building close to the entrance of the wigwam. 'So what was that about? If it's Owen that's after us, he must be kicking himself about teaching us all this!'

Dax pressed his lips together for a moment and then spoke. 'If he's coming after us, he's doing it because he thinks it's the best thing. The right thing.'

'So why didn't we go to him at the checkpoint?' asked Gideon. 'What did you see, Dax?'

'Nothing. It just . . . wasn't safe.'

'You saw something, didn't you?' persisted Gideon. 'Or heard something. What? Come on!'

Dax gritted his teeth. 'I don't know! It's just that . . . it doesn't seem safe to go to Owen yet.'

As he spoke the vision of the throat slitting flickered through his mind again and he thought he saw Lisa blink and step back. She dropped her eyes and said, 'Leave it, Gideon! You'll just have to trust us.'

Mia stepped over to Dax and put her warm hand on his shoulder. 'We all love Owen,' she said. 'We really do. We'll sort it out with him when the time is right.'

They found dead bracken and put a spongy mattress of it on the floor of the wigwam and then laid Dax's plastic sheet and their various bits of warm clothing around it.

Dax felt it was safe to make a small fire—the cover of the trees above them should hide it from view, if a helicopter passed overhead again. It was made quickly and efficiently, on a patch of bare earth in front of the shelter. They sat beside it and roasted more beechnuts. The smell was wonderful. Gideon found more water from a nearby spring that trickled down the slope on a course for the river, and collected it at the point where it naturally sopped through more cleansing sphagnum moss. They boiled it for several minutes and drank it as soon as it cooled enough, pouring it first into Dax's and Gideon's metal flasks. The beechnuts were tasty and filling and Dax discovered the four remaining Polos to finish off the meal.

'It's going to be a tight squeeze in there,' said Lisa, peering into their wigwam as the last light faded from the chinks of sky among the leaves above them. She shone the torch around it. 'Bags I go on the other end from Gideon. He's guffing for Britain again.'

Gideon looked hurt and then let out a stout trumpet. 'That reminds me,' said Dax. 'Nobody leave any evidence in the bushes either. Bury *everything*—OK?'

Lisa pulled a face. 'It'll only be three at a time in the shelter anyway,' said Dax. 'One of us will have to keep watch in the doorway. And when I'm sleeping I'll be in fox form again. Help to keep you all warm.'

Gideon said, 'Aw! What would we do without you? Being all fluffy and toasty as you are!'

Dax chucked the empty billycan at him and he

snatched it to a stop with his mind and then spun it casually in the air. Dax felt his scalp tickle again and brushed away an insect which wasn't there.

Lisa abruptly sat up straight and dropped her hands into her lap. 'Listen, everyone,' she said seriously and they all snapped to attention at her tone. The billycan thudded to the ground. 'Have any of you felt anything at all odd, in the last hour? Anything at all?'

There was silence and then Mia coughed and said, 'Um . . . it's probably nothing, but my head has felt tickly once or twice.'

Everyone stared at her and then Gideon said, 'I've had that too. I thought it was midges or something.'

Lisa looked at Dax and he nodded. 'I thought so,' she said. 'I saw you flapping at your hair just then and then I realized.'

'What?' said Gideon. 'What is it?'

Lisa looked around them all gravely. 'We're being dowsed,' she said.

13

'I know this is going to sound ridiculous,' said Lisa, as they all stared at her, 'but you need to imagine something. Right now.' She looked distinctly uncomfortable and shuffled her feet. 'You need to imagine you are covered, completely, by a pyramid—and that the pyramid has mirrors on every surface.'

Gideon snorted. 'You what?'

'Don't,' snapped Lisa, 'make me repeat myself. Damn well just do it, Gideon! All of you. NOW!'

They continued to stare at her for a second or two, and then dropped their eyes as they tried to do as they were told. Dax pictured the mirrored triangles on every plane of the pyramid, gleaming in the soft light of the fire. It rose to its tip just above his head and its base was at his toes. For some reason, his pyramid was also revolving slowly.

'Everyone done it?' said Lisa. They nodded. 'Gideon?'

'Yes! I am capable of imagining a pyramid, you know!'

'Right over your head, yes?'

'Yes! Now tell us what all this is about. What's going on? And why is it always me that has to ask?'

'Keep imagining while I talk to you. Someone is trying to find us and they're using a technique called dowsing,' said Lisa. 'It's a kind of remote viewing. You lock in to certain . . . wavelengths . . . they're a bit like radio frequencies. Energy patterns and stuff. Oh, brilliant! I sound like a healer now. Sorry, Mia, but you know I don't *do* wifty-wafty!'

Mia smiled. 'No—wifty-wafty's doing *you* though,' she countered, smartly.

'Anyway,' Lisa went on. 'People like me, who find things, can do this dowsing thing. You can do the walking around with hazel twigs business, looking for water and suchlike—or you can look at a map and if someone tells you a bit about what they're looking for you can usually pinpoint it on the map—because even the map, though it's a bit of paper made in a printing press with thousands of others just like it, still carries these wavelengths. I don't know how. I think the really top-end finders, like me,' (Lisa didn't even think of being modest) 'we just have to think about something that someone's trying to find— maybe touch the person who's looking or just know them really well, like I know you lot, and that's enough. The image comes, of where the thing is, even if you've never been there or seen it on TV or anything. That's remote viewing. And if you're really good you can even find the map co-ordinates.'

Dax swallowed. 'Does this mean we've been viewed?'

Lisa pursed her lips thoughtfully for a moment, and then said, 'I don't think we have been viewed. Not properly. I don't know how I know—maybe it's *them.*' She made a sweeping gesture above her head and they knew she meant the crowd of spirit people who trailed around after her, trying to get her attention. 'They do sometimes chime in with something useful. Anyway, I don't think whoever is trying to dowse us has actually worked out where we are. They know we're alive—that's the first thing you work out. Dowsing the dead is a very different feeling. Now they'll be trying to find out more—but if we keep doing the pyramid thing, that *ought* to keep them out.'

'But what happens when we go to sleep?' asked Gideon. 'We can't keep visualizing pyramids then!'

'I know,' said Lisa, biting her lip.

'The sentinel will have to do it for all of us,' said Mia, unexpectedly. 'Don't look at me like that, all of you! What do you think I'm fit for? Just mending sprained wrists? I read a lot, about all of the things we do. One of us—as long as everyone trusts them completely, can be a sentinel: sit guard for the others and visualize the pyramid over all of us. It'll work just as well.'

Lisa shrugged. 'It makes a sort of sense.'

'In a wifty-wafty way?' said Mia waspishly, which was quite unlike her. They all laughed and Lisa had the grace to look a bit sheepish.

'Well, that'll work out fine, as we're all doing a watch anyway,' said Dax. 'I'll start—do the first couple of hours.'

The other three looked at each other and then Gideon spoke up. 'No, mate. You sleep first—and sleep a double shift.'

'Why?' said Dax, surprised.

'Because you're using up a lot more energy than we are,' said Mia. 'You're leading us and hunting for us—and flying for us. You've got to be more tired—and we can't have you crashing out before we get to your bolt-hole.'

They didn't look as if they'd be argued with. 'And I,' added Mia, 'will be doing my share of the watch tonight— no arguments!'

Dax felt a warm glow and it wasn't just from the fire. He realized that they meant to look after him as much as he meant to look after them. And they were right—he was bone tired, and he'd had to stop himself eating more than his fair share of the food, he was so hungry after all the shifting.

'You'll help Lisa and Mia get off to sleep, too, if you can go all furry for them,' pointed out Gideon. He took the first watch as Lisa and Mia curled up under the wigwam on either side of Dax who was radiating heat in fox form. He relaxed into sleep more quickly than he expected to, feeling safe under their shelter and Gideon's imaginary pyramid of mirrors.

Gideon kept the fire going and boiled some more water for the morning while he kept watch, and in the depths of his sleep Dax could hear the occasional hiss and rattle as his friend stoked the glowing sticks, along with night noises of the wildlife around them. After two hours Gideon swapped with Mia, who continued to gently feed the low fire and hold them all safe under her own pyramid. Hers seemed faintly lilac to Dax as he slept on, close to the top layer of waking.

Then Lisa took her turn, and halfway through her

watch Dax opened his eyes and stared up into the dark ceiling of the shelter. He gasped and sat up, shifting back to a boy, and said, 'What the hell was *that*?'

Lisa looked over her shoulder, her profile silhouetted by the faintest firelight and a luminous glow of early dawn. 'Oh hell,' she said. 'I was hoping it was just me.'

He eased outside the shelter, careful not to wake Gideon and Mia, and sat down next to her by the fire.

'What did you see?' she asked. She looked as rattled as he felt.

Dax struggled to describe the thing that had hovered in the darkness above his head. 'It was a sort of . . . sphere. Perfectly round. Inside it was moving—kind of *squirming*—like something trapped inside a glass tennis ball. And the way it moved was . . . like a mathematical puzzle or something. Symmetrical but—curly. Moving in and out of itself.'

'What colour was it?' asked Lisa.

'No colour really—sort of grey and black and . . . more grey. It was like . . . *dark* light. Does that make any sense?'

'Yeah.'

'It faded away as soon as I sat up. Is that what you saw too?' She nodded, looking worried. 'What was it?'

She bit her lip. 'I should have worked harder on my pyramid,' she said. 'I let it in.'

'I don't think it had anything to do with your pyramid,' said Dax. 'This wasn't like the first time. Do you think it was another kind of dowsing?'

'Maybe,' said Lisa. 'It felt like something watching us. Something not good. We should ask Mia when she wakes up. I haven't done that much reading about all our stuff. You know I don't like to encourage them. I only learned about the pyramid thing from another girl in Development back at the college. It was working, though—I could feel it. Could you?'

'Yes—I could,' said Dax, surprising himself with how certain he felt. 'Mia's was . . .'

'Lilac!' said Lisa at the same time as he did. 'Yeah—it was. And Gideon's was gold. It *did* work. Whatever got through mine must have been something really strong. That's what worries me.'

'Do you think it knows where we are?'

Lisa sighed and poked at the fire which glowed a dull red. 'I don't know any more. I'm too weirded out by everything. I think we're OK for now. We've got to get to your place tomorrow though, Dax. I think we're too easy to track out here. If anyone's using heat-seeking stuff, they'll find us, won't they?'

Dax hadn't thought about this. He'd been more concerned with supernatural stuff than hi-tech gadgets, but Lisa was right. 'I'll put the fire out,' he said. 'We'll be all right now. We all have to be up in an hour or two anyway. As soon as it's light enough to see properly we'll go. Get some more sleep now.'

But Lisa wouldn't. She said she was stark staring awake and kept him company until the sun's first pale rays began to filter through the trees. Then they woke up

Mia and Gideon. Neither of them knew anything about a strange floaty orb thing. Mia agreed that it didn't sound good, but could offer no ideas on what it might be.

Everyone wanted breakfast but there was nothing to eat except a few leftover beechnuts and Dax didn't want to waste time hunting and cooking before they set off.

'If we get going fast we might be able to get a late breakfast at the Owl Box,' he said, more cheerfully than he felt.

They destroyed the shelter and scattered it around in the undergrowth before burying the remains of the fire, now cold and dead, in fresh soil and leaf litter. With no breakfast to kick-start them, they were not a happy band, but they were all a little spooked by the orb thing and ready to get moving.

'Do we still have to imagine we're under pyramids?' said Gideon, grumpily. He had a very healthy appetite and it was unnatural for him to wake up and not stuff his face.

'Yes,' said Lisa. 'It may not have worked for the orb thing, but I'm sure it was working for the other kind of dowsing.'

'All right,' said Gideon as he skidded down a steep wooded bank towards the dark channel of the river.

They followed the water as closely as they could, helping each other over the small streams that rushed down the hill to join it from time to time. At one of these they collected water in Gideon's billycan and had a bit of a wash.

'No drinking,' said Dax. They had finished all the boiled water at breakfast.

'It's probably fine, anyway,' said Gideon, 'coming out of a fresh spring like that.'

'Can't take the risk,' said Dax. 'We'll have tap water before the end of the morning.'

They moved on and as the sun rose higher Dax thought it was time for another falcon flight, to check around and ahead. He could find the village from the air and work out how much longer their journey would be.

High above the wooded cleave where his friends clambered on unseen along the river bank, Dax could see the twists and turns of the valley. He glided to thirty metres above the canopy of the trees, causing some panic among the small woodland birds below him. In minutes he had reached the village and he tried hard to work out where the Owl Box was from what he'd seen on the map. There were two buildings along the track off the road which was engraved in Dax's mind. Pennylost Lane. A track off Pennylost Lane. He recognized the lane because it zigzagged markedly on the map, taking travellers down and down, back and forth along the steep sides of the deep valley. The track off it looked like broken lines because trees blocked his view of it. Good. The more trees the better.

He dropped lower and followed the track until he saw a small patch of thatched roof. The only other building off the track was clearly derelict and had no roof at all. The thatched building had no smoke rising from the chimney. If this was Caroline's cottage—the place she'd meant him to run to if he was in trouble—then it didn't look as if Caroline was there. This must be her holiday home, as Dax had always suspected.

He turned on the wing and flew back up the valley until he found a spot which he guessed the others would be approaching by now. He dropped into a small clearing and shifted to a fox to sniff them out. He had to backtrack a little way, and found them a quarter of a mile upstream.

'Did you find it?' asked Lisa, hopefully. She looked very relieved when he shifted again and put his thumb up.

'It looks like a thatched cottage of some sort,' he said. 'I reckon we'll get there in an hour or two.'

By the time they reached Pennylost Lane, climbing awkwardly on the steep wooded embankment alongside it, their stomachs were rumbling so loudly that everyone could hear everyone else's. 'Lord, I hope there's some food there,' moaned Gideon. 'I might have to eat my jumper if this takes much longer.'

'If your belly gets any noisier there won't be any point us staying off the road,' muttered Lisa. 'They'll be able to hear you from the village!' Gideon said nothing but his stomach made a rude noise.

At last they found the muddy track which led to the cottage. They followed it, speeding up with excitement, and five minutes later they rounded a bend with tall wild hedgerows on either side of them and high branches stretching overhead, and saw a five-bar wooden gate set into a stone wall. Beyond it lay an unkempt garden with a cobbled path that led to the front door. *The Owl Box* was printed on a china plate beside the door. Gideon and Lisa whooped with relief. Dax had imagined this place for so long that seeing it for real was very odd. The building was a converted old stone barn, with a low thatched roof and pretty leaded windows. The front door was like a stable door, opening in two halves. Dax found his hands were shaking when he took the key and chain from around his neck and pushed it into the lock. It slid in easily and turned stiffly. There was a clunk and the door—top and bottom—opened quietly inwards.

They stepped inside onto a flagstone floor and looked around them in delight. It *was* delightful. The interior was all warm wooden beams, rising in cathedral style to the high ceiling which slanted with the shape of the roof. The walls were exposed stone, softened and cleaned to a pale yellow when the building had been converted and restored. The open fireplace was laid ready for a blaze with kindling and screwed up newspaper in the iron basket and matches to one side of the hearth. Grouped around it were a battered leather sofa and three worn brocade armchairs, all liberally heaped with mismatched cushions. A thick red rug stretched between them on the flagstones. A small kitchen area of green-stained pine cupboards, sink, and hob, stood along the back wall, and an open door to their left led into a white-tiled shower room and toilet.

The loveliest feature, though, was the turning wooden

stairway which led up to a mezzanine floor—a broad timber balcony across half the width of the building. From below they could see two wrought-iron single beds with an old oak trunk between them. A silk-covered lamp stood on the trunk—another one on the matching chest of drawers at the top of the staircase. Early autumn sun poured in from two slanted skylights in the roof.

Gideon was moaning with delight. Not at the beauty of the Owl Box, but at what he'd just found in the kitchen cupboards. Rows and rows of tinned food of every kind were stacked high on its shelves. Gideon held up one tin of custard and another tin of treacle pudding.

'I think I'm going to cry,' he said.

14

At first, when he drifted awake, Dax thought he was looking at the embers in the fireplace. Then he remembered that they had not lit a fire, worried that the smoke would give them away to a sharp-eyed local or a passing military helicopter. They had just put on the electric central heating. Still—there were definitely small red-silver lights in front of the armchair he'd curled up in. Lisa and Mia had bagged the beds, Gideon was on the sofa, and he had taken the armchair, shifting to a fox to make it a more comfortable fit. Dax sat up and stared. Then a shiver ran across him, making the fur at the back of his neck bristle.

I've been expecting you, he said, in his head, to the creature that lay by the fireplace. The wolf got to its feet and fixed its eyes, glowing silvery-red in the dark, upon the fox's. *Tried,* it said. *Tried.*

You mean you tried Lisa? Dax sensed its frustration as it gave a curt nod of its dark shaggy head. The wolf had tried to make contact through Lisa before, but it didn't always work. *She's having a bit of trouble with the Loved Ones' Buffer,* Dax explained and it nodded again. *What can you tell me?*

Three.

Dax frowned as he tried to work out what the wolf was saying. If the wolf had been a living creature, there would have been a helpful scent coming in along with the telepathy, but his spirit friend had no smell. *Three? OK—three things? What?*

Laughing man, sent the wolf. *Bad comes from laughing man.* Dax nodded, hoping he was understanding. *The eagle is protection.* Dax sighed, wondering why everything the wolf said to him had to be a riddle, but he nodded, encouragingly. *Small maker of things,* sent the wolf, before sighing itself. *Small maker of things . . . helps.* As before, its messages seemed to take an immense effort and already it was harder to see, drifting like mist.

Dax repeated the three things back to the wolf in his head and it gave another nod, before turning and walking away. Strangely, Dax could hear its claws clipping faintly on the stone hearth as it disappeared into the dark fireplace. Instantly he shifted to a boy and walked across to the kitchen in search of a pen and some paper. He switched on a dim light above the cooker hob and quietly rifled through the bottom drawer of bits and pieces and unearthed a felt tip and an envelope. He wrote down the three things before he could forget them. *1. Bad comes from the laughing man. 2. The eagle is protection. 3. Small maker of things helps.* He studied the words under the hob light and tried to make sense of them. *Laughing man? Eagle? Small maker of things?* As usual, none of it made a blind bit of sense. Yet. He could only hope to work out the clues in time.

Dax left the envelope on the side, switched the light off, and returned to the armchair. Back in fox form, he willed himself to sleep. He had no idea what would happen tomorrow, but he knew that a good night's sleep would help with whatever came. He curled his tail round to his snout and settled into the saggy cushion of the armchair and sleep reclaimed him quickly.

He was aware of voices but slept on persistently until the smell of toast and baked beans woke him. He shifted back to a boy and peered around the wings of the old armchair to see Mia and Gideon in the kitchen.

'We found bread in a freezer!' said Gideon, with glee. They had spent the previous day resting and eating the assorted delights from Caroline Fisher's store of tins, but hadn't found anything in the fridge or freezer. It was switched off.

'There's a chest freezer out the back!' said Gideon, indicating the small lobby beside the shower room which led out to a back garden, wild and surrounded by trees, with a stream tumbling across rocks at its far corner. 'It's been left on and there's loads of stuff in it. Oh, man! This is so, *so* cool! She won't mind, will she? Us eating all her food?'

'No, I'm sure she left it here deliberately,' said Dax. 'She seemed to know that we'd need it one day. Not bad for a non-Cola, eh, Lisa?'

Lisa leaned over the wooden balustrade of the balcony above, still brushing her hair and wearing a fresh pair of pale pink jeans and a matching fluffy jumper. 'I could've slapped her when I first met her,' she said. 'Who'd have thought a journalist would turn out to be such a godsend? Oh—it was *so* good to sleep on a mattress last night. I would almost have sold her my story for that!'

'Yeah—good for *you*!' muttered Gideon. He'd kicked up a fuss yesterday when the girls claimed the beds.

Dax switched on the TV. It had only four channels, and BBC2 was very grainy, but he felt they should keep an eye on the news, in case their disappearance was being reported. Throughout the previous afternoon and evening they had tracked every news bulletin they could find, but nothing had been mentioned about four runaway children.

They all sat down to watch the morning news with plates of beans on toast and mugs of tea with the long-life milk from Caroline's cupboards. Lisa made a face when she tasted hers, but drank it anyway. 'Tea,' she said, 'is what gets us through.' There was no mention of them on the network news and they all sighed at the end of it. Then the BBC South-West presenter clicked onto the screen and her lead story made them all freeze.

'Thousands of homes across Somerset were without power last night after fire apparently melted *a pylon near Taunton,'* declared the presenter, earnestly.

'South-West Power says it hopes to restore electricity to the 55,000 homes affected within twenty-four hours. The fire is believed to have had a knock-on effect on a number of pylons across the area, and police are investigating the cause.

'Our reporter, Jo Palmer, is close to the scene, by the Taunton Deane services on the M5. Joanna . . .'

The scene switched from the warmly lit studio to a drizzly shot of a young blonde woman by a hedge. Jo Palmer looked intently into the camera as she nodded. *'Anna,'* and went on, *'It's all a bit mysterious at the moment, because we haven't been allowed close enough to the site to see what's happening. We do know that enough damage has been done to the pylons across this area to knock out power to more than 55,000 homes. What's odd is that we can't see the damage—we also haven't had any reports of smoke in the area, which is leading some people to speculate rather wildly. The power actually cut out in the early hours of this morning, and some locals have said they saw something rather strange in the air, just behind this area of hedging and trees which screens the pylons from the road. Joining me now is George Barker, who runs the local pub.'* She turned to a middle-aged man who was smiling nervously. *'George—tell me what you saw.'*

'Well,' gulped George, *'it was a sort of ball of light—not very bright and quite small—up in the air. There was this sort of bluey light over the hedge and this ball thing came up through it. I thought I was just seeing things, but my missus saw it too.'*

Dax and Lisa gasped and looked at each other.

'Did it move anywhere?' went on Jo Palmer, her brow furrowed with studied interest.

'It just sort of hovered,' said George. *'And then it vanished . . . into thin air . . . '* He stared intensely into the sky and Jo Palmer turned back to face the camera.

'As you can imagine, Anna, the UFO spotters have become very excited!'

Back in the studio the presenter smiled indulgently and she and the reporter allowed themselves a chuckle. The presenter then composed her face into one of mild concern and probed: 'Are there any fears that this could be a terrorist incident?'

Joanna mirrored her colleague's expression. 'There has been no official word that police are investigating that possibility, but certainly it has been raised by people we've spoken to. Until the police allow us a closer look and an interview—and right now they're not even allowing the TV crew chopper to fly overhead—well, it's impossible to speculate. We hope to bring you more later.'

As the presenter thanked her and moved on to a story about road building, they stared at each other. Mia switched the TV off. Gideon was still holding his fork of cooling beans in front of his mouth. He gulped. 'Before any of you asks, it wasn't me!'

Lisa gave him a sneery look. 'Gideon—don't get yourself excited. We know you can't do that much damage.'

Gideon immediately rounded on her, stung, his fork clattering back on his plate. 'How do you know? Eh? You think you're so cool just because you can find lost socks and there's always some dead old bag wittering in your ear! You don't know anything about real power. They're not bothered about you, are they? Or you!' He suddenly scowled at Mia, too, who folded her arms and glared back at him. 'It's *me* they're after! And they've got good reason to be, even though it's not me that's been crunching up their crummy pylons. You want to see what I can do? Do you?'

They stared at him in silence as he stood up and fixed his eyes above their heads. At first there was no sound but Gideon's agitated breathing and then there was a faint metallic twang. On the floor above them, behind the wooden balustrade, not one but *two* metal bedsteads, complete with mattresses and the bedding they'd found in the airing cupboard, were floating high enough to bump gently into the wooden beams at the top of the ceiling.

Dax felt very uneasy. It wasn't that he hadn't thought Gideon could do this—it was the way the metal of the bedsteads was beginning to sing. The wrought-iron legs were vibrating so intensely that a musical hum was coming from them—and now the bedclothes and pillows were beginning to writhe about, curving and curling as if possessed by the spirits of angry snakes. There was a hot, electrical smell in the air.

'Gid,' said Dax. 'Gid—mate. Stop it.' But Gideon was angry and Lisa was angry too.

'Cut it out, you idiot!' she hissed at him, tugging sharply at his arm. He didn't respond, holding his concentration and pressing his lips together. Lisa's expression also intensified and then she leaned towards him and murmured, 'You want to know what I'm getting from the beyond? Eh? Do you? Do you? And I'm not just talking about your Auntie Pam—I'm talking about your grandad and your nan and your Uncle Pete and your little mate from the nursery—Joshua—the one who died of meningitis, and your first-year teacher, who called you Curly Top and took you to the first-aid box when you fell out of that tree and—'

'Lisa!' Mia looked horrified. 'You can't use this stuff! It's not right. Stop it!'

But Lisa's eyes were still locked onto Gideon's face, which was flushed and sweating, and the beds still shook and whined and the linen and pillows still writhed, and now cutlery from the kitchen surface was beginning to ping up through the air and stick to the iron bedsteads, as if they were giant magnets.

'You know these people—don't you? Don't you? Not just some old bag wittering in my ear after all, eh? I know stuff! I get stuff like this *all the time*!' Lisa's expression was almost vicious. 'They're telling me you have to STOP! You have to STOP NOW.' Her voice rose to a shriek that gave Dax goosebumps down his spine. 'You're putting us all in danger! STOP! STOP! STOP!'

Gideon's eyes snapped away from the spectacle upstairs and onto Lisa. He looked furious and his teeth were chattering. She was almost nose-to-nose with him now and suddenly something in him seemed to snap. He shoved her away so hard that she fell back into the sofa and as she did so there was a tremendous crash. The two beds had dropped back onto the wooden floor upstairs, followed by the clink and rattle of cutlery tumbling back down through the air.

A few seconds' silence followed. Then Lisa, sitting up and brushing toast crumbs off her sleeve, remarked, 'Well, I'm glad we managed to clear the air on *that*.'

Mia and Dax both let out shaky sighs, too shocked to laugh. Gideon sat back down and rested his head in his hands, drawing in long slow breaths.

'What did you mean, Lisa—about him putting us all in danger?' asked Dax, his unease still very much with him.

'Did I say that?' She looked slightly dazed. 'I probably did. It was a bit . . . blurry. You know . . . heated.'

'You're not kidding.' Dax looked at Gideon, who was now as pale as he had been pink and flushed a minute before. 'Mia?' She nodded and moved across to Gideon, touching the back of his head. The boy let out another long breath and started to look a better colour.

'I think what Lisa is picking up,' said Mia, in her lovely calm voice, 'is that if we use our powers too much, we're creating a kind of beacon. Like radio waves—what we do probably sends a kind of interference into the atmosphere, and certain people may be able to pick that up.'

'Like whoever was dowsing for us?' asked Dax.

'Yes,' said Mia. 'And maybe whoever sent that strange orb thing. We don't know, do we? But . . . ' She stood back from Gideon and let her hand drop. He gave her a small smile of thanks and picked up his mug of tea with a trembling hand. 'To be on the safe side, it's probably best that we don't do any Cola stuff. Was that man on TV describing the same thing you both saw?'

Lisa and Dax nodded. 'That's what it would look like from a distance, I think—so it can't be coincidence,' said Dax. 'It's something to do with the pylons and Gideon.'

'So why didn't I see it?' muttered Gideon.

'You might yet,' said Dax. 'It might not have been there for me or Lisa.' He shook his head. 'I need to shift to the falcon and keep an eye on things from the air from time to time.'

Mia shrugged. 'I know you think that, but it's probably just like sending up a flare, every time you do it. We need to be dull and quiet here for a while, until we've worked out what's happening and what we're going to do. Even healing Gideon just then—a really little heal—that might be sending out a signal. Don't you think, Lisa?'

Lisa nodded. She looked at Gideon and seemed faintly guilty. 'Look . . . I'm sorry about all that stuff,' she muttered. He didn't reply, but stared into his mug. 'I don't normally do that sort of thing, you know. But . . . I got a warning from my . . . ' she wrinkled up her nose and looked acutely embarrassed, 'I got a message from . . . I have this . . . helper.'

Suddenly Gideon whooped with laughter, tipping back into his chair. He pointed at her, singing out like a playground chant: 'You've got a spirit guide! You've got a spirit guide!' Dax grinned at Lisa's rising blush.

'I have *not* got . . . I mean it's not like . . . '

Gideon was now rocking back and forth, giggling. 'Ah! *Brilliant!* Lisa Hardman, hard girl of the medium world! What's he called? He must be a Native American,

yeah? They're always Native Americans! Let me guess—
He-Who-Fights-With-Teatowels! Or no—Waltzes-
With-Rabbits? No, no, no . . . Run-Like-Deer, Poop-
Like-Cat!' Lisa picked up a cushion and whacked him
hard across the head with it.

'Her name,' she said, testily, 'is Sylv.'

Gideon gave another hoot of laughter. 'Sylv? What
kind of Native American name is *that*?'

Dax was intrigued. 'How long have you had her?'

Lisa huffed and folded her arms. 'She's been knocking
around right from the start,' she muttered.

'But . . . let me guess,' said Dax. 'You just ignored
her.'

'Well—duh! Of course I did. What would I want with
a spirit guide when I don't want any spirits, eh? I've told
her to push off countless times.'

Dax shook his head at her. 'I'm surprised she puts up
with you. You are *such* a nasty girl.' She stuck her tongue
out at him and even Mia laughed.

'Sylv's all right,' conceded Lisa. 'She's got a great
sense of humour and her language is shocking.
Sometimes she keeps the maddest dead people off me
for a while, when I get really tired. Anyway, what I was
trying to explain, Gideon, is that she was warning me,
more or less, about what Mia said. We'd better hope you
haven't already blown it with that stupid bed business.
Male ego—honestly!'

'Dax,' said Mia softly and, with the look on her face,
he at once felt that familiar twinge of responsibility. She

was looking at him again, as if he knew the answers. 'Do you think we're safe here?'

He didn't know what to say. Eventually he got up and went to the window and they all seemed to be waiting for his response. It wasn't much comfort when it came.

'I don't know if we're safe anywhere.'

15

After they'd cleared up the breakfast things they searched for maps. Dax wanted to look at the areas where the pylons had been damaged. They found an old radio with batteries that were still working and put that on, to listen in to the local station for any more news, and also put the TV back on, with the sound down, keeping an eye on it for more information. At last Mia unearthed a dog-eared motoring atlas and they found the first pylon location by the service station on the outskirts of London, not far from Gideon's house, and then traced the route of the M5 around Taunton until they found the motorway services area mentioned in the TV report.

Dax sat back on his heels and gulped. It looked horribly close to where they were. No distance at all by air. They looked at each other, wide-eyed.

'There's one question we haven't really answered,' said Gideon. 'If this isn't me, which we know it isn't, even though,' he shot Lisa a look, 'I am clearly *capable* of it—if it's not me, then who is it?'

'Maybe it really is a fault with the electricity grid?' said Mia, hopefully.

Lisa shook her head firmly. 'You didn't see it. It was

like a load of melted toffee. A real mess. And I didn't see any sign of fire, did you, Dax?'

'No—and I didn't smell it, either. I would've smelt it from miles away.'

'So who then?' persisted Gideon. 'And, more to the point, why?'

'What worries me is how close these events have been to Gideon,' said Dax. 'If they'd happened up in Scotland we wouldn't be in this mess.'

'Mess?' said Lisa, crisply. 'I think we're handling it pretty well, actually.'

'Yeah right,' muttered Gideon. 'Right up to the point where we run out of food. And don't forget, you say Dax can't hunt! And even if he could, Mia wouldn't eat it. And I haven't had any chocolate for more than twenty-four hours, and that's really not good.'

'We obviously can't just stay here forever,' said Dax, trying to think clearly amid Lisa and Gideon's bickering. 'But if we can stay away from Ow— from *them* for a bit longer, we might be able to find out who, or what, *is* melting the pylons. If we could prove it's nothing to do with Gid, then we'd probably be OK. I mean, they don't *want* to lose us, do they? They want to study us and all that, so they don't want us . . . you know . . . neutralized.'

They all looked gravely at him and he realized he might have been the first to say out loud what they had all thought at some point. Just how dangerous did a Cola have to get before *neutralizing* them was the safest course of action?

'We've got family,' said Lisa, quietly. 'They'll be asking questions. They'll be worried. That's got to count for something.'

'Right, so, we know it's not me,' said Gideon, briskly, and Dax knew he was worrying about his dad, left stranded and confused in the shopping centre. 'And we think it's some kind of paranormal power, but we don't know who or why.'

'We haven't got enough information,' sighed Dax. 'We need to know how many pylons have been melted and where they all are. It looks like it's all being covered up as much as possible. I really think I should fly over the area—see what I can see.'

'Too dangerous,' said Lisa. 'If you *are* giving out a sort of beacon signal, then you could be traced all the way back here.'

'Oh, this is getting us nowhere!' said Dax, exasperated. He went to the front door and they all looked at him, tensely. 'Look—I'm just going out into the garden! Nobody can see me from the air; it's covered in trees.' Lisa nodded. He went out and left them still looking at the map.

He wandered to the little brook that tumbled across the far corner of the garden, glancing up at the chinks of sky between the leaves as if something *was* silently hovering over them, tracking them down. Think! He needed to think, the way that Owen would think. But Owen was a man in his thirties, a government agent and a skilled survivalist. *An assassin*, said a small voice in his mind. *And you're a twelve-year-old boy who can kill a rabbit when you really have to.*

There was a snap away to his right and Dax was suddenly on full alert, his fox senses throttling up inside him—hearing, scent, sight, and instinct. Was there someone further out in the trees? *You're just nervous— spooked,* his human common sense told him. He stood quietly and looked around, lifting his nose to the air. Something . . . something familiar. Probably just Gideon creeping up on him. His head cracked left in a split second. There—in the trees—a glimmer of light, like something reflecting on glass. He felt his heart begin to hammer in his chest, and fought the urge to shift to a fox: if anyone *was* watching him that could be even more dangerous.

Keeping his eyes on the area where he had seen the glimmer, Dax frowned and sent Lisa a message, hoping she wasn't too distracted to pick it up. *Lisa—send Gideon out after me. Quietly.* For what seemed like ages nothing happened and he sent the message several times. Then Gideon emerged from the back door and looked around the garden. He caught Dax's urgent expression and mouthed '*What?*' Dax motioned for him to come over and Gideon did so, trying to tread lightly.

'I think there's someone out there,' said Dax, his throat tight with nerves. They both paused, silent, and just when Dax was beginning to think he'd imagined it, there was another glimmer and another snap in the thick woods to the right of them. 'We've got to check it out,' said Dax.

They moved in an arc around the garden, clambered over the low stone wall boundary and crept into the woods towards the source of the noise and the light. Dax picked up a scuffling sound and that scent again— *familiar*. But how? Could it be Owen? No—he would never have made a sound. He and Gideon moved swiftly between the trees, quietly rolling their steps as Owen had taught them and pausing behind the thicker trunks to listen. Their watcher was moving away from them now, in some haste. Occasionally they could hear a rustle of leaves or the snap of a twig and Dax caught the scent more and more strongly. It was like following one of those ribbons of smell that led to a hot pie on a window ledge in a *Tom & Jerry* cartoon. As they got closer, Dax felt less scared. Like a predator. He pictured one of Owen's agents, maybe someone a bit less experienced, getting ready to report back by radio. They had to get him and stop him—maybe even take him prisoner and use him to bargain with. Dax's thoughts were getting feverish; Lisa would laugh out loud at him—how on earth would he and Gideon overcome a grown man?

But then, as they came to the top of a hillock among the trees, he caught a movement below him. Instantly he realized that there was a hollow in the tangle of roots beneath their feet—and whoever it was was hiding there. He was picking up a scent of fear rather than aggression, which made him feel more confident. He pulled up short, motioned downwards to Gideon and gave him a meaningful look. He counted to three with his fingers and then both he and Gideon leapt down and turned into the hollow.

Their stalker yelped as they grabbed him, arms and legs scrabbling wildly in the dirt. 'Got 'im! Got 'im,' yelled Gideon, piling all his weight onto their captive, who seemed to be shielding his head with a large grey backpack. As Dax tried to haul it off him, he kicked out at Gideon's leg and Gideon grunted: 'Yeah? You want some? You want some?' and kicked him back.

There was a squeak and Dax fell backwards down the slope with shock. In less than a second he had realized who it was. There was another squeak and a little cursing in very mild language considering how much kicking and counter-kicking was going on.

Dax ran back up the slope and dragged Gideon off. 'Wait! Stop!' His disbelief rang shrilly in his voice. 'I know who it is! I know who it is!'

As Gideon reluctantly pulled away, the head behind the backpack began to shakily emerge. A grubby face came into view, two large grey eyes staring short-sightedly at them both while a hand felt around ineptly for spectacles which had fallen into the dirt.

'What on earth are *you* doing *here*?' gasped Dax, utterly astounded.

Their stalker grinned weakly and sniffed. Gideon looked round at Dax, confounded. 'Who is it?'

Dax started to laugh. 'It's my friend. It's my friend Clive!'

'Gideon! Did you have to kick him quite so hard?' asked Mia, as she sponged the dirt off Clive's bruised shins. Clive stared at her, his mouth slightly ajar, surfing wave after wave of the Mia Effect. Totally in love.

'Well, I didn't *know* he was Dax's mate, did I?' said Gideon. 'We both thought he was a—a—baddie of some kind,' he finished lamely. 'And why was he running away in the first place, eh? Eh?'

Dax poked at Clive and then moved his head around until the boy focused his eyes normally again. 'Why did you run away?' asked Dax.

'Well—I didn't know who was with you,' said Clive. 'I was approaching it all tactically.' Gideon snorted and Mia glared at him. Dax sat down in the armchair beside the sofa where Clive was reclining, still shaking his head in amazement at the sight of his schoolfriend, here, with his Cola friends. It was weird. Like finding out your maths teacher went ballroom dancing with your dad. 'It could have been enemies in here with you,' Clive went on. 'You might have been held captive . . . or . . . or something. And . . . well, I couldn't get my glasses to work properly with my binoculars, so I was trying to use the binoculars without them, and I couldn't really see that well. I didn't actually know, for sure, that it was you.'

'How long have you been out there?' demanded Lisa.

'Oh—only since this morning. I got a bus to the village, after the coach dropped me off—and then camped out for a bit, watching the house.'

'But how on earth did you find us?' Dax could feel his

brain doing a strange sort of yoga—trying to bend around the amazing fact that Clive—*Clive*—had tracked them down.

'Oh, that was easy,' said Clive. He leaned forward, shooting a loving glance at Mia, who was now drying his soggy, pummelled legs with a tea towel, and reached for Dax's throat. With a flick of his fingers he pulled out the key, still on its chain around Dax's neck. Dax looked down at it, confused. Clive laughed—the laugh he always did when he knew he was cleverer than anyone else in the room. Not smug, but pleased; relieved. 'Look closely at it,' he urged and Dax undid the chain so he could turn the key over in his palm.

It was a fairly ordinary looking key with the manufacturer's name and circular logo engraved at the top, on both sides. As Dax turned it he saw a glint of something black and shiny, embedded into the engraving. 'What's this?' he held it up.

'Tracking dot,' said Clive, airily, pushing his corduroy trouser legs back down. 'Strongly magnetic. You've been sending out a signal since the day before yesterday—but only to me. Nobody else could have picked it up.' The Colas were stunned. They gaped at each other. 'To be honest, Dax, I'm disappointed in you! I thought you would have checked. Seeing that a load of people must be after you, didn't you think there might be something stuck to your shoe or somewhere? This is junior school stuff!' They all began to look uneasily at themselves, checking for something small, black, and strongly magnetic. 'Look at the things you always wear—like shoes and watches and jewellery and stuff,' advised Clive. 'The heel of the shoe is a favourite one.'

They all did, sitting down and turning up the soles of their trainers urgently. Clive laughed. 'It's all right. You're all clean,' he said. 'I've already swept you. Only Dax was bugged and that was mine.'

Dax sank back into the armchair. 'OK—let me get this straight. You put a tracking dot thingy on my key, and then you got a signal of wherever I was going—and then you followed me here. Why? I don't understand.'

Clive beamed. 'Well—it was partly an accident really. Just lucky I spend so much time on the internet and all that and get loads of birthday and Christmas money, rather than socks or soaps shaped like footballs or CDs of pop songs . . . ' Clive noticed that they were all, now, screwing up their faces in confusion. 'OK—it's like this. I had just got a SatNav tracker and some tracking dots through in the post when I saw you, Dax. I thought it would be a laugh to try one out with you—and I was going to tell you, but then . . . then you were a bit strange, weren't you? All *"I don't know where I'll be or if I'll ever see you again, Clive,"* kind of thing. And,' he gulped, 'well— this'll sound weird, but I got a sort of . . . intuition that you might have some trouble.'

Lisa cackled. 'Yeah—well weird!' she said.

Clive looked embarrassed, but carried on. 'So, just as I was going I thought I'd put the dot on you. I could see if it worked, and, if you did go off somewhere, I could tell where you were.'

'What are you?' said Lisa. 'Some kind of computer nerd stalker?'

'Lisa, don't,' said Dax, and she bit her lip obediently.

'Anyway, I saw that you went off pretty quickly after I'd gone. By the time I got back and checked the tracker monitor, you were right out of the county and going north-east. You must have been flying.' Dax nodded, fascinated. 'So, you know, that was a bit worrying, but I thought I'd leave you to it. You know what you're doing and all that. Then I started just doing stuff around my lab.'

'Your lab?' gasped Gideon.

Dax waved impatiently. 'He's got a big bedroom and half of it is set up as a laboratory and workshop,' he explained, as if this were completely normal. 'Go on, Clive.'

'Well—I was just doing stuff and then I got an email from one of my newsgroups. You know—you register with them about a certain subject you're interested in and you get emails about anything interesting that crops up on the internet about the thing you're interested in.'

'Sounds interesting,' said Gideon.

'So I've been signed up to all kinds of weird stuff since . . . well, since all of you lot happened,' went on Clive. 'I get news on psychic stuff, healing—all that new age guff. Sorry.' He smiled at Mia and Lisa. 'And shapeshifting, of course, although most of that is nonsense; all role-playing games and stupid teenagers who wear a lot of black eyeliner. Anyway, there was this ping, and some new stuff came through. On telekinesis. And pylons.'

There was a total hush. Dax was the first to break it. 'What? What do you know?'

Clive was pink with enthusiasm now. 'Well, remember we had that power cut, Dax? Last Sunday night?' Dax nodded. 'Well, I think that's when it started. And there was more than one power cut, let me tell you. A lot more than anything you heard on the news. It's been hushed up. As far as I've been able to work out, there have been . . . ' he did a swift calculation in his head, ' . . . twenty-eight pylons melted so far.'

'Twenty-eight?' gasped Gideon. 'Pigeons on a *stick*!'

Clive gave him an odd look. He wasn't used to Gideon's weird exclamations. 'Twenty-eight,' he repeated. 'At least. Across the south and south-west of England. They're trying to keep it quiet and they're even stopping all air traffic over it. A lot of the stuff that came through was about UFOs, of course. Loads of people think it's first contact with extraterrestrials. Terrorists is another one, but nobody believes that. Not spooky enough. Then there was this little bit from someone going on about mind power and saying that environmentalists are hitting back at the big power companies by getting in telekinetics to knock over their pylons. Tosh! I never laughed so much in my life. But I got to thinking about Gideon and started to wonder about you all. Then I got my map of Southern England out and—well—look.'

He reached across to his bag behind the sofa and

pulled out a folded map. He spread it out across the rug in front of the fire and they all leaned in. Stuck to the map, in efficient Clive style, was a rash of perfect red dots, charting the melted pylons. Nobody spoke, but, as they took in what they were seeing, the room seemed to get colder.

Travelling across the map from right to left, the dots indicated a line, beginning in the north of Hampshire, travelling up to the south-eastern end of Berkshire and then sloping down across Wiltshire, before appearing to leap—with a gap of a hundred miles or more—into South Devon, a few miles outside Exeter, before a final visit to Taunton in Somerset. The last red dot marked out the motorway services area that the TV report had come from that morning.

'Very weird,' said Clive, tapping the edge of the map thoughtfully. 'At first I just sat at home, surfing the web, trying to find out as much as I could about it all. And then the transponder would beep at me and I'd know you'd changed direction a bit, or gone over a county border. Wherever you went, a few hours behind you—power cuts. Squashed-up pylons. No overhead traffic. Government operatives all over everything like ants, according to the information on the net. It had to be you guys! No wonder the suits have been running around, going bonkers. I'm amazed I got to you first. What's Gideon been up to?'

16

It took the whole of lunch to convince Clive that it wasn't Gideon. Munching on ravioli from one of the tins, Clive eyed him sceptically. 'So why is this destruction following you all?'

'Someone or something else is doing it—*not* Gideon,' said Dax. 'We need to find out—so we can find Owen and clear Gideon and get back with all the other Colas in the new college.'

Gideon was glaring at Clive. 'Why would I *want* to do it? What would be the point? I love *Coronation Street*. Why would I knock out the power to my own telly?'

'Maybe it's subconscious . . . like a poltergeist,' enthused Clive. 'You know . . . those invisible spirits that chuck stuff around, usually in the bedrooms of sulky teenage girls.'

'Yes—we *know* what a poltergeist is,' muttered Lisa.

'Well, I expect whatever it is will catch up with you soon,' said Clive, cheerfully. 'And either explain itself—or incinerate you. It's definitely chasing you—the map proves it. Maybe it *is* an alien! Using the power grid to travel by . . . ' Clive's eyes widened as he marvelled at this possibility. 'One or two people claimed to have seen a small light bobbing around in the sky nearby. Mind you, people normally claim that.'

'There may have been,' said Dax, and told Clive about the orb he and Lisa had seen.

'But why would an alien want to follow Gideon around?' snorted Lisa. 'Surely it could find more exciting things to do!'

'But that orb thing *could* be a UFO,' persisted Clive.

'It was only the size of a tennis ball!' spluttered Lisa. 'Not exactly *War of the Worlds*!'

'How do you know? Just because it was novelty-sized, doesn't mean it couldn't be *more deadly* than an entire fleet of motherships,' said Clive, talking like an advert for a soon-to-be-released sci-fi blockbuster.

'No,' said Dax. 'It's not that. I don't know what it is, but it's not an alien, I'm sure of it. I want to fly out to see all these pylons, but we think we might be getting tracked—supernaturally, I mean. By someone who can pick up whenever we use our powers.'

Clive nodded. 'Makes sense,' he said. 'Must be a lot of electrical disturbance whenever you do your thing. Oh! That reminds me!'

He jumped up, dropping his fork with a clunk, and went again to his backpack, which was almost half the size of its owner. Out of it Clive tugged two long cardboard tubes. He undid one of them and quickly shook out a shining river of tin foil. He pulled a reel of thick white sticky tape out of his cardigan pocket and walked over to the kitchen window, the foil drifting after him with a ghostly whisper.

Clive worked quickly, pulling the fine wooden blind down and closing it, and then tearing and folding a double layer of foil, which he pressed to the wall around the window frame. He held out the reel to Mia who was closest. 'Please,' he said and Mia began to hand him strips of tape, her eyebrows raised. As the others watched, mystified, Clive securely taped the foil across the window opening until no light showed through. He moved on to the small window to one side of the front door, and then began the same strange ritual, closing the curtain on the window first and then sealing it from the edge of the sill to the top of the curtain rail with more doubled up foil.

'What are you *doing*?' demanded Lisa, at last.

'Don't just sit there,' said Clive. 'Get the other roll and do the rest of the windows with me. I should have done it as soon as I got in. It's to stop them tracking you with lasers. Any laser or infrared technology trying to track heat or movement in the house won't be able to get through the metal. Shut the curtains first, though. If they get close enough to see the foil they'll guess something is up.'

'You don't say,' murmured Lisa.

'Come on.' He chucked another reel of tape at her, which she caught deftly. 'It may not look great but it works. We'll probably be able to leave the skylights; can't reach 'em anyway. Then I need to get out and sensor the garden and the lane. Dax—can you help me?'

Dax was so impressed he was speechless. He followed as Clive went outside with his backpack, from which he pulled more high-tech gadgets. There were eight twin sets of 'sensors' as Clive called them. Small black units which could be set up anywhere, facing each other, to create a laser beam bridge between them. If the beam was broken by something passing through, a remote alarm, set up back in the Owl Box, would go off.

'How did you get all this stuff?' asked Dax, in awe.

'I get most of it from the internet, some from magazines. I make a few things myself too,' said Clive, modestly. 'It doesn't cost all that much and Mum and Dad don't mind paying for stuff like this—helps my engineering projects. They think I'm a genius.'

'You are,' said Dax.

'Some of it doesn't work and it's just a con, but I've worked out the good suppliers now.' He set one of the black units into a gap in the boundary wall, facing out across the track that led to the Owl Box. Dax set up its twin at the same height, nestled into the soft earth bank opposite. They set another laser trap further back up the track, just past the intersection with Pennylost Lane. Then they worked around the boundary of the garden with the remaining six pairs, covering every access point they could think of.

'What happens when a fox or a bird or something goes through?' asked Dax.

Clive shook his head. 'Won't trigger it. The lasers are set too high up for wild mammals and birds shouldn't set it off. Anyway, the movement is different and it's supposed to be able to tell the difference. If one of us has to go out for some reason, we just have to remember to drop to our hands and knees to go underneath. Hang on—I'll just check this one.' He pulled a small oval container with a round metal lid with holes in it out of his trouser pocket.

'Talc?' said Dax, astonished. Clive nodded and turned the lid before upending the bottle and giving it a gentle shake. A fine cloud of talcum powder drifted down to the path, and, as it passed the laser units, fragments of the fine red beam were briefly revealed.

'It's working,' said Clive and twisted the lid shut again, with a waft of tea rose perfume.

As they walked back up to the front door, Clive paused and began rummaging once again in his bag. 'Ah,' he said. 'Good. I thought I'd packed this.' In his hand was a reel of fine cord. He pulled a bit of it out and Dax could see it was transparent—almost invisible. 'Where's your rubbish?' asked Clive.

'In the bin, in the kitchen,' said Dax. 'Why?'

Clive led them back inside, where the lamps were now on, with all of the windows now mantled in tin foil. He went to the bin, flipped the lid and grunted with satisfaction. Then he began hauling out all their discarded tins. He took about a dozen of the squashed, sticky containers to the sink and began to rinse them out under the tap. Lisa was staring at him as if he'd gone mad.

He looked at her over the top of his glasses and said, 'You could help, you know.'

She gaped at him and everyone else grinned. It was hard to imagine Lisa *ever* doing washing-up (she'd neatly avoided it so far). There were servants to do that in her world. Nevertheless, she shrugged and began to help him. A few minutes later Clive was punching holes into the sides of the washed tins with a metal corkscrew. They stood watching him, fascinated, as he then threaded six at a time on either end of about four metres of the transparent cord. He took it back out into the garden, the tins trailing him noisily, and began to place them close to the gate, carefully, among the overgrown grass— six on either side of the path. He placed the uncluttered cord that connected the two clusters of tins across the path, snagging it lightly on stones on each side, so that it was suspended three or four inches above the ground. He stepped back and looked at it.

'Go down to the gate and walk up,' he said to Lisa. She did so, stepping high where Clive told her to on the way down, and then turning to retrace her steps. 'Don't look at your feet,' he said. 'Just walk normally.'

Lisa walked normally. After four strides there was a loud clatter as the tins were abruptly tugged together. Lisa's foot had caught the cord. She laughed. 'Not bad,' she said. 'Not bad. But won't it give away that we're hiding here?'

'By the time you hear that,' said Clive gravely. 'The game will be nearly over. It's a back-up, if they get past the lasers. It will only give us an extra few seconds, but it's something.'

Dax shivered. He looked up into the sky above them and wondered how close 'they' were. As if in answer to his thoughts, there was a remote vibration—a thudding in the air. Dax gulped. The others couldn't hear it yet, but he knew what it was.

'Inside,' he said. 'Now!' They bolted in, scared. By the time they'd shut the door everyone could hear the approaching helicopters. Two—maybe three, thought Dax, his fox hearing acute, even through the muffled windows and walls. They sat silently on the chairs and sofa, gazing up to the high skylight windows. Mia was squeezing Lisa's hand, her violet-blue eyes huge with fear.

'Keep going, keep going,' muttered Gideon, as the black outline of a military chopper came into view overhead. It hung in the air above them like a malevolent insect and Dax felt sick. If it came to a chase, he could shift to a falcon and escape, he was sure of it. But what about his friends? He couldn't desert them. Helplessness washed around inside him.

After what seemed like half an hour, but could not have been more than thirty seconds, the helicopter moved away from their view. For another five minutes they sat, tense and silent, listening to the coming and going of the search above their heads.

'They must be working their way back and forth across the countryside,' said Dax, at length. 'Just working across it until they pick something up. Could they have picked us up, Clive? From up there?'

'Only if they really got lucky,' said Clive. 'Their heat-seeking stuff shouldn't be able to get through all that thatch and old stone. And the chances of lasers getting down through those skylights is slim. None of us was directly underneath. I can't see how they could . . . but . . .' He shrugged. 'I know quite a lot about this stuff . . . but I don't know everything.'

Half an hour after the last sound of the helicopters had died away, they began to feel slightly less tense. They switched the television back on to check the news, but only a daytime quiz show and some DIY programmes were running.

They let the sound of the quiz show burble quietly in the background—it seemed vaguely comforting as they sat around the unlit fire and tried to work out what they should do next.

'There's no point in trying to run,' said Dax. 'We're far more likely to get caught if we're moving across the country again, than if we stay here. I'm sure we'd have heard the alarms go off by now if those helicopters had dropped any patrols down to find us. They can't know we're here.'

'So how long do we stay here? This is driving me nuts!' complained Lisa.

'I think we have to have at least a full day without any helicopter noise before we can risk moving outside again,' said Dax. 'Oh, I *wish* I could get out there! Fly around a bit and see what's happening!'

'I wish we had Barry with us,' said Gideon. 'That really would be a help.'

'Who's Barry?' asked Clive.

'He's one of our friends at Cola Club,' said Dax. 'A glamourist.'

Clive blinked. 'Glamourist?' Dax could tell he was picturing someone dressed in a glittery frock and high heels and had to grin. He had thought exactly the same when he'd first heard the name.

'No—it's not what you're thinking.' He laughed, in spite of his jangled nerves. 'Glamourists mess around with what you can *see*. A glamour is a trick which makes you see something differently. So if you're like Barry, you're the kind that can disappear—really vanish into thin air.'

'You're kidding!'

'No—Barry can do that. Well, mostly. He's always got such a stuffed-up nose that you can hear him whistling and glugging through it half a mile away.'

'And he's always falling over stuff,' added Gideon. 'He's about as graceful as a three-legged hippo on stilts. It takes away the element of surprise.'

'What other kinds of glamour are there?' asked Clive.

'Well, there's the illusionist kind,' explained Dax. 'Still messing with what you can see—that type can make you see stuff that isn't there. The illusionists did a whole firework display for us last year. Didn't cost the college a penny.'

Clive took a moment to imagine this. 'So . . . so you saw fireworks which weren't there?' he asked, at length.

'Well, *we* did—*and* heard them!' said Gideon. 'Dax didn't though. Dax has got immunity.'

'Immunity?'

Gideon sat up and clapped Dax on the back. 'Spook Williams *hates* that! He can't get one over on Dax, because Dax is a part-time fox and that means he's resistant to glamour! He can usually even see Barry, if he puts his mind to it—but Spook can't get anything past him at all!'

'Spook? What kind of a name is that?' asked Clive.

'I think his real name is Spencer,' said Mia, much to everyone's surprise. Nobody knew that Spook had a 'real name'. 'He told me once,' she said, looking slightly embarrassed. 'He made up Spook when he came to Cola Club. He says it's his stage name and he wants everyone to know him by it, because that's the name that'll be famous.'

Gideon and Lisa snorted with laughter.

'Spook is going to be the best-known magician on the planet, apparently,' Dax told Clive. 'He's totally in love with himself and can't wait to be famous.'

'He's not all that bad,' said Mia kindly, but Lisa touched her shoulder and reminded her: 'He wears a *wizard* cloak! In his own time! With sequins on it!' Everyone snorted with laughter again and Mia sighed and gave up.

'Who else have you got then, in the Cola Club?' asked Clive, intrigued.

'Well, there's over a hundred altogether,' said Dax. 'Healers, like Mia, mediums, psychics, dowsers, telepaths—like Lisa. She can do all of that stuff.' Lisa made a face, somewhere between pride and annoyance. 'There are a couple of telepathic brothers—Jake and Alex Teller—they're a good laugh. They're brilliant mimics as well. They have us creased up when they do Spook in his snogging the mirror routine.'

'And there's other vanishers, like Jennifer Troke,' added Gideon. 'She hangs out with Barry a bit, and gets him into trouble in class. Everyone always blames Barry though.'

'I'm looking forward to seeing Jessica Moorland again,' said Mia, softly. 'She's a good friend. She's like Lisa—a medium. But she can't read minds or find lost things like Lisa can. All the other healers are lovely too. It's like they're family.' Lisa rolled her eyes, but she patted Mia's arm.

Clive hugged his knees and looked wistful. 'I would *love* to be at Cola Club,' he said. 'You're all so lucky!'

'Yeah—lucky enough to be trapped in here with a pylon-melting monster and half the British secret service trying to find us!' muttered Gideon. He and Dax went upstairs to look out through a gap in the tin foil, in case they could see any pylons in the distance. They couldn't.

'I'm sorry about all this, mate,' said Gideon, quietly, as Mia and Lisa went on telling Clive about Cola Club in the room below.

'Why should you be? You didn't bring us here.'

'Maybe you'd be better off turning me in though,' mumbled Gideon, sitting down on one of the beds. 'This sounds like it could be really dangerous ... what Lisa's been picking up and all the stuff that Clive's told us. I don't want you all getting hurt because of me. You should let me give myself up.'

'I can't do that,' said Dax.

Gideon looked at him sharply. 'You found out

something bad, didn't you? When you went off to the roadblock? What?'

Dax put his face in his hands. 'Gid—Owen is . . . he's not just an ordinary bloke.'

'Well, I know *that*,' said Gideon.

'It's just that he's—he's killed people, you know.'

Gideon looked at him levelly. 'He's been a soldier, I reckon. That's what soldiers do. Sometimes. Doesn't mean he's a murderer.'

Dax shook his head. 'I know—I know. But what I heard made him sound so—ruthless.' He related the conversation he'd heard in the van and saw his friend swallow nervously.

Gideon thought for a while and then spoke quietly, glancing down to be sure nobody else was listening. 'What does your fox instinct tell you about him?' he said.

'I don't know. I'd have to see Owen or at least smell him to pick up anything. But I don't know if I can risk that now. And you definitely can't. What if he really would do *anything* for his country? Anything at all.'

Gideon looked dismayed. 'Dax . . . you've always thought Owen was the best.'

'I know,' said Dax, his misery dripping off his words. 'I know.'

There was a shout of horror from below them and they hurtled downstairs to see Lisa scrabbling for the remote control.

On the television screen in front of her was her own face.

17

Lisa brought up the volume as Dax, Mia, and Gideon were also pictured, staring cheerfully out of the screen from old school photos.

'. . . *children are believed to have gone off on a camping trip in the North Devon or Somerset area,*' said the female newsreader, as four old school photos of themselves stared out at them. *'But they haven't been seen for several days and their parents are now desperate with worry. Earlier today, the father of one of the boys, Gideon Reader, made an emotional plea for his son to come home.'*

Gideon groaned aloud as the report moved to a small stage area where his father sat at a table next to a uniformed chief constable, looking grey and strained. '*I only want to say,*' Michael Reader mumbled, as a number of camera flashes lit him up, '*that if you can hear me, son, I just want you to come home. You're not in trouble. I'm really, really worried about you—and your friends—and I just want to know you're OK.*' He paused and the chief constable beside him murmured something in his ear. He nodded and said, wearily, with his eyes not quite on the camera, '*And if there's anyone out there holding Gideon—stopping him coming home—please—please—let him go. Let them all go.*' He lowered his head into his hands and the scene ended, returning to the newsreader, who looked solemn.

'*Police are asking anyone who may have seen these children to contact them on the emergency number on the screen now,*' she said. '*They also say that they're not sure if one of the children is still with the others. Dax Jones, who has dark hair and is about five feet tall and slimly built, may have left the party and could be alone. It's thought, also—rather unusually—that the children may have a pet bird of prey with them. Police say that the public need not approach the children, but should call them immediately if they have any information. Now . . . other news . . .*'

They stared around at each other. Mia switched the sound back off. Gideon looked very shaken. 'I can't believe they got my dad to do that. Dax—you did give him the note, didn't you?'

'Yes,' said Dax. 'I did. But he won't know what to do, will he? He won't know about what's happening.'

'I'm glad they didn't get *my* dad on,' muttered Lisa, angrily. 'I'd've freaked out!'

Mia looked grave but didn't mention her dad at all. 'They're clever,' she said. 'They know you might be travelling as a bird, Dax. So they're getting people to look for three children, as well as four. And that bird of prey bit . . . they're clever. This is Owen, isn't it? Maybe Mrs Sartre too. I don't know what to think about them any more.'

'If we could only get a message out,' sighed Dax. 'To Mrs Sartre, maybe—make them all understand that it isn't Gideon doing the pylons in.'

'But how can we prove it?' said Lisa. 'We can't, can we? He could be public enemy number one to them. And I'm telling you, they'll lock him away. Underground. Put drugs in him or something. Wires around him . . . '

Gideon sniffled and said, 'I didn't know you cared . . . ' Lisa narrowed her eyes at him and Dax was pleased to see he was messing about. Scared, but still messing about.

Nobody felt much like food, but as the afternoon stretched towards teatime they opened some more tins of hotdog sausages, spaghetti hoops, and boiled potatoes.

'Lord—what wouldn't I give for a fresh salad,' sighed Lisa. Then she gave a small scream. Like a signal from an alien world, the telephone had begun to ring.

Everyone froze. The phone was on a table by the front door, and they'd barely glanced at it since they arrived, knowing it was traceable and useless to them. Slowly, as the ringing continued, they looked around at each other. After six rings, to their surprise, there was a click, and a tinny voice announced: *Sorry—Caroline's not here right now—although she wishes she was! I don't know when I'll be back next, so call me on my mobile if you need me soon—otherwise leave a message after the beep.* She rattled off her mobile number and then there was a long beep and after a pause, someone began to leave a message.

'Hi, Caroline—this is me, Caroline—leaving me a message because I always forget stuff when I get down to the Owl Box. REMEMBER to clean up as soon as you get in. You know how wild animals sneak in sometimes.'

They all looked at each other, and Dax felt his heart speed up with excitement.

'So anyway,' Caroline's voice went on. 'If there *are* any wild animals knocking around, eating my grub and listening to this—you'd better clear out before I get there. Get a shift on. There are some . . . er . . . guests on their way, too, I think. And they might get in before I do, and I'd hate them to find the place crawling with you lot! They might not be as soppy about furry creatures as I am. So get out fast, please. That's all, Caroline—you forgetful woman!'

There was a click and the peculiar message ended.

'Was that for us?' whispered Gideon.

Dax walked to the answerphone and pressed the PLAY button. They listened to the message again. 'Yes,' he said. 'They're coming. They must have found out about this place and worked out we might be here— that's why she called. She's warning us. Come on. Get your stuff. Take some food. Be quick.'

They erased the message that Caroline had left them. 'We don't want them giving her a hard time,' Dax explained.

'We need to split up,' said Lisa, suddenly. They all looked at her and Mia shook her head, worried.

'We do,' insisted Lisa. 'Mia and I need to go off with Clive. Clive needs to put Gideon's clothes on—and his awful hat. And keep his glasses off.'

'Um—excuse me—I can't *see* without my glasses!' complained Clive.

'Well, you'll have to manage! We need to be a decoy,' said Lisa, firmly. 'They're looking for four or *three* children. We can be three children, and we can maybe lead them away from Dax and Gideon. Shame we haven't got a pet falcon, really. Still, maybe we can keep feeding peanuts into Clive's backpack and making cooing noises.'

Dax bit his lip. He wasn't sure about splitting up. Lisa poked his shoulder. 'I'm right, Dax! I know I am. I've got enough money to get us on another coach or train up north. And if we make sure we're seen by security cameras or something, then they'll come after us after a few hours. It'll give you and Gideon a chance to get away. Go down into Cornwall or something.'

'And then what?' wailed Dax, suddenly overwhelmed by it all. 'What do we do after that? Any ideas, anyone? Because I'm all out of them! I don't know what to do!'

Lisa paused and Dax realized her eyes had gone hazy. She was rubbing her left shoulder again and nodding abstractedly. 'Go,' she said. 'Something must be *seen*. I don't know what that means—but you will work it out! I know you will.'

'Is that what Sylv is telling you?' asked Gideon, without any teasing in his voice this time.

'Yes. Sylv says you two go south. There's something that has to be . . . *seen*. You can't go to Owen yet. He's not . . . reachable.'

'Yet?' said Dax. 'Do you mean he *will* be reachable? Is it safe—I mean—Lisa! Is he on our side or not?'

Lisa looked pained. 'I really don't know,' she sighed. 'I

don't! It's all confused and messy and I'm tired and . . . '
She took a sharp breath and stood up straight. 'We have to
go now—and I am taking Mia and Spock here, with me.'

Dax nodded, finally convinced. Clive changed quickly
into Gideon's clothes and Gideon said no thanks to his
corduroy trousers and knitted cardigan in exchange,
and put on his spare jeans and sweatshirt. Lisa pulled
some of her money out of her pocket and gave it to Dax.
'Remember—no powers unless you really have to,' she
said. 'Just in case.' Mia hugged them both and Clive looked
at Dax, nervously, from under the peak of Gideon's hat.

'You really want me to go with them?' he asked.

'I know Lisa's a bossy madam,' said Dax, with a grin.
'But she's tough. She'll look after you.'

Clive looked offended. 'Look—*I'm* Spock, apparently.'
Dax could tell he was secretly delighted with the
nickname. 'I'll look after *them*!'

'Won't your parents be trying to find you, too?' asked
Gideon. Clive shook his head.

'Nah. I was supposed to be at a BAYS get-together
this week. British Association of Young Scientists,' he
explained. 'They think I took myself off there.'

'So what happens when this place calls to say you
haven't arrived?' said Gideon.

'They won't. I emailed them from my mum's email,
saying I was sick. Then deleted the evidence. And if they
email back it won't get through. I put their name onto
the junk email list. Their messages will go straight in the
bin. Mum'll never look there.'

Gideon shook his head. 'I know you're not a Cola,' he said, 'but you should be.'

'Time to GO!' said Lisa, by the door.

She, Mia, and Clive went first, Clive only pausing to shake Dax's hand and say, 'Good luck. We'll duck under the beams as we go, so we shouldn't set them off.'

Mia hugged them both again, giving them a warm pulse of energy to help them along. After the door closed behind them, Gideon and Dax stared at each other for a moment and then lifted on their backpacks, heavy with tins. Fortunately there had been two tin openers in the kitchen drawer, so both parties had taken one.

They made to go, but then Dax paused. 'Wait—I need a pen and paper,' he said. In the kitchen drawer they found more paper, pens, and envelopes. Dax knelt on the floor and wrote a note. 'For Owen,' he said to Gideon. 'Just in case. It might help.'

Dear Owen, he wrote. *I know you're looking for us, and you're probably really angry with me, but I promise you, we only did this because we had to. You have to know that Gideon is NOTHING to do with the pylons. It's not him. Lisa thinks if you get Gideon he'll be put in an underground bunker because he's dangerous. But you have to believe he's not. We are staying away until we can decide what to do.*

Please trust us. We will try to get in touch when we think it's safe. Tell Gideon's dad he's OK.

Yours sincerely

DAX

PS. Please don't put Gina on TV.

Gideon read the letter and nodded. They sealed it, and wrote Owen Hind on it, and then, as an added security measure, melted some hot wax onto the seal, using a white kitchen candle. Then they left it propped up by the phone. Maybe ten minutes passed while they did this. It was ten minutes too long. Just as they lifted their bags up again a high-pitched whine cut through the air and a red light flashed urgently on the black box beside the door.

One of Clive's laser beams had just been broken.

18

They stared at each other, wild-eyed. 'Could it be Lisa and the others? Going out?' gasped Gideon. Dax shook his head. He could already hear the hiss and whine of radio communicators and more chopper noise in the distance. They hurtled out of the back door of the Owl Box, keeping low to the ground and leaping across the boundary on the side of the garden furthest from the track. Had the others already been caught? wondered Dax, as they belted into the woods behind the garden, his legs shaking so much he could hardly run on them. He thought not. Somehow they had slipped away. He was sure there would have been a telepathic warning to him from Lisa if they had been caught.

But now it looked as if he and Gideon would be. He felt like a total idiot for stopping to write a letter! What was he thinking?

They ran on, deeper into the woodland, but Dax could not shake the sound of the radios. There was another sound too—one that made him feel sick—an animal noise. They must be moving in, on down the track towards the Owl Box. Even as he thought this there was a distant clatter of what could only have been Clive's tins. They were at the door.

'Faster! Faster!' he gasped at Gideon, although neither of them was managing too well. Shocked and scared, they were staggering more than running. The closest bit of woodland, thankfully, sloped downwards, taking them out of view of the team of agents descending on their hideaway. Ahead, it rose again. Dax remembered from his last flight that they were in a steep and heavily wooded cleave. He and Gideon would have to scale a very high hill and get down the other side before they were a mile away from their pursuers. If these men were half as well trained as Owen, he didn't reckon they stood much chance.

'I'm going to have to shift,' he panted, as they began to climb up the next slope, grabbing at the fine branches of the trees and the thick networks of ivy across the steeply angled ground.

'What? Go ahead?' puffed Gideon.

'No! Of course not! I'm not leaving you,' said Dax. 'I'm going to fly back again.'

'Why? They could see you! They might shoot you out of the air!'

'No—I'm not going right over them. I'll fly around them and off in the other direction a little way. Then I'll shift back into a boy and run away from them, as noisily as I can—draw them away. I need your old socks.'

'What?'

'Give them over! Now!'

Gideon didn't argue, although he peered at Dax as if he was going barmy while retrieving some muddy socks from his bag. Dax took the socks and sniffed them. 'Euurgh,' he winced. 'Perfect. Just the job. Get to the top of this hill and wait for me under the trees. I'll make a falcon cry when I come back, so you can wave.'

Before Gideon could say any more, he was flying up between the branches. Above the canopy he could see two of the black military helicopters, hanging low over the Owl Box. Between the trees he could make out flickers of colour and light and realized that dozens of men must be deluging down the track and into their bolt-hole. He flew low, close to the tops of the trees, and skirted the area, well aware that Owen could be down there, or in one of the choppers, scanning with his binoculars. He saw no worrying glints of glass and swooped down to land between the trees just north of the track—close enough. Close enough.

As soon as he'd shifted back to boy form his old panic began to stir and tickle in his chest. The dread. It wanted to come out to play, but this was not the time. Dax took a long, steadying breath and with it came the unmistakable scent of dogs. Search dogs this time, rather than foxhounds. All the same to him, though. Dax had nearly died in the jaws of hounds only months ago and the dread of them had still not left him. He could hear them now, their barks shrill and sharp against the thudding of the rotors overhead. It made him feel sick and weak. He had to ignore this. Had to. Dax began to run noisily along, staying parallel with the noise and scent a few metres away from him. He sensed a quickening in the dogs; the urgency of their baying increased and they were turning towards him, he could hear it, pulling their handlers along. There were shouts of excitement. Dax shouted too.

'Gideon!' he bellowed. 'This way! This way! Get up, Gideon!'

He turned north again and ran as fast and as noisily as he could, heading for a small clearing in the trees where he could take flight. The dogs were getting louder. He reckoned he had about five seconds before he was seen. As he ran he dropped Gideon's smelly socks behind him. Moments later they were seized in the wet jaws of the lead dog, as a falcon shot high into the sky above. It stooped, dropped, and turned in the air, low above the trees, and Dax made his way back to Gideon.

He gave a shrill falcon screech as he coasted down, eyes ready for the slightest movement of his friend's fair head. Gideon was huddled under a tall pine tree, and stepped out to wave. Dax dropped heavily on to his shoulder and Gideon yelped.

'Ow!'

'Sorry,' said Dax, as soon as he was back in boy form. 'Couldn't find anywhere else to land.'

'What did you do with my socks?' asked Gideon, rubbing his shoulder.

Dax explained and Gideon chortled. 'Saved by smelly socks! You really think they'll believe that we're both down there, just because the dogs found my socks? Brilliant!'

'Well, they're bound to have stuff that belongs to

us—that smells of us, for the dogs to follow our scent,' said Dax, still with a faint shudder. 'Hopefully they'll go in the other direction for a while yet, before they work out they were tricked. If Owen's with them that won't take long. We have to keep moving.'

After two hours it seemed as if they'd been stumbling, climbing, scrabbling, and sliding through woodland forever. Twice they fell into a bog and staggered out slicked in dark mud. The sounds of the search, though, receded, and Dax began to hope they really had got away. Another hour took them to the edge of a long, sloping escarpment of heather and gorse, with very little tree cover. Wild ponies grazed in the valley below them—exposed and highly visible.

'We can't go across here yet,' said Dax. 'We'll have to wait until it's dark. Make camp for a while and get some rest.'

'Are we far enough away?' asked Gideon, scanning the sky warily.

Dax considered. They'd been moving for three hours, but it was still possible for a helicopter to catch up with them in minutes. So much of their journey had been up and down hills.

'Probably not,' he said. 'But we can't go any further south now. We'll have to wait. Come on—let's rest and eat. It'll be about three hours, I reckon, before it's dark enough to go across.'

'We'll fall in a bog,' said Gideon. 'We won't even see it coming! We can't use torches, can we?'

'No. But I'll shift to the fox, and then I can see and I can lead you,' said Dax.

'Even though Lisa said not to?'

'I don't think we've got much choice now,' said Dax. 'No need for you to use yours though.'

They settled down under some small trees, tucked far back into the undergrowth. Gideon got out a tin of corned beef and a tin of mandarins in juice. They ate the meat and fruit and drank the juice, saying very little, and then lay down on Dax's well-used plastic sheeting. It was a warm evening, and there was no need to light a fire. Just as well, thought Dax, because neither of them had the strength. They were both exhausted and Gideon seemed really low. They fell into a troubled sleep, Dax shifting first to a fox, so he could keep his ears cocked for trouble.

He dreamed of Lisa. She and Mia and Clive were on a train, heading north. Then he dreamed of Owen. Owen was laughing and shaking his head at Dax as if to say he was on to him. 'Are you working straight?' Dax was asking him.

He opened his eyes and found himself not so very surprised to see the orb again, floating over Gideon's sleeping face; curling in and out of itself in perfect symmetry, like a mathematical puzzle. Dark light. Dax sat up, still a fox, and it seemed to spin around at him, like a baleful grey eye—although it looked the same from every angle. Dax liked the look of it even less this time. *GO*, he told it, in his head. *You are not welcome here.* It blinked away into thin air.

He shivered, wishing it could have been the wolf who'd come to visit them, rather than that weird thing. He checked through the wolf's last warning to see if it made any more sense now. At least part of it he understood. *Small maker of things helps.* Of course, that was Clive. And he had certainly helped. Without his wacky alarms they would almost certainly have been caught by now. He smiled to himself—which would have looked strange to anyone who'd been watching the fox beside the sleeping boy. Who would have thought that Clive, of all people, would end up on the run with them? Where was he now? He hoped his dream had been accurate—sent by Lisa maybe, to let him know they'd got away.

He focused his mind back on the other two messages: *Bad comes from laughing man* and *The eagle is protection.* Nope. None of that made any sense. He was pretty sure there weren't any eagles on Exmoor. Buzzards and kites and kestrels, yes—but no eagles. And who was the *laughing man*? Could be anyone. He shrugged. It was no help.

Gideon woke up half an hour later, when it was almost dark enough to go. He found Dax sitting, brooding, back as a boy. 'I was dreaming,' he said.

'About Lisa?' asked Dax, instantly.

'No! Why would I be dreaming about *her*?' said Gideon, grimacing.

'Just wondered . . . I was dreaming about them all, on a train. I hope it's true.'

'I was dreaming about Catherine and Luke,' said Gideon, softly. A tawny owl hooted somewhere above him and a lone bat flickered past in the sky, hunting moths. Dax looked at his friend. Gideon didn't normally mention Catherine and Luke much.

'I dream about them a lot,' Gideon said. 'I dream about getting Luke away from the water—that he's safe. At home with me and Dad. And sometimes Catherine's there too. And it's all been a mistake and she's fine, really. She's not bad at all. All laughing, like she used to be.'

Dax didn't know what to say. Catherine had turned out to be the most dangerous, callous person that he had ever encountered. Worse, even, than Patrick Wood. Patrick would have killed Dax and Caroline Fisher for his own convenience. Catherine would have killed every single Cola—including her brothers—for hers.

'Then I wake up,' concluded Gideon, 'and remember how useless I really was. Sometimes I wish I had never met either of them at all. But that's not fair on Luke. I let him down.'

'I'm so sorry, Gideon,' said Dax. He couldn't think of anything else to say.

'Never mind. They're dead, aren't they? And that's that. I guess.'

Dax didn't tell him about the orb. He was distressed enough already.

As the velvety night sank over them they rose and packed away their stuff. Away from the town it was truly dark, lit only by the stars which studded the sky like chips of diamond above them. Dax shifted to the fox and Gideon rested his hand on his best friend's furry head as they picked their way down into the wide, shallow valley, heading further south. Where to? Dax hadn't a clue. He remembered Lisa's words. *'You will work it out, Dax. I know you will.'* Yeah. Right.

Gideon walked silently beside him, humming occasionally and, from time to time, longing for chocolate, out loud. 'It's been days,' he said, wistfully. 'Days!'

Exmoor ponies shuffled away from their path, munching at the dry turf in a loud rhythm. They seemed quite unconcerned by the odd pairing of human and fox. As the night wore on they passed through more wooded areas, across further expanses of heather moor, down deep valleys, across shallow gurgling brooks and up and over more hills. Once, a herd of deer froze before them in the starlight, like an elegant painting. The chief stag looked Dax squarely in the eye before shaking his antlers and turning. Then they all turned and ran delicately away.

'Wow,' breathed Gideon.

As the sky began to grow lighter in the east, Dax scanned the horizon for somewhere to shelter. They were back in the middle of open moor and needed to find tree cover soon. He felt nervous. They needed to move faster. The search patrol back at Pennylost Lane would surely have widened out by now. He had expected to reach the far side of the moors by this time, perhaps to find a small village—a road or railway which would take them down into Cornwall. But all he could see was endless undulating moor and the occasional small rocky hill, sometimes crowned with an ancient standing stone.

'How much further, do you think?' asked Gideon, as if he was reading Dax's thoughts.

Dax shifted back briefly, so he could speak. 'I don't know. We need to get to cover soon, though. We'd better speed up.'

Half an hour later, he knew they were in trouble. Still surrounded by rolling moor, Dax felt the fur on his neck prickle, and turned round. On the eastern horizon he could see a black speck. He couldn't hear it yet, but he was sure he knew what it was.

'What?' said Gideon, staring after him edgily. Dax shifted to the falcon and rose easily on the early morning thermals, high, high above Gideon. As soon as he turned on the wing to face east, his vision immeasurably improved, he could make out the familiar shape of the military craft. He stooped, curled down and was back beside Gideon in seconds, shifting to a boy.

'Chopper!' he gasped. 'Run! Over to that!'

He pointed to a small round hill ahead of them. At its top stood another of the strange stones—ancient monuments thought to have been put there by Stone Age man. They pelted towards it, glancing back at the black speck in the morning sky, which was slowly growing larger. The stone was five metres or more in height and seemed to be bent over, halfway up, with a smaller rock tipped against it at the base. Inside the inverted V between the stones was enough space for Dax and Gideon to squeeze into. They ducked down and crawled in as fast as they could, hauling their bags in behind them. Granite, thought Dax. Probably granite. Good. Surely no sensors or heat-seeking stuff could get through *that*.

They crouched wordlessly, their scared breathing rattling against the dark stone, and strained their ears for the approach of the search patrol. The thudding in the air came and went with the light breeze, but it was growing louder. Soon it seemed to be thundering overhead, cutting through the air like a giant blender. Dax and Gideon found they were screwing their eyes shut, like small children hiding from monsters.

They kept them shut until the horrible sound began to fade away. In a few minutes it had gone altogether.

Gideon puffed out his cheeks and wiped his mouth. 'Blimey. That was a close one. Looks like we're stuck here for the day.' He was right. The sun was up now, and if they tried to move from their shelter they would be easily seen. 'Good job we've got supplies.'

There were probably enough tins of food and bottles of water to see them through two days, if necessary, thought Dax. He peered out of the side of their stone tent, then leaned across Gideon and looked out of the other. Miles and miles of open moor lay around them. The only cover was another small hillock with another stone on it, a quarter of a mile away. If there had been a dozen more like that, running in a neat path south, they might have risked running between them—but Dax could see only one.

He settled back with a sigh. It was going to be a very dull day and his head felt thick with weariness and perhaps the start of a cold. He shivered. 'Let's sleep,' he said, and they both settled down again. When he next awoke it was late morning and Gideon was sitting up, moaning softly, his back to Dax. 'What?' hissed Dax.

'Oh no,' sighed Gideon miserably. 'It's my dad.'

Dax sat up so fast he cracked his head on the stone slant above him. 'What?'

'They've dropped my dad out there—he's down there. He's calling me. I can see him. Dax—I can't do this any more.' Gideon looked round at Dax and his eyes were red and wet. 'He's been calling me for the last ten minutes. I thought I was dreaming it at first. It's just him, on his own. I think I have to go. I really think I have to go.'

Dax rubbed his temple and stared out past Gideon's shoulder. 'Where?' he said.

'Down there,' said Gideon, with a wobble in his voice. Dax could tell he'd had enough. Maybe it *was* time to give in now; maybe Owen had found the letter and they believed that Gideon was innocent. Maybe . . .

'Wait!' Dax seized Gideon's elbow, as he was about to spring out of their cover. 'Don't move!' Dax lay flat on his belly, and eased out of the lowest angle of the stone, straining his eyes to see Michael Reader roaming the moors in search of his lost son. Nothing. He could see nothing. Neither could he hear the man's calls.

He glanced back at Gideon, wondering if he was in a sort of sleepwalking state, but Gideon was making eye contact with him, and looked totally awake. He was pulling his bag onto his back and shaking his head at Dax. He'd had enough.

Dax looked around once more and there it was. Yes. There it was. In the stretch of moor just beyond the other small hill, the air shimmered and waved. It was not nearly hot enough for this to be a heat haze. Dax inhaled deeply and then shook his head in amazement, before hauling Gideon back under the shadow of the stone.

'It's NOT your dad, Gid. Don't go anywhere.'

'But I can see him!' wailed Gideon.

'No—you can't. That's not your dad. It's an illusion. Do you know who's really out there? I can smell that stupid gel he puts in his hair.'

Gideon gasped, his eyes wide.

'Yep,' nodded Dax. 'It's Spook Williams.'

19

He must be somewhere on the other side of the small hill, thought Dax. He wondered if Spook had actually seen Gideon, and thought probably that he hadn't. Whoever he was with—and it must surely be the military search patrol or part of it—would have descended on them by now if Gideon had been seen.

Gideon looked at him bleakly. 'What are we going to do?'

'You are going to stay here—and *I* am going to see our old classmate,' said Dax, through gritted teeth. Trust Spook to betray them. Dax could imagine how nauseatingly self-important Spook would be feeling, helping out a crack squad of Owen's soldiers. He shuddered.

'They'll see you,' said Gideon, miserably. 'They might shoot you. Why don't I just give myself up? I'm tired. I don't care any more.'

Dax rounded on him. 'What—so we put ourselves through all of this for nothing? No way! Don't you even *think* about it, Gideon. Imagine what Lisa would say.'

Gideon winced and Dax realized he'd said the right thing. Gideon wouldn't be able to stand Lisa knowing he'd wimped out. 'All right. Sorry. I know you've all done a lot for me.'

'And you would for us,' said Dax. 'Now, lie down and stay still. I don't know how long I'll be. Try to stay calm.' Gideon nodded.

Dax looked outside again and saw that the shimmer in the air had moved slightly east. He knew he'd have to be very fast. He was thankful that some low cloud had crept across the sky. If he went up fast, he could get through it and be barely visible. He shifted, flexed his fine wings, and shot into the air, up through the fine shroud of water vapour, within four seconds. Had he been seen? Looking down, he thought not. He could see six or seven men below, crouching low to the ground, and periodically running along, knees bent, keeping down, travelling north-east of their hiding place, not towards it.

Walking east towards them, shivering slightly with his efforts (and it must take some effort to keep his mirage steady for that long, thought Dax) was Spook Williams. Dax could see his dark red hair, and realized he was wearing the same army-style clothing as the others. Oh, how cool would Spook think he was? Dax shuddered inside his bird body at the thought.

He observed how the men spread out, working across the land in an organized grid, checking the thicker clumps of heather and shallow moorland hollows for runaway boys. They had not yet seen the stone shelter that Gideon lay beneath, but surely would, at any time—if he didn't do something right now. Decided, Dax flew a little way south of them and then dropped like a stone, inverting his aerodynamic body like an arrow, pulling up and putting his talons down again only seconds before hitting the ground. As soon as he felt the heather beneath him he shifted to a boy and began to run, upright and clearly visible, to the south.

Once again, he called urgently to a phantom Gideon. Immediately he sensed, rather than saw, the turning of many heads. He heard the chatter and whistle of radios and then a shout. They were giving chase. There was a small drop in the moor ahead of him—a shallow basin no more than ten feet across. It would have to do. Dax waved his hands, as if motioning Gideon on ahead of him, and then leapt into the middle of the shallow basin of grass, ducking just out of view of his pursuers. As he did so he shifted back to the falcon—then coasted very low across the tufts of vegetation, turning and scudding a hundred yards west of where he'd been seen, before shooting high beyond the clouds again. He prayed he hadn't been spotted, but thought that even if he had, the patrol would still be chasing the imaginary Gideon south.

Clearing the cloud, he looked down through the occasional gap in the mist to see that his hunch was right. He could see the excitement building up in the patrol. They had been hunting for days, and were probably delighted that it was nearly all over. They moved upright now, running with great confidence. Then Dax caught sight of Spook, who wasn't running at all, but poised, preening himself, beside the small hill with the standing stone, just south of his and Gideon's. A burst of fury ran through Dax, from the vicious tip of his beak to his tail. Noting that none of the patrol were looking back at Spook, he dropped, fast, aiming for that dark red head.

He struck Spook so hard, at more than ninety miles an hour, that the boy toppled over on his back without the breath to even shriek. Even so, Dax hadn't given him the full impact. He didn't want to knock him out. He wanted to talk. Oh yes—he wanted to talk. As Spook swayed up onto his knees, a thin trickle of blood running off his scalp and down his forehead, Dax shifted quickly to a boy and yanked his adversary by his arms, round to the far side of the standing stone, out of sight of the patrol below them.

'You scumbag!' he hissed into Spook's shocked face. As soon as he realized who his attacker was, Spook began to recover his usual swagger.

'You!' he sneered. 'Oh, you're in so much trouble, Dax Jones. There's talk of you being expelled from Cola Club, did you know that?'

'You traitorous, slimy git,' said Dax, through gritted teeth. 'I bet you couldn't wait, could you? To do what you could to snitch on us.'

'Snitch on you?' snorted Spook, getting back to his knees and dabbing at his forehead. 'What do you think this is, Dax? Bunking off school for a laugh? Who do you all think you are? The Famous Five? Gideon, Lisa, Mia, Clive, and Daxy the dog? Yeah, that's right! They've found your mate Clive too—with Lisa and Mia. You're the traitor! Not me. You're putting all the other Colas at risk by what you're doing. They're going to be watching us all, all the time now. And that's *your* fault.'

'They were watching us all the time, anyway!' spat Dax. 'I wouldn't have expected you to work that out on your own, though. What did they offer you, eh, Spook—to betray your own kind? Your own TV show?'

Spook was known to have been rehearsing a show for months. To boost his illusionist glamour, he liked to use real tricks too, and was given to throwing showers of glitter out of his sleeves and wearing an assortment of flowing shiny capes at weekends. He'd written to various TV channels suggesting a show based around a talented young magician. He'd never received a reply. Dax was fairly certain his letters hadn't even reached the channels.

'They asked me to help,' said Spook, curling his lip. 'And I was happy to do it—for my country.'

He looked so pompous that all Dax wanted to do was punch him. So he did. Spook shrieked this time and Dax immediately regretted it. What if the patrol heard? His enemy was on him, though, before he had time to listen for them, dragging him down onto the wiry grass and punching back. Dax took a smack to his face before he writhed away from the bigger boy with a sharp knee into his ribcage and Spook gasped, winded.

'Now you just listen to me,' panted Dax, aware that Spook could shout out for help at any time. 'You don't know what you're doing—I bet they haven't even told you what's happening, have they?' Spook was holding his ribs and fighting to get his breath back, but he gave Dax a mutinous look which told him he was guessing right. Nobody had fully briefed Spook. 'I'm telling you this—if we don't make a stand for each other when things start going bad, then it could be any one of us, buried in an underground bunker. Do you get that? You're in just as much danger as Gideon! You could probably do as much damage with your Cola powers as he can. Do you get that? Or are you just too thick?' Spook stared at him, looking confused. 'If it comes to it, we would have to do this for you, too. Like you'd ever deserve it!' Dax went on. 'Tell Owen—we'll always be sticking together. They take on one of us—they take on all of us!'

'Owen?' grunted Spook. 'What's he got to do with it?'

Now it was Dax's turn to look confused. 'He's running the search patrol—isn't he?'

'No!' Spook looked at him as if he was an idiot. 'Why would a *teacher* be running it? It's being run by some government suit called Chambers.'

The name seemed vaguely familiar to Dax. He frowned, kneeling on the turf, trying to make sense of this. He had definitely seen Owen at the roadblock on the Minehead road.

'Where's Gideon?' Spook asked, suddenly. 'And what's he supposed to have done?'

Dax sat down, leaning against the stone behind him, touching his lip, which was swelling. He saw no reason not to tell Spook, who also leaned against the stone, delicately prodding his ribs and wincing, but showing no sign of calling for help—yet.

'They think he's been melting electricity pylons all

over the country—knocking out the power. Causing blackouts. It's not him, though.'

Spook looked at the blood on his hands. 'So why hasn't he just called Control and told them?' he said. 'I mean—hello-o! You can't live out on the moors like a pair of Neanderthals for ever. Well—correction—*you* probably can, and good luck to you. But Gideon can't. He'll croak without chocolate.'

As much as he loathed him, Dax realized that Spook was probably right.

'Well.' Spook got to his feet, with a hearty grunt. 'Can't sit here chatting all day, delightful though it is. Tell me where Gideon is and we can get it over with. You know you're beaten. And what have *you* got to worry about? Nobody's scared of foxes or budgies, are they?'

Dax restrained his urge to punch Spook again. 'Gideon's nowhere near here,' he said. 'I heard you all from miles away—well, actually, I could smell your hair.' He wrinkled his nose. 'How much more gel do you think you can get in it?'

Spook ran his fingers across his head and glared at Dax. 'They're not even close,' Dax went on. 'So they might as well give up. Find Owen, if you really care about the Colas. Tell him what I told you. We'll be in touch—but he'll have to do something to make us trust him before we come back in.'

He sounded far tougher than he felt. If Spook only knew it, his words had hit home. Dax wondered again if he had done the right thing, taking his friends on the run.

Before Spook could say anything else to unsettle him, he was airborne again, flying high overhead and moving south, hoping to convince Spook that he was heading back to Gideon. If the boy had any sense at all, he would check the neighbouring standing stone—but, looking back, Dax was relieved to see that Spook didn't have *that* much sense. He was running back down towards the patrol, waving and screaming and pointing up at the falcon as it disappeared into the cloud. Good! He flew on for several minutes until he could no longer see any sign of the search patrol, then he curved a graceful arc to the west and made the return trip in a wide circle, avoiding flying back over the patrol. Once he heard the familiar chopping of a helicopter to the south, but it was moving further down country. They had bought themselves a little more time.

Gideon was looking pale when Dax flew back under the stone tent.

'That was close,' said Dax, cheerfully, but his friend didn't smile.

'I saw something,' he said, with a gulp.

'Yeah—Spook Williams, like I said. Did you see me thump him?'

Gideon shook his head. 'After that. I saw something. In here.'

Dax stared at him. He didn't look well at all: there was a sheen of sweat on his face and he was trembling.

'What? What did you see?'

'It was weird. A kind of—ball thing. All squirmy. I didn't like it. It was . . . I think it was . . . '

Dax felt cold. He nodded.

'You've seen it too?'

'A couple of times now. Don't you remember? Lisa and I told you about it that morning—when we were still in the woods.'

'Oh yeah,' said Gideon, faintly. 'We haven't been doing our pyramids, have we?'

Dax sighed. He was sure that no kind of pyramid would keep out that sphere of dark light. It wanted something from them. Nothing they'd want to give it, he was sure.

'I saw it while you were sleeping last night,' he said. 'I would've said, but I didn't want to worry you.'

'What do you think it is?' asked Gideon.

'I don't know,' said Dax. 'Nothing good, that's for sure. Come on. We need to go off west—we can't stay here now. They're searching down in the south, so we might have time. Maybe we can get to the coast. There might be caves we can go in or something.'

Gideon nodded. Dax really didn't like the look of him. As he pulled the Exmoor map from his bag and spread it out, he hoped his friend could make it through another long trek. He didn't feel that great himself. His nose was stuffed up and he thought he probably *was* getting that cold. Brilliant!

'I reckon we're about here.' He pointed to the lower part of the moor. 'Look—*tumuli*—that's these standing stones, isn't it? Some have even got names—that one's the Hanging Stone. Lovely. Oh—this is nicer. The Lost

Maid. Wonder what ours is called. Come on—we should go now, before they come back.' He shuffled backwards from under the stone, pulling the map with him.

He stood up and allowed himself a stretch as Gideon scrambled out too. Gideon looked up at him and then his eyes stretched wide and his mouth fell open.

Before Dax could ask why, his arms were roughly gripped and yanked behind him. Before he could even cry out, a thick material engulfed his head and he was pushed to the ground and pinned down. Before he could curse himself for his stupidity, he knew.

Owen Hind had found them.

20

There was no point in struggling. Dax knew it. The heavy material over him meant that neither kind of shift would do any good. He couldn't escape. He almost laughed. Astounding supernatural powers overcome—with a sack. Still he punched out angrily at the dark material and shouted for Gideon.

Owen Hind leaned heavily on him and said, his voice muffled by the cloth over Dax's head, 'Gideon's OK, Dax. He's all right. He's just fainted.'

'What?' Dax struggled to sit up and now Owen let him.

'What's going to happen if I take this sack off you, Dax?' he said, his muffled voice like steel. 'Am I going to lose you again?'

Dax closed his eyes in dismay. Now that Owen was here, he felt weak and stupid. If it meant leaving Gideon behind, he couldn't flee, even if he wanted to.

'I really could do with your help with Gideon now,' said Owen. 'Are you going to shift and escape if I let you out?'

'I'm not going anywhere without Gideon.' Dax sounded stronger than he felt.

'Good. That's what I thought you'd say.'

Owen pulled the sack off, and lifted his heavy grasp. Dax blinked and took in the scene around him. Gideon was lying on his side, only pale slits of eye showing through his lids, shaking and white.

'What's wrong with him?' Dax clambered across to his friend, whose legs were still under the stone tent.

'I think he's just exhausted—and in shock perhaps. Maybe it was seeing me coming up behind you that did it.' He checked Gideon over. Owen was dressed in dark green combat gear, with a black jacket full of pockets, into which assorted gadgets seemed to be stuffed. His thick long hair was tucked into a tight fitting woollen black cap and he wore dark glasses. It was hard to tell how angry he was—Dax couldn't smell much and the glasses hid Owen's expression.

'I don't think it was seeing you,' Dax said, hesitantly. 'He—he saw something else . . . before. I think he was freaked out by it.'

'What did he see?'

'Um . . . a sort of . . . orb thing.'

'Go on.'

'Well—it's hard to explain.'

'DAX!' Owen snapped off his sunglasses and when he locked his blue eyes with Dax's they were icy. 'I need you to tell me exactly what's been happening. It would have helped, of course, if you'd done that from the start, instead of running around the country like an idiot. What were you thinking of? Now—stop fluttering about and tell me about this orb. I am *all out* of patience.'

Dax gritted his teeth. He felt as if acid was pouring through him, melting every strand of pride and self-worth inside him. Slowly, he described the orb thing; how it had come to him and Lisa first, and, just in the last hour, to Gideon. When he'd finished, Owen offered no opinion on what it might be. Instead he picked a communicator off his belt and called in to the patrol. There was a tinny squawk of surprise and shouts of urgency at the other end.

'On *my command*,' stressed Owen into the communicator. 'No guns, no assault. It's under control here. Confirm!' There was a burst of confirmation.

'I can't believe you got *Spook* in to help,' muttered Dax, still stinging and raw. His heart kept speeding up and slowing down. He was bewildered about what to do next, but with Gideon lying helpless at his feet, he couldn't take flight.

'I didn't,' said Owen, curtly. Dax stared at him.

'Chambers is running the search patrols,' Owen went on. 'I've been tracking you alone. I wanted to get to you before anyone else did. Make it easier for you than they would.'

Dax gulped, wondering what Owen meant. The single word that came into his mind was *assassin*. The energy began to sap out of him and he leaned against the stone. Owen was checking inside it now, and pulling out Gideon's backpack.

'What are you going to do with us?' said Dax.

Owen dropped Gideon's pack at his feet and rested

his hand on the hunting knife in his belt. 'I'm going to do what's best for everyone,' he said, curtly.

Dax stared at the knife. He felt himself reeling back months and months to the point when he had once believed Owen was going to kill him. Then it had been a gun, but Owen had not killed him. Owen had saved his life and nearly died trying. But now he believed the safety of his country was at stake . . . would he work straight?

'Are you—are you going to . . .?' Dax breathed, feeling faint himself now.

Owen stared at Dax and his right hand tightened on the sheath of the knife. Then he looked down at it and began to laugh. He laughed and laughed. He fell to his knees laughing, colour rushing into his face and tears beginning to stream from his eyes. 'Am I going to . . . ?' he gurgled, between the torrents of mirth, 'Oh, Dax— you are priceless!'

Dax felt as if cold, wet, concrete was pouring over him—he was immobilized by the horror. In an instant the wolf's warning had sliced through his brain—*Bad comes from laughing man.* Oh no, oh no, oh no . . . Dax only realized he was moaning this aloud when Owen began to stop his laughing and look at him curiously.

'You . . . ' muttered Dax, stepping back away from him. 'You're the laughing man. Bad comes from the laughing man. Bad comes . . . '

Owen was back on his feet now, and frowning. 'Dax? What are you talking about?'

'I've been warned!' yelled Dax, a sob in his voice. 'I

know! You're the laughing man . . . bad comes from the laughing man.' He stepped back further, misery and fear buffeting him like waves. *No—this could NOT be happening again! Why must this always happen? Why must he be betrayed by the people he loved?*

'Dax—stop! Calm down. Whatever you think I am, I am *not* the bad guy.' Owen was talking to him calmly now, struggling to keep the urgency out of his voice, but Dax's nose cleared and he could smell the stress on him. He felt himself instinctively flicker towards the falcon shift, but held on, desperate about Gideon.

'Dax—don't! Don't shift!' Owen's eyes darted away over Dax's left shoulder. 'Dax—for the love of God or anyone you hold dear—DO NOT SHIFT.'

'Why NOT?' yelled Dax, fiercely. 'Why should I come with you? I don't trust you any more! I don't trust you! I can live alone—you know I can. What do I need you for?'

'Dax,' Owen held up his hands, 'just behind you— about two hundred metres away—is the search patrol led by Chambers. They want to take you back to safety—but they *will shoot you* if you shift. I can't stop them! Do you understand me? Do you?'

Dax laughed mirthlessly but it sounded like a sob. 'Oh, that's good. *It's behind you, Dax!*'

At this point there was a moan from Gideon, and his best friend sat up, looking around him in bewilderment. 'Dax?' he slurred.

The second Dax's eyes went to his friend Owen was upon him. The force of the man was tremendous, knocking him over and locking him tight with his arms. They rolled down the slope and as they did so, Dax shifted to a fox and began to twist and claw and bite at Owen's hands and arms.

'Dammit, Dax,' grunted his captor. 'Have you got a taste for my blood or something?'

They slid to a stop and Dax heard himself emitting desperate growls and whines, waiting for the blade across his throat as he struggled to escape from Owen's armlock. Then his vision cleared and he found himself staring— *staring*—at Owen Hind's scratched and bitten forearm.

On it was a black tattoo of an eagle.

When Dax shifted back to a boy, Owen wondered why he was apologizing. The boy's face was streaked with tears and grass and mud, but he was definitely apologizing, as if in huge relief.

'Protection!' he choked. '*The eagle is protection*. Owen, I'm sorry. I'm really sorry. I thought you were the laughing man.'

Owen sat up. He picked up his communicator again, quickly barking to the approaching patrol that everything was under control and to drop all arms. Then he wrinkled up his forehead and peered at Dax. 'The Laughing Man, Dax, is up *there*!'

'What?' Dax stared blearily back up the slope to where Gideon was getting unsteadily to his feet, leaning against their stone shelter.

'At the top of the tor, you donkey! The standing stone! That's what it's called. The Laughing Man. It's marked on the map. When you look at it from one side, the stone's all bent and looks like someone doubled up laughing. *I* was laughing, by the way, because it looked like you thought I was going to bump you off. *Again!* Dax—you and I really have some issues! And what is particularly funny, is that in trying to see that nobody *else* bumps you off, I might well have lost my job. Well—sorry if I'm boring you!' Owen stared back up the slope, following Dax's gaze. Gideon stood watching them both, hugging his arms across his chest nervously.

'Laughing Man . . . ' Dax was murmuring, and now the hackles on his neck began to rise as the warning made a whole new kind of sense. 'Bad comes . . . from the Laughing Man.'

He and Owen exchanged one glance and in a second both were charging back up the hill to Gideon. As soon as they moved Dax could smell the electrical charge in the air. He could hear a shrill singing coming from the rock and barked commands from the approaching patrol, which was now heading up the slope behind them, moving steadily and cautiously.

Gideon raised his hands into the air, like a conductor about to start a concert. 'GIDEON! NO!' bellowed Owen. 'DON'T DO ANYTHING. DON'T USE YOUR POWERS!'

Dax heard the horrible sound of ammunition being readied behind them; a chorus of metallic clicks. He didn't dare to look back. *Bad comes from the Laughing Man.* The orb appeared slowly this time, moving in a figure of eight around Gideon's upheld hands. He looked at it in awe.

'This isn't good,' Dax heard him mutter.

'What the hell is that?' said Owen, echoing Dax's words of two nights ago.

'I don't know—but it's not good,' said Dax.

The sphere glowed again with that eerie dark light and even three metres away, Dax could see its writhing, precisely ordered tentacles, moving in and out in endless mathematical perfection.

'Don't come any closer,' said Gideon and his voice was calm—faraway. 'It's dangerous. Owen—you have to tell those men to stay back. They're in danger too.'

Suddenly, with such force that the atmosphere seemed to suck out of their ears as it went, the orb shot high into the sky. There was a crackle of gunfire behind them and then a flash and a cry. Dax didn't even look. The orb had risen thirty or forty metres into the air and was spinning faster and faster, a blue halo growing around it. Dax realized this was his chance. He leapt at Gideon one second before Owen did and they collided, hauling the dazed boy away from the Laughing Man. Just as they did so there was a sharp whine—something falling, terribly, terribly fast—followed by a thunderous crack and a thick rush of air and Dax felt the shocked earth rear up under his feet. The three of them tumbled down the hill, hitting knees against chests and elbows against jaws until they lay still amid the tufts of heather.

For a few seconds there was silence and then Dax

heard crackling and caught a hot aromatic scent. The heather all around the Laughing Man was on fire and the Laughing Man no longer saw the joke. He lay snapped in half on the blazing earth, precisely where Gideon had stood.

'First of all, Dax, I need to understand,' said Owen. 'I need to know why you felt you couldn't come to me. Surely it wasn't just that telling-off I gave you back at home!'

'No. Of course not,' said Dax.

Owen and Dax sat in the back of a military truck. Dax was wrapped in an army blanket and drinking steaming hot cocoa. Owen was sitting very still and watching him intently.

A helicopter thudded overhead; troops moved around the tourist car park at the edge of the moors; and the paramedics who were still checking Gideon talked cheerily to the tired boy a few feet away outside. Communications chattered and chittered endlessly in Dax's sensitive ears, but he shut them out and tried to drink his cocoa. He needed to hear Owen now, nothing else.

'What was it, then? Did you even *think* of coming to me?'

Dax looked levelly at Owen. 'I did come to you.' Owen blinked in surprise, and then put down his own mug, resting his elbows on his knees, tilting his head to one side, trying to read the boy's face. 'So what happened? Why didn't we speak?'

Dax didn't know how to say it. He closed his eyes. 'I heard something—something Chambers said.'

'Go on.'

'About how you would work straight—do what you had to do, even though we were kids—for the good of the country. That he'd seen you slit throats . . .'

Owen pressed his lips together and his stare dropped to the metal floor. 'Dax . . . you have to understand . . . I wasn't brought in to Cola Club because I know how to take a woodwork class. I—look, you saw this, yes?' He pulled back his sleeve, revealing the livid bites and scratches that Dax had given him just an hour earlier. The tattoo of the eagle flew determinedly amid the wounds. 'This is a tattoo that you will only see on a very few, highly trained British soldiers. Yes—I have killed men. Possibly women too. I am not proud of it—but I'm not ashamed either. This eagle means protection. I protect my people—and there have been times when I have had to kill to do it. You—and all the Colas—are my people. I am your protection. Do you understand?'

It was the look on Owen's face that made it right. For the first time since he had known him, Dax saw Owen *beseech* him. Dax sat up and nodded. 'I do understand.' He was about to apologize, too, but the door opened and Gideon clambered in, looking much better than he had when they'd first been brought in to the makeshift camp.

'Oi—I hope you aren't telling him stuff without me! Start back at the beginning again!'

Owen chuckled and poured more hot cocoa from

a flask for Gideon. 'We were just getting a few things straight—about how we lost sight of each other for a while. I think we're OK now, aren't we, Dax?'

Dax beamed and nodded and felt relief trickle through him like a cool shower on a scorching day. Being right with Owen meant more to him than he could explain.

'Right then,' said Owen, and his own relief was evident in Dax's nose. 'We got the news that you had gone within half an hour of the stunt you pulled at the shopping centre.' He shot them both a wry look. 'I have to say, that was pretty good.' He paused, shook his head and then went on, 'But your poor dad, Gideon. For a few minutes he was convinced you'd thrown yourself off a six-storey building. It was only when he'd mentioned you had a backpack that we worked out that Dax must have come along with you and you'd done a switch.'

'We left a note,' Gideon mumbled.

'Yes, I saw it,' said Owen. 'Obviously, there was a lot of distraction that day, with another pylon meltdown too—then Dax and Lisa got spotted at the site and we guessed you were all together. Everyone was even more certain that Gideon was either losing control of his powers somehow—or else trying to make a very big point! I really hadn't believed it until then, but I couldn't come up with any convincing argument against bringing Gideon in. And, of course, Dax had been acting up too.'

'But I didn't do anything!' said Gideon, but Owen waved him quiet.

'I *was* leading the patrol tracking you down, but I

handed it over to Chambers yesterday and decided to track you alone. I didn't agree with his methods. The TV thing was wrong—and I would never have involved Spook Williams or any other Cola.'

'Where is he?' muttered Dax.

'He's here—in one of the other trucks with Chambers. They caught up with Lisa and Clive and Mia too. You seem to have become some sort of Pied Piper, Dax.'

'Not me,' he said. 'Lisa. She knew that Gideon was in trouble, and then she realized that Mia was too.' He glared at Owen. 'Something should have been done about that way before we got there! I can't believe you let her take all those hangovers off her dad! That was awful.'

'I can't believe it either,' said Owen, rubbing his hands tiredly through his unruly hair. 'To be fair, she hid it extremely well from her tutor. We knew her dad had a problem—he's not the only Cola father who has felt the need to drink—but we didn't know she was trying to heal him every day. She didn't ask for help in letting the symptoms go because she wanted to protect him. That's something we'll sort out now, Dax. I understand why you went to get her—and I would have done the same.'

Dax nodded, feeling better.

'Anyway, we managed to track you as far as Exeter—after a quick detour to Bristol, thanks to Lisa's mobile phone trick. We set up roadblocks along the main routes out of the town.'

'I know,' said Dax. 'I saw you.'

Owen looked at him, smiling faintly. 'So that was

where you heard Chambers? I thought I saw something in the sky above the hill—but it could have been any kind of bird. Then we got a call—a sighting up in Minehead. The patrol moved off on it straight away, but I still organized a helicopter search of Exmoor. I just had a hunch. Then I called it all off and sent them across to Minehead and then on to the Taunton area.'

'Why?' asked Dax, intrigued. 'Did you think we'd gone there?'

'No. I was certain you hadn't. Paulina Sartre asked me to. She had told Chambers about the Minehead sighting. She was lying. She wanted me to go after you alone.'

Dax and Gideon sat up and stared at him. That their college principal might be involved in such trickery hadn't even crossed their minds. Paulina Sartre was a seer and a dowser, like Lisa, who had found most of the Colas through her extraordinary sixth sense. Of course she would have been called in to help find them immediately, but evidently she had her own ideas about what should be done.

'So she knew where we were?' asked Dax.

'Not at first. She was only getting vague stuff—but she knew you were all together and OK. She didn't start to really place you until last night, after you'd split up from the others, but she always felt you were all in Devon. She said she thought she'd made some kind of contact on the second night.'

Dax nodded, grinning. 'We felt her. Our scalps went tingly—mine and Lisa's—like when she touches your head. Then we had to start thinking of glass mirror pyramids.'

Owen nodded back, apparently unsurprised. 'Yep—pyramids are quite effective. Takes a lot of concentration, though. You can't keep it up. Just get Gideon thinking about chocolate and you're done for. Speaking of which . . . ' He leaned over and pulled something oblong and purple from a box—a large bar of Cadbury's Dairy Milk.

Gideon moaned with delight and seized it. 'Thank you! Thank you *so much*!'

As he wolfed it down, sparing a chunk or two for Dax when he thought of it, they listened to the rest of Owen's story. Paulina Sartre had told Owen to speak to Caroline Fisher, sensing a connection between Dax and the journalist. This was the main thing she had picked up from her dowsing. So Owen had gone to see Caroline, back in Hampshire. She wouldn't tell him anything until he finally convinced her that Dax's life was in danger.

'I can't believe how stupid I was,' he told them. 'Of course, her flat was bugged; had been for months, ever since we let her go after you saved her life. Chambers got to hear our conversation minutes after we had it.'

'But you and Chambers are on the same side, aren't you?' asked Gideon, through a mouthful of melted chocolate.

'Only just. I didn't trust his men not to panic if they saw Dax shift or you spin a TV or something. They've seen a lot of weird things—but nothing quite as weird as you two at work. I would have approached your hide-out on my own, but I couldn't stop Chambers sending in a whole unit and I couldn't get ahead of them, so I just had to go in with them. Would have been a shame to miss your note! Candle wax too, eh?' Dax and Gideon exchanged slightly embarrassed looks.

'Then, after we realized you'd got away from the cottage and the dogs lost your trail, I took off to track you alone. I found the remains of your camp on the edge of the woodland. Pretty good, you were—but I could see the way the ground had been scuffed up to cover your tracks, and there were prints of a boy and a fox in the boggier parts of the moor. I spotted you both some way off early this morning, and just tailed you for a while. Then the patrol came through and I didn't want to lead them to you—so I had to wait for a while. I saw you flit overhead at one point, Dax, and thought I'd blown it— but then you landed again and starting scrapping with Spook. It was like old times. By then I'd seen the standing stones and realized that Gideon was under one—I just had to wait for you to come back to him.'

Dax and Gideon exchanged a defeated look.

'Don't be too hard on yourselves,' said Owen, draining the last of his drink. 'I'm actually quite proud of you both, in spite of all the stress you've caused me. You picked up a lot from our bushcraft lessons, didn't you? You put me to a lot of effort! And if it hadn't been for Mrs Sartre and a line of buckled-up pylons pointing the way, I might not have found you yet. There were more near Exford in the early hours of this morning.'

'But Gideon will be safe now, won't he?' said Dax. 'Chambers knows it's not him—yes?'

Owen sighed. 'No. All Chambers knows is that two of his men were electrocuted an hour ago, just as Gideon was holding up his hands and playing with some kind of mini UFO. Then an ancient slab of rock split in half and the ground caught fire.'

Dax and Gideon groaned.

'So what will happen now?' mumbled Gideon, putting down the remaining chocolate. 'Is it underground bunker time?'

'Well, they'll have to go through me first,' said Owen. '*I* know it's not you, Gideon. But whatever it is—it's something *to do* with you. The melted pylons have mostly happened close to where you've been, within a few miles. And there's something else, too.' He reached under the narrow bench seat in the back of the truck and found a plastic folder. He unzipped it and pulled out a sheaf of glossy photographs. They were all of pylons—scores and scores of different pylons, all statues of tangled metal, surrounded by emergency trucks. 'Notice anything else?' asked Owen and they stared down at the images spread out on the truck floor.

Finally Gideon raised a shocked face to Dax. 'Is that really what I think it is?'

In every photograph, scorched into the earth somewhere close to the pylon, was the letter G.

22

'It's like some kind of joke!' said Gideon. 'Like someone trying to pin the blame on me.'

Dax said nothing, but watched the hedgerows and trees begin to blur through the darkly tinted window. They were on a sort of small coach—a government vehicle, armoured and packed with computer gadgets (Dax could hear them endlessly whistling and clicking). Gideon was too angry and stressed to feel sick this time. Owen and Chambers sat further towards the front, in earnest discussion. Occasionally their voices would become heated and Chambers would glance sceptically back over the seats at them, as if he didn't believe anything Owen was saying. Dax recognized the smartly dressed head of the Cola Project from earlier that year; he had led the patrol which had come in to deal with the destruction of Tregarren College. He knew all about Dax's shapeshifting abilities. His was the voice Dax had recognized talking to the other man about Owen slitting enemy throats, in the van at the roadblock.

Only one other person travelled with them and he was sitting right at the back. Spook was gazing idly out of the window. He hadn't bothered to speak to either of them yet. When Dax had glanced back at him, he'd looked unutterably smug, still wearing his borrowed army gear.

The vehicle they were travelling in was sleek and comfortable, with plush navy upholstery, soft lighting, a long, tinted, skylight window in the roof, and wide seats which could convert to beds if needed. A TV monitor hung over the aisle up front; the driver was in a sealed-off area, behind a bulletproof screen. At least, Dax guessed it was bulletproof. From the outside, you couldn't see into the black vehicle at all. It was like the tour bus of a famous band, with mirror windows. Ahead of it and behind it drove several army trucks. They were all heading north. They weren't being taken home, but to the new college, somewhere in the Lake District, Owen had told them. It wasn't totally ready, but the security was in place and all the Colas had been called there now. Most would arrive tomorrow and the day after, but Dax and Gideon would meet Mia and Lisa there in a few hours.

'A big G! Honestly! It's a joke, isn't it?' Gideon was still going on. Dax pressed a button on his armrest and his seat eased back with a gentle hiss.

'I'm going to get some sleep,' he said.

Gideon looked cheesed off. He obviously wanted to complain a bit more, but Dax was shattered. He turned over, his back to his friend, and closed his eyes. The walking, the hunting, the stress, and shapeshifting so many times in a few days, had drained him almost dry. Even the hot soup and thick buttered bread they had been given hadn't helped. Most of all he needed sleep—

real sleep, where he didn't have to be on alert all the time.

It was difficult to let go. He took several deep breaths and reminded himself of the wolf's message: *the eagle is protection.* Owen was here. The wolf trusted him and so must Dax. They'd be OK now. Finally, lulled by the hum of the engine and the soft conversation between Owen and Chambers, which he had made a decision *not* to listen in to, Dax began to sleep. Really sleep. He sank beneath the layers of slumber, his head nodding gently on the tipped-back chair, in rhythm with the wheels on the road. Sleep. He slept on for two hours, fully, deeply, and woke to the sound of raindrops on the glass overhead. Clouds had rolled in with the late afternoon.

Spook had moved down and was now sitting in a seat across the aisle from them; he was looking at them both and narrowing his eyes. Gideon woke up beside Dax and stared back. 'Whadayouwant?' he grunted.

Spook pursed his lips and tipped his head to one side. 'I reckon you two should tell me what happened when Owen got you,' he said.

'Yeah, right!' snorted Gideon.

'I think you owe me!' said Spook, self-importance all over him like a rash. 'I put myself on the line to get you two back.'

Dax hooted with laughter. 'Oh—my hero!'

Spook scowled at him. 'I was on *holiday*! I had to cut it short and roam around some empty moor for several hours, magicking up Gideon's dad!'

'Oh, get off it!' said Gideon. 'When they let you dress up like a soldier I bet you nearly wet your pants! Strutting about like you think you're it! Don't forget—we *know* you.'

Spook glared and the air around him shimmered. Dax sat up and shoved his shoulder. 'Don't even *think* about it, you stupid idiot!' he hissed.

Gideon gritted his teeth and Dax grabbed his wrist. 'No!' he said, urgently. Spook had slumped back into his seat and the shimmering was gone. Gideon shook his head.

'Sorry, mate,' he said. 'He just did my dad, wearing a dress.'

Dax shot Spook a scornful look. 'You are so full of it. Why should we tell you anything?'

Spook folded his arms. 'What was it you said to me about us all being in this together?' he said. 'I thought we were meant to look out for each other—that's what you said. So you should tell me, in case I need to be on my guard. Stuff's been happening to Gideon and you said I'm as dangerous as he is! What if it starts happening to *me*?'

Gideon stared at Dax. 'You said *what*?'

Dax sighed. 'Well—it wasn't quite what I said.'

'He's so *not* more dangerous than me!' huffed Gideon.

'Oh, for crying out loud! It's not a competition!' Dax covered his face with his hands and Gideon and Spook bickered on.

'You are nothing more than pumped-up special effects!' sneered Gideon.

'Better than you, mate! I can stop a whole army in its tracks if I want to! You might be able to drop a dustbin on one of them, maybe. Really scared, I am!'

Dax dropped his hands and raised his head. He snatched a breath sharply. 'You should be,' he said, his eyes widening as he stared up through the skylight above them. Every hair on his body prickled and his throat tightened with fear. Travelling with them, measuring its speed exactly with the movement of the vehicle, hovering six inches above the glass, was the orb.

They all looked up in silence. Owen and Chambers talked on, oblivious to the smell that seemed to fill up Dax's head—hot, electrical, dangerous. Spook's eyes were wide and fearful and Gideon seemed frozen in his seat.

'Not again . . . ' he moaned. 'Not again.'

The three boys stared up, mesmerized, as the orb, writhing and glowing darkly, remained in its position, speeding along in tandem with them. The rain seemed to bend around it, never colliding with it. Then, just as Dax opened his mouth to shout for Owen, it shot up out of sight.

They had maybe three seconds in which to stare blankly at each other.

Then came a crash so loud and sudden that Dax felt as if his ears had been boxed with iron gloves. Suddenly there were shards of glass flying everywhere, the shriek of rubber tyres on the road, a series of crashes behind them and one, with a sickening jolt, right into the back of them. Dax saw Spook's head connect with the seat in front of him, and blood spring from his nose as he slumped to the floor, unconscious. Gideon was crouching in his seat, shouting, and Owen and Chambers were yelling and struggling towards them when there was a sudden searing white light, which could not be shut out even when Dax screwed his eyes shut in terror. With it came loud buzzing cracks and noises like scraping metal, shrieking and shrill amid the stinging shower of rainwater and glass.

'DAX! GIDEON! GET DOWN!' bawled Owen, and as he moved across towards them the metal roof of the coach above him suddenly dented in, as if a giant flat iron had been smashed into it. Owen ducked away, with athlete's reflexes, but was still caught a glancing blow on the temple. He fell back with a cry and tried to move towards them again, but now there was a horrible metallic twisting noise, coupled with an unearthly groan above them. Dax found himself crouched in the aisle between the seats, staring up in horror. What appeared to be a huge liquid silver tentacle was snaking down towards him through the shattered skylight, trailing fine silver hairs which sparked and snagged in the wet air. The hot smell of warped electricity, bent into this unnatural shape, was choking. Dax realized, with amazed, appalled clarity, that the orb thing had found another pylon and was melting it into a useful, moving body—something with which it could poke and prod, pinch and grab. And it meant to grab Gideon.

2 3

The glowing silver tentacle pulled away for a moment and then punched down into the coach like a piston. Dax felt it pass within an inch of his head and heard Gideon shout. Before Owen could move one more step towards them, the boy was hooked through the wreckage of the coach roof so fast that his limbs flailed behind him, like a broken doll. Dax felt himself scream his friend's name, but could not hear it. The noise of shrieking metal seemed to have deafened him. He felt Owen reach for him, to try to shield him from another fishing tentacle of molten metal, but he was gone by the time the man's hands fell onto the seat. He was up, out, soaring into a glowering sky that buzzed and crackled through his peregrine frame. Mad currents of disturbed air threw him around, and he had to fly high to get above the turbulence of the terrible scene below. Rain pelted at him, dragging on his feathers as he turned in the air and looked down, scanning desperately for a sign of Gideon.

Please, don't let him be dead. Please don't let him be dead. He repeated the words feverishly as he circled, eyes travelling to the scene below. The single carriageway road they had been driving on was mayhem. The army trucks behind the coach lay in a zigzag, cannoned into each other; one was on its side, the driver struggling to get out of the shattered windscreen. The coach lay at an angle, leaning into trees on the verge, its roof torn open like a tin of sardines. Men were running from one vehicle to another, ducking down out of view and raising guns towards the incomprehensible thing that towered over them, weaving and buckling and groaning.

The pylon had been yanked across from its footings, through a roadside hedge, and bent over. Its base still seemed to be anchored, but the vertical struts that held the power cables were waving like the branches of a palm tree, snapped cable wires skittering through the air with sprays of sparks. One of the struts seemed to have been stretched longer, like an arm, and was pistoning repeatedly into the tarmac surface of the road. Further away in either direction, cars and lorries were at a standstill, some people getting onto their bonnets to get a view of what was happening, others cowering inside.

Dax dropped down, feathers prickling with the intense electrical charge in the air, and saw Gideon, on his knees, two or three metres away from the strut of metal that was thumping into the tarmac. Wires snapped and whipped around him in showers of blue sparks. Chunks of black road surface were erupting into the air with every punch of the possessed metal strut. Now Owen and Chambers clambered out of the ruined coach, dragging the unconscious Spook between them. They deposited him on the ground and began to run towards Gideon, but as if sensing this, the metal strut stopped its ferocious pounding and suddenly curled back up into the air again, a fluid tentacle once more, jerking once and sending a circle of electrical bolts hurtling around Gideon. Around and around him they raced, like the spirits of naughty children in a playground. Gideon knelt, shaking and bleeding, in the centre of the circle, his hair beginning to stand up on end, but he shouted over to Owen.

'Don't come any closer! You'll be electrocuted!'

Owen drew up, his hands at his head, his face desperate. Chambers tried to get his radio to work, but it, along with every other electrical thing on that dark, wet road, was dead.

Dax wondered why Gideon hadn't been electrocuted. Surely that thing must've packed thousands of volts into him when it picked him up? But Gideon seemed relatively unharmed, apart from the bleeding from the broken glass. Dax turned in a circle above him and realized that there was a kind of dome over him. His eyes were cool and his face still with concentration, despite the tremors running through his body. He was holding it all off with his telekinetic power. The cable wires still cracked crazily in the air around him and now Dax remembered Lisa's vision—the metallic noises and smells—the tower. She had likened it to the Eiffel Tower but it was surely the pylon she had been seeing. And there were the wires. What would follow was . . . *despair.* Something worse was yet to happen.

Dax had a wild instinct—could he get through? If

so, he could perhaps do *something*. Change the ending of Lisa's vision. He would *not* let this all end in despair. Gideon was holding off an incredible force, but his mind could surely only welcome Dax? It would let him through, he was sure of it. Dax stopped thinking and arched into the air, dropping down beak first. He heard Owen shout: 'Dax! No!' He expected to feel a pressure, like the surface of water, but in fact he sliced into the dome and down to Gideon's side without any problem.

'Hi, Dax,' said Gideon in a strange, flat voice. Dax knew he was only just able to divert enough attention to him to talk. 'I think it could all be over soon. Maybe you should get away while you can. I can't hold this off much longer.'

Beyond the madly circling balls of lightning Dax could see Owen and Chambers arguing over what to do next. A small group of the search patrol men had gathered behind them, staring at the incredible scene which whirled around Gideon. As he desperately tried to think of some way to help, Dax became aware of more movement behind them. He realized the malevolent ribbon of molten metal had now curled away from Gideon, leaving him in his electrical circle, and was grasping the tilted wreck of the coach. It scooped it high into the air with a grinding whine and a sprinkling of glass and threw it directly at the men below.

Owen and Chambers didn't stand a chance.

'NOT THIS TIME!' bellowed Gideon, so loudly that Dax fell over, with a flutter of wings. There was silence—

an eerie, thick silence—and Dax realized the coach had *not* fallen. It was suspended three or four feet above the shocked heads of the patrol men and their leaders. Chambers stared up, his mouth open. Owen's eyes were closed, waiting for the end. When it failed to arrive, he opened them again, peering up in amazement.

'Make . . . them . . . move!' gasped Gideon and Dax saw that sweat was pouring off his face. The weight on his mind must be incredible.

The bolts of lightning had vanished. Dax shifted to a boy and bellowed, 'MOVE! MOVE! MOVE!' The men staggered out in all directions and then there was one more terrific crash as the coach hit the road.

Gideon collapsed and lay on the wet tarmac, staring up. Dax shook him but he continued to stare. Dax followed his gaze and saw the orb, a few feet above them. It had released the ruined pylon from its possession and now seemed to look down at them.

Gideon got up on one elbow. 'I know you,' he hissed, his lip curling. 'I KNOW YOU!' He sat up. 'I KNOW YOU! I KNOW YOU!' he yelled, getting to his feet. 'I WILL COME FOR YOU! I WILL GET YOU! I KNOW YOU!'

Dax shivered and stared at the orb. It seemed to contract into itself, its dark light turning dimmer.

'I—KNOW—YOU!!!' roared Gideon.

The orb winked out of existence.

24

From the top of the hill they could see it, an imposing country house, whitewashed and three storeys high, with rows of tall glittering windows and a high-pitched slate roof. It was set in many acres of lush green countryside and surrounded by the steep and rocky inclines of the Cumbrian hills. Small waterfalls tumbled down the fells and calmed themselves in winding brooks which wove across the meadows, disappeared into woodland and then re-emerged to loop and curve through the soft swells of turf where sheep grazed peacefully. One of the brooks led to a large, beautiful lake to the east of the house, cascading into it through rough steps of granite.

As the Jeep drew closer, Gideon and Dax sat up as high as their seatbelts would allow, staring hungrily at their new home. Lights shone in many of the windows, and Dax's fox smell believed it could already detect hot beef casserole and freshly baked bread. He felt like crying. For many reasons. He probably wouldn't do it, but he felt it.

Gideon was smiling too now, and Dax was so glad to see it. After the events of the last few hours, he had wondered if Gideon would ever be normal again. The carnage on the road had been covered in special forces in minutes, it seemed. Some of the patrol who had nearly died under the coach were treated for shock. Even Chambers had been unable to speak properly for at least half an hour. When he had found his voice, he had come over to Gideon, whose cuts were being dressed in the back of an army ambulance with Dax at his side, and he had shaken his hand solemnly.

'I don't know what the hell that was,' he had said, 'but I know you just saved our lives. I won't forget it, Gideon. I don't think I would have believed what you just did if I hadn't seen it.' Dax was immediately reminded of Lisa's last message from Sylv. 'Something needs to be *seen*!'

Chambers looked at them both for a few seconds, weighing them up. He took a pen out of a pocket and began to click the button on the top of it in and out repeatedly, thinking. His hands were less than steady. Dax remembered the pen clicking from the last time they had met, above the ruins of Tregarren. 'I know you're just children,' he said, finally. 'But you've had to grow up fast, so I guess you'll understand this. The road ahead is going to be rocky. You're growing up and developing more and more Cola power and we don't know what this is leading to. There will be arguments and disagreements. But Hind was right about you two. You have my trust and I hope— some day—that I'll have yours.'

They looked at each other and then nodded at him solemnly, not knowing what to say. Chambers clapped them each on the shoulder, causing Gideon to wince slightly, and the paramedic who was tending him to shoot Chambers a disapproving look. Chambers had nodded again and then moved away.

'Ready for some supper then?' said Owen, bringing Dax back to the present as they wound down the gravel track towards the house. Behind them another Jeep followed, containing Chambers and three of the armed patrol men. They were taking no chances.

'Oh yes,' they murmured.

'Is this where we'll be staying from now on?' asked Gideon. 'It looks really posh.'

'Yes—this is Fenton Lodge. A country estate. It dates back about five hundred years—rebuilt a few times—this is the Georgian version. It was in a right mess when we found it; virtually derelict. But it's in a perfect position for us. Very safe. And beautiful, don't you think? They've done an amazing job inside, too.'

Dax gazed at it, his heart beating hard with delight. The house was lovely and it felt so good to be going back to the other Colas. He couldn't wait to see the other students again, to sit in normal lessons with Mrs Dann, to mess around with Gideon and Barry, to hear Lisa and Gideon bickering and watch Mia's smile as she sent everyone healing energy to calm them down.

'Are you sure it's safe?' he asked, not wanting to break the spell, but glancing at Gideon for reassurance. 'You really think you've seen that thing off?'

Gideon nodded. 'Oh yes,' he muttered vehemently.

Dax stared at him some more. In the last few hours since the violent events on that rainwashed road, Gideon had said no more than that. Dax had prodded him gently for more information but he shook his head every time— as he did again now.

'I don't want to talk about it,' he said. 'Not yet.' The smell of him was strange to Dax. Gideon smelt fearfully angry. But he was in control; the anger was contained and held inside him, like ammunition. Every instinct in Dax told him to wait. Gideon would tell him when he was ready.

The Jeep had now reached the bottom of the track and paused at a pair of huge metal gates. Dax saw they were wrought iron, flanked by tall stone pillars giving on to high stone walls on either side, which snaked away as far as the eye could see. Metal posts ranged along the top of the wall, supporting thin wires, which he guessed were electrified. Owen brought the window down and reached across to a key pad under a small metal hood on a post beside the track. He punched in a number and then peered into the hood. Dax saw a blueish light sweep across his face. A retinal scan. Everybody's eyes were as unique as their fingertips and this is how Owen was recognized and allowed in. There was a pause as Owen moved back into his seat and sent the window back up and then the gates slowly opened, in the white glare of two security lights that shone down from the stone posts. As he drove through, two men emerged from small wooden shelters on either side of the path. They were carrying rifles and in uniform. Owen nodded at them, and they stepped aside, nodding back and eyeing the two boys in the back sharply. Behind them, Chambers's Jeep went through the same procedure.

The gravel drive stretched straight for half a mile, ending in a circular area by the tall oak front door of the country house. 'Fenton Lodge,' Dax murmured to himself, getting used to the words. They climbed, stiff and tired, from the vehicle and Owen, resting a hand on their shoulders, guided them up the stone steps. Before they reached the door, it was flung open and Lisa hurtled out to greet them. Mia followed, more hesitantly, beaming with delight.

Lisa thwacked into Dax and gave him a rough hug; then did the same to Gideon before pulling herself back quickly and looking rather embarrassed. Mia reached them and squeezed one hand of each in both of hers.

'It's so good to see you,' she said, without any self-consciousness. 'We were so worried.'

A wonderful scent of hot food poured out of the open doorway along with the golden light from a chandelier which hung, twinkling, in the reception hall. The floor was covered with gleaming pale yellow stone and a grand oak staircase swept upwards in a curve, past a tall stained-glass window. Antique furniture was dotted about and a giant mirror in a gilded frame clung to the wall above a carved stone fireplace.

'Come on! We've got food for you!' Lisa yanked them across the hall and through a door to a large dark-red room, in which a long table was already set with plates, cutlery, baskets of bread, dishes of butter, and glasses of juice and water. A teapot sat steaming on a china pedestal, surrounded by mugs, and Mrs P, the chief cook at Tregarren College, carried in a tureen of beef casserole. Dax and Gideon groaned with pleasure.

'It's good to see you both! At last—people to feed!' she smiled, happily.

Dax, Gideon, Lisa, and Mia sat at the table with Owen and Chambers, who had followed them in, as Mrs P went to fetch the vegetarian stew for Mia. Dax realized the table was set for two more people and just as he was wondering who they would be, the door opened and Paulina Sartre stepped in. Dressed in soft folds of green, her pale auburn hair swept up on her head, she gazed at them with concerned grey eyes, framed with gold-rimmed spectacles, and smiled. She looked tired and much thinner than the last time he'd seen her, thought Dax, with a pang of concern. He realized he must be at least in part to blame for this. Paulina Sartre carried a huge weight of responsibility for all her students and the past few days must have been terrible for her.

They said hello, shyly, remembering how the principal had been dowsing them; keeping track of them as best she could. As she took her seat, the door opened again, and Dax cried out with amazement.

'Clive!'

His friend grinned and pushed his glasses higher up his nose. He was wearing his usual mad attire—nylon blue trousers with a crease ironed into them and a tight checked shirt that looked as if it had once been owned by his grandad and shrunk in the wash. 'Hello, you two! You took your time getting here,' he observed, sitting down next to Dax.

Dax gaped at Owen and Chambers, who smiled back, nodding. 'Clive's going to stay with you all for a while,' explained Owen. 'A sort of honorary Cola. We explained to his parents that he has some . . . '

'Unique abilities!' chorused Dax, Gideon, and Lisa, with a giggle.

'Yes—that's the wording,' laughed Owen. 'And, of course, he has. His parents already knew he was a genius, so they agreed to let him board with you all. They think you're all geniuses, by the way. Clive is at the government's most illustrious Genius School—which is no less than he deserves. I loved the tin foil, Clive!' Clive looked very pleased and sniffed happily. 'He's also very useful as a kind of control,' went on Owen. 'I wouldn't say he's exactly your average twelve year old, but I hear he's reassuringly dud when it comes to all the psychic tests. Just what we need.'

Over their stew and bread and butter, they exchanged the news of the last thirty-six hours. 'We only just got away!' breathed Lisa, dramatically. 'We ran through the woods and got to the village, just as the bus to Minehead was pulling in. We all got on and kept our heads down as the helicopters were coming in overhead. We couldn't believe nobody stopped us. They picked us up at Minehead, though, just as we were getting off again. I thumped one of them, but it was no good. We kept hoping you and Gideon had got away. And you did! It was ages, wasn't it, before Owen found you? Sorry, Owen . . . ' She gave him an apologetic look. 'But I really didn't know if you were on our side this time. To be honest, I still wasn't sure really, until Dax and Gideon just showed up.'

'For the record,' said Owen, putting down his fork and looking around at them all, 'I am *always* on your side. So is Chambers here, even though he does look kind of sinister.'

Chambers nodded and smiled around a mouthful of beef and carrot.

Dax told them about the events earlier that day, and Mia looked pale with horror as he described Gideon being hooked out of the coach. 'What happened to Spook?' she asked, at one point. 'Where is he?'

'He's coming tomorrow,' said Owen. 'Broke his nose in the crash and got knocked out. He's fine, but they're keeping him in hospital overnight.'

'That'll teach him to mess with me and my dad,' muttered Gideon. Mia looked shocked.

'He'll be fine—here tomorrow and back to his usual self,' said Owen and they all groaned.

The meal continued and the words that flowed between them all, as the dishes were cleared away and two huge warm lemon meringue pies were brought in, were healing words, Dax thought. Perhaps Mia had something to do with it, but nearly everyone said sorry at one point or another. Even Lisa.

'I'm sorry I told Dax not to trust you,' she said to

Owen. 'It's not that I thought you were against us, exactly, it's just that I could sense danger whenever I thought of you. I could see you and Dax fighting and I couldn't imagine what could make you both do that.'

Owen and Dax had shot each other a look. They both still had bruises from their roll down the hill below the Laughing Man.

'Just a bit of confusion!' said Owen. 'And me laughing at the wrong moment. I'm sorry I put a sack over your head, Dax.'

'Sorry I bit you,' mumbled Dax, but he was too much in lemon meringue heaven to put much feeling into it.

'I'm sorry I didn't tell you about Dad,' said Mia, softly. 'I worry about him so much.'

Paulina Sartre, sitting next to her, touched her shoulder. 'He's getting some support now, *chérie*,' she said, her French accent gentle. 'We can't have you worrying all the time. I promise you he will be better—and happier— if we can possibly make it happen.'

'What are you sorry about, Gideon?' said Lisa, poking at him with her foot.

'Not dropping that coach on Spook,' he muttered.

'And you, Clive?'

Clive beamed across his pudding spoon. 'Not a thing! I've had a brilliant time!'

After the meal they were taken upstairs to their new rooms. Dax and Gideon had barely enough energy to climb the grand staircase. The first floor was carpeted in thick wool, the colour of summer grass, and everything smelt of fresh paint and new flooring. The corridors had light oak panelling to waist height, and pale apricot paint above it, with soft semicircles of light glowing along the walls, every few feet. Dax and Gideon were in the same room.

'I'm in with someone called Barry—he's coming tomorrow,' said Clive, moving to the doorway of the room next to them. 'Is he all right?'

Dax and Gideon chuckled. 'When you can see him!' said Dax. 'He's the vanishing glamourist, remember?'

Clive looked thrilled. Dax thought they'd make an extraordinary pair of room-mates, with Clive's sharp scientific mind and Barry's blunt common sense.

They stepped into their new room and sighed with happiness. Opposite them was a bay of tall windows, with a stone frame and many small panes of glass, set in lead. The floor-to-ceiling velvet curtains were deep blue and held back with gold ties, revealing a curved window seat, padded with the same material. A round silver tin was on the windowsill. Outside was dark now, but promised to be a vista of lovely Cumbrian countryside when dawn broke. As far as Dax could tell from their drive in, every view would be fantastic.

The walls were freshly plastered and painted cream. A bed was on either side of the window, standing on the polished wood floor against the walls to their left and right. Each was covered in crisp white bed linen, which had the familiar scent of lavender that Dax had last picked up at Tregarren College. Beside each bed was a pale blue mat and a small two-drawer chest, with a golden-shaded lamp, a blue water glass, and an alarm clock set on top. At the foot of each bed, much like their last room, was a chest for boots and shoes, and on the wall behind them, beside the door, was a large, long wardrobe. Dax peered inside it and found it full of clothes—not uniforms but casual T-shirts, jumpers, and jeans in their sizes. He wondered if their new uniform would be the same as the old one. Perhaps it was still being made.

'Bathroom's down the hall, second on the left,' said Owen, putting his head around the door. 'Everything OK?'

'Yeah!' they said. Gideon sank into the window seat and picked up the tin. He opened it and chirruped with approval. It was full of home-baked biscuits, still slightly warm from Mrs P's oven.

'I can't believe you're even thinking about it!' said Dax, who felt as if he was ready to burst after their supper.

'I'm thinking about it . . . tomorrow,' said Gideon.

They showered in the freshly tiled bathroom, brushed their teeth for the first time in days, and hurried back to their room, intent on sleep. The first sleep in a proper bed for many nights.

Dax lay back on his pillow, wearing new pyjamas and a contented smile. He might never have been here before, but he felt as if he was at home. He and Gideon were both asleep within a minute.

2 5

'I can't help wondering,' said Lisa, at breakfast the next morning, 'where they're going to put everybody. This place isn't anything like as big as Tregarren.'

'Maybe there are more buildings out the back,' suggested Dax, as they worked through plates of bacon, eggs, and beans. Mrs P was determined to feed them up after their recent adventures. She had shuddered when Gideon told her about the rabbits and the beechnuts.

'Could've poisoned yourself out there, you could!' she scolded.

There were more buildings out the back. As the day passed, Gideon, Dax, and Clive explored the grounds together and discovered a long, low building of local stone which housed a gymnasium and an indoor swimming pool, much to their excitement. There was a kind of adventure playground area, too, among some tall trees, with rope ladders, logs, swings, and climbing frames. It had been built within the last few weeks.

The woods and meadows called to Dax and he longed to shift and explore them properly, leaping across the streams and waterfalls as a fox and flying low down the valley as a falcon, but he didn't dare. He had reached the conclusion that all their recent misadventures had arrived just after one of them had flexed their Cola powers. The last one had happened right after Spook had thrown an illusion. It couldn't be coincidence.

They wandered through the country house and found there was a lofty library, lined with books from floor to ceiling, three classrooms with rows of desks and whiteboards on the walls, a small science lab, and a wood and metal workshop. A ballroom had been converted to a school hall, with a few chairs already laid out in rows, and there was a basement area, which they couldn't yet get down to, where the Development classes would take place. Everything was bright and freshly decorated.

In the afternoon there was excitement as other Colas arrived. Barry came first, his dark hair longer and his middle a bit thicker. He was introduced to Clive, whom he eyed with amazement when he found out he wasn't a Cola. 'Wow!' he said. 'Someone normal!'

'Um . . . I wouldn't go that far,' said Dax and Clive shoved him before leading Barry off to show him his room. Dax thought he'd never seen him so happy. Another glamourist came next: Jennifer Troke, lugging a suitcase along and staring about through her round glasses in wonder. Lisa and Mia bore her away to their room. It was bigger and there were three beds in it.

Then Spook arrived, sullen when he saw Gideon and Dax sitting on the stone steps at the front entrance, but excited in spite of himself. He ran up the steps, wearing a thick plaster bridge over his nose and one of his ludicrous silky black capes over his shoulders. They wondered how on earth he could have got hold of one, having spent the night before at a hospital.

'He probably always carries one, in case there's an emergency and a TV producer shows up,' snorted Gideon. 'Then he gets changed in a phone box and becomes the Great Stupido.'

'The Great Stupido! Now *that* we can work with!' Dax and Gideon looked up in surprise, to see Jacob and Alex Teller. The brothers were telepathic between each other, but, more entertainingly, also fantastic mimics. Jacob, the older of the two, theatrically shook back his nut-brown hair and locked his blue eyes dramatically on something in the middle distance. In a perfect copy of Spook's voice he proclaimed: 'I *am* the Great Stupido! Watch my hands! Watch my hands!' He swivelled them about in the air. 'I will make you see amazing things! A huge, oversized, swollen ginger thing! What can this be? Behold—my head!' He flounced up and down the steps, wafting about an imaginary cloak and Dax, Gideon, and Alex fell about laughing.

The brothers picked up their bags and looked around them. 'Looks great,' said Alex, who was the younger brother, slighter and fairer than Jacob, with the same merry blue eyes. He glanced at Jacob and then back at Dax and Gideon. Jacob nodded and Alex said, seriously, 'They asked us to come and help find you. They wanted us to do your dad's voice, Gid. And yours, Dax. We said no. We didn't want to cheat you.'

'Were we right?' said Jacob, earnestly.

'Yeah,' said Dax. 'Don't worry—Spook did the snitch duty!'

By the end of the afternoon there were ten Colas at the new place. The only further arrival had been Darren Tyler, a quiet boy who was a friend of Spook's—another illusionist. At four o'clock they were all called into the hall, where they sat down on the small row of chairs.

Paulina Sartre and Mr Eades, a grey and humourless man from Tregarren, were there as Owen ushered them in. Mrs Sartre smiled at them, resting one elegant arm along the top of a grand stone fireplace, and the room was still with expectation.

'It is so good to have you all together again, safe,' she said. 'It has been a difficult time, yes? But we have got past the difficulty. You are safe here. The house— its walls and ceilings—have been lined with tourmaline and other crystals which repel unwanted attention from outside forces.' She looked meaningfully at Gideon. 'The security system here, also, is second to none. I look forward to you all settling in and resuming your classes.'

Lisa looked at Dax, perplexed. 'But where's everyone else?' she whispered.

Paulina Sartre paused and Lisa went slightly pink.

'You might well ask, Miss Hardman,' she said, quietly. There was silence for a few moments and Owen, perched against a wooden table behind her, sighed and looked at his feet.

'The fact is, you are the only Children Of Limitless

Ability we now have,' said Paulina, gravely. 'You ten. That is all.'

There were gasps of shock. They stared at each other.

'After the terrible events at Tregarren College, you were all taken home to recover, yes?' Mrs Sartre continued. 'And recover you did. *You* did. The rest of the Colas, sadly, did not. What was taken from them that night was never returned to them.'

There was an appalled silence and then, realizing that no more of their friends would be joining them, Mia and Jennifer began to cry. Dax thought of all the hilarity around the tables in the old college refectory; of the Saturday mornings when fifty-odd Colas would descend on the local village to lark around and spend their pocket money; of the messing about in the common room and the laughter and the excitement. He saw the faces of so many children who had been amazing and exceptional and now might never return to Cola Club. Blighted by Catherine. It was as if he'd been hit with a brick.

'We keep hoping their powers will return one day,' sighed Mrs Sartre, 'and we will keep monitoring every one, but for now, you are all that is left. You are the true ten.'

Gideon looked up. Dax caught a sudden pulse of that cold, steady anger in him again. 'No,' he said. He spoke firmly. 'Not ten. Not the true ten. The true eleven.'

Everyone stared at him.

'Who is the eleventh, Gideon?' asked Owen.

Gideon took a deep breath and gulped. 'The true eleventh,' he said, 'is Luke. My brother is alive.'

26

Anyone else—any ordinary person—would probably have tried to explain to Gideon that because he so *wanted* it to be true, he was just lying to himself; making himself believe the impossible.

But these were not ordinary people, and so many extraordinary things had happened to them now, that nobody tried to talk Gideon out of what he said.

Dax hardly dared to say it, but he had to ask. 'Do you mean that the orb thing—that thing that came and got you—that was Luke?'

'No, of course not,' said Gideon. 'Although . . . maybe partly. It wasn't his *will*, I know that. But I think he was caught up in it. The orb was her . . . my *sister.*' His mouth curled with disgust around the word. 'Catherine.'

Once again, there was a shocked silence. Dax felt his skin crawl and his hands grow cold.

'But she's not coming back, you don't have to worry,' said Gideon. 'She wanted to find me—and all of us—and finish the job. But she couldn't. I think Luke was stopping her. And she knows I saw her and she's scared now. Scared and hiding.'

'Do you know where she is, Gideon?' asked Owen.

'No.'

'Well—she can't get to you here,' said Paulina Sartre. 'I promise you, Gideon. In this house you are safe. You all are. Now—go to the dining room. There is tea. Drink it hot, with sugar! You are all in a shock, I think.'

Dax and Gideon took their mugs of tea outside, leaving the others talking in hushed tones. Catherine! She had tried to kill them all. They had thought she was dead, buried under oceans of sea water. But she wasn't, was she? Not if Gideon was right.

They climbed into an elder tree, which spread its horizontal dark branches above the adventure play area. Dax handed Gideon the mugs when he was settled, and clambered up after him. On the branch they drank their tea and said nothing, listening to the breeze stir the leaves around them.

Eventually Gideon spoke.

'I think I kind of knew, all along,' he said. 'It was there in dreams. I just didn't get it for a while. Didn't think I got that stuff.'

'How do you feel about it?' asked Dax.

'I don't know. I'm OK, I think. But I'm never going to feel right. Not until . . . '

'Until what?'

'Until I find Luke. Until we're the true eleven.'

Dax said nothing. He didn't know if the true eleven would ever stand together. He could only guess about the future. Nothing in the past year had been remotely what he had expected.

He leaned back against the trunk of the elder and felt its energy seep into him, strong roots anchored deep in the earth and leaves stretching from the branches, reaching ever skyward. This was where he was meant to be now, he knew it. With this mug of tea. With this friend.

Whatever comes, I won't be sorry for this, he thought.

The light wind curled around the elder, carrying a wisp of steam from Dax's mug south-east. The steady breeze moved down and down, through the middle of the country, across to the Hampshire coast and out over the sea, never pausing.

At the rise of a foreign land it curled through forests and valleys, spread over flat wide sands and raised goosebumps on the neck of a twelve-year-old girl, who held a still hand.

And closed her eyes.

ACKNOWLEDGEMENTS

Special thanks to Andy Hinton and Mike Riley at the Hawk Conservancy in Weyhill, Hampshire, for excellent peregrine falcon advice, to David and Mary Kingston for MOD and paranormal advice, and to Neil White for special ops/military advice (and very fine pancakes).

ALI SPARKES

Ali Sparkes was a journalist and BBC broadcaster until she chucked in the safe job to go dangerously freelance and try her hand at writing comedy scripts. Her first venture was as a comedy columnist on *Woman's Hour* and later on *Home Truths*. Not long after, she discovered her real love was writing children's fiction.

Ali grew up adoring adventure stories about kids who mess about in the woods and still likes to mess about in the woods herself whenever possible. She lives with her husband and two sons in Southampton, England.

HAVE YOU READ THEM ALL?

THE SHAPESHIFTER